SPECIAL EDITION

CELEBRATION

1000

CHRISTINE FLYNN

LOGAN'S BRIDE

Holiday Elopements

ISBN 0-373-09995-9

50375

AVAILABLE THIS MONTH FROM SILHOUETTE SPECIAL EDITION®

#991 MAGGIE'S DAD
Diana Palmer

#992 MORGAN'S SON
Lindsay McKenna

#993 CHILD OF MINE
Jennifer Mikels

#994 THE DADDY QUEST
Celeste Hamilton

#995 LOGAN'S BRIDE
Christine Flynn

#996 BRAVE HEART
Brittany Young

THE WHITAKER BRIDES

Sam was losing her composure.

Logan didn't say a word. He simply pulled her into his arms and held her head to his chest.

"My family's falling apart. I don't know what to do," she whispered against the steady beat of his heart.

The pain in Sam's voice tore at Logan. The small sob she muffled against his shirt had him tightening his hold. "Don't worry about it right now," he told her. "Just lean on me for a while."

"I can't do that, Logan."

"Why not?" he growled.

"Because I want to so much."

The admission was not what Logan had expected. Nor had he expected his own reaction to it. He had no business feeling protective about this woman. "Do it anyway," he whispered. And, damning the consequences, he lowered his lips to taste the salt of her tears....

Dear Reader,

Book #1000?! In February, 1982, when Silhouette Special Edition was first published, that seemed a far distant goal. And now, almost fourteen years later, here we are!

We're opening CELEBRATION 1000 with a terrific book from the beloved Diana Palmer—*Maggie's Dad*. Diana was one of the first authors to contribute to Special Edition, and now she's returned with this tender tale of love reborn.

Lindsay McKenna continues her action-packed new series, MORGAN'S MERCENARIES: LOVE AND DANGER. The party goes on with *Logan's Bride* by Christine Flynn— the first HOLIDAY ELOPEMENTS, three tales of love and weddings over the holiday season. And join the festivities with wonderful stories by Jennifer Mikels, Celeste Hamilton and Brittany Young.

We have so many people to thank for helping us to reach this milestone. Silhouette Special Edition would not be what it is today without our marvelous writers. I want to take a moment, though, to mention one author—Sondra Stanford. She gave us Book #7, *Silver Mist*, and many other wonderful stories. We lost her in October 1991 after a valiant struggle against cancer. We miss her; she brought a great deal of happiness to all who knew her.

And our very special thanks to our readers. Your imaginations and brave hearts allow books to take flight— and all of us can never thank you enough for that!

The celebration continues in December and January—with books by Nora Roberts, Debbie Macomber, Sherryl Woods and many more of your favorite writers! Happy Book 1000—to each and every romantic!

Sincerely,

Tara Gavin, Senior Editor

Please address questions and book requests to:
Silhouette Reader Service
U.S.: 3010 Walden Ave., P.O. Box 1325, Buffalo, NY 14269
Canadian: P.O. Box 609, Fort Erie, Ont. L2A 5X3

CHRISTINE FLYNN

LOGAN'S BRIDE

SPECIAL EDITION®

Published by Silhouette Books
America's Publisher of Contemporary Romance

To Betty Flynn, my other mother. With love.

 SILHOUETTE BOOKS

ISBN 0-373-09995-9

LOGAN'S BRIDE

Copyright © 1995 by Christine Flynn

This edition published by arrangement with Harlequin Books S.A.

Printed in U.S.A.

Books by Christine Flynn

Silhouette Special Edition

Remember the Dreams #254
Silence the Shadows #465
Renegade #566
Walk upon the Wind #612
Out of the Mist #657
The Healing Touch #693
Beyond the Night #747
Luke's Child #788
Lonely Knight #826
When Morning Comes #922
Jake's Mountain #945
Logan's Bride #995

Silhouette Romance

Stolen Promise #435
Courtney's Conspiracy #623

Silhouette Desire

When Snow Meets Fire #254
The Myth and the Magic #296
A Place to Belong #352
Meet Me at Midnight #377

Silhouette Intimate Moments

Daughter of the Dawn #537

CHRISTINE FLYNN

is formerly from Oregon and currently resides in the Southwest with her husband, teenage daughter and two very spoiled dogs.

The Whitaker Brides

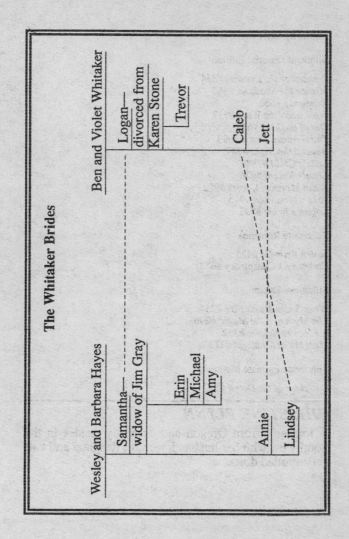

Wesley and Barbara Hayes

Samantha—
widow of Jim Gray

Erin
Michael
Amy

Annie
Lindsey

Ben and Violet Whitaker

Logan—
divorced from
Karen Stone

Trevor

Caleb
Jett

Prologue

For as long as Logan Whitaker could remember, gossip had been the lifeblood of Leesburg, Texas. Most of the people in the small rural community knew everyone. Everyone knew everyone else's business. And everyone had an opinion about what everyone else was doing. In a way that scrutiny was as much a form of protection as invasion, for anyone new was looked over as carefully as an applicant for membership in the most exclusive country club. Nothing got past the old men who smoked their pipes out in front of Arnstad's Drugstore, or the ladies who ran the café. Not that Logan had much to do with those ladies. Or that he associated with the men, for that matter. When it came to talk, Logan paid little attention to anything he heard, and he contributed even less. All he cared about when he made his weekly twenty-two mile trip into town was taking care of his own business.

Since his patronage was pretty much limited to two stores plus the post office and, when his hair started curling down over his ears, the barber, he could usually be in and out of Leesburg in an hour—provided his standing orders at Meiers Market and Leesburg Feed & Hardware were ready. It wasn't that he was antisocial, though he knew many thought him so. Nor was he a recluse or a loner, though he was aware some people had stuck those labels on him, too. He'd just never been one to poke his nose in where it didn't belong, especially when he always had a dozen other things he needed to be doing, not one of which was being accomplished with him away from his ranch.

There was an undercurrent about the talk today, however. An excitement that felt like anticipation. Logan usually ignored any speculation he overheard about the town itself. Specifically, about how it was going to have to grow if it didn't want to wither up one of these days and disappear like dust in a dry wind. People had been speculating about the health of the businesses anchoring the community for as long as he could remember. And for as long as he could remember, nothing much had changed. The fact that it *hadn't* changed in the thirty-eight years since he'd been born, on the very ranch he now owned, was exactly what he liked about the place.

Ordinarily that was all the thought Logan would have given the matter. By the time he'd pulled his keys from the front pocket of his jeans, his concerns would have turned to the weather, beef prices, his men and the never-ending list of backbreaking chores that came with running one of the largest cattle ranches in west Texas. Yet, as he pulled his hat low against the early September sun and loaded the last of his purchases from the feed store into the bed of his dusty black pickup truck, he was having a hard time dismissing what he'd just heard. According to the feed store owner, the mayor had brought in some hotshot from Los Angeles to develop a chamber of commerce for the town. She was being introduced at the town council meeting tonight at seven.

"She's the sister of that young gal who took over May Bradley's dress shop couple years back," Gil had said. "Real citified type, but she's sharp. Real enterprising, too. Wasn't in town two days before she'd been around to most of us, talking about a publicity brochure and getting some businesses into those boarded-up buildings on Main. Seems the mayor's going to live up to his promise and get some money coming in here after all."

Hard muscles bunched beneath Logan's frayed work shirt as he hefted the last bag of feed pellets to his shoulder. Tossing the fifty-pound sack into the bed as easily as most men shrug off a suit jacket, he glanced across the street at the Lone Star Tavern. The clock in the window next to a glowing neon beer sign indicated it was almost five o'clock. He had two hours to get back to the ranch, get one of the boys to run the medication he'd picked up out to those late-dropping calves with the scours, and get back to Leesburg. He'd never been to a town meeting in his life. But something about Gil's comments made him uneasy. It didn't matter that it would be midnight before he'd get to the spreadsheets on his desk. As much as Logan believed in minding his own business, when someone got serious about messing with what mattered to him, it was time to check out what was going on.

Chapter One

Everything would be better soon. It had to be, Samantha Gray coached herself, as she glanced uneasily about the sea of unfamiliar faces in the rustic old library's cramped meeting room. She had promised her children the move to Leesburg would work out; that they would be happy with their new home once they settled in. As rough as the past year and a half had been on them, it was a promise she couldn't bear to break.

It was with the weight of that promise resting on her slender shoulders that she smiled at the balding man demanding her attention and attempted to scrape up the enthusiasm she'd managed to fake this morning in front of Amy, Michael and Erin. She'd known starting over wasn't going to be easy. That was why she'd tried to convince her children they should look upon the move as an adventure—an undertaking that had made her feel like an absolute fraud since there wasn't a single adventuresome bone in her own body. If she craved anything it was stability. Routine was good. *Uneventful* was her favorite word. Still, she had honestly felt that if she were adaptable they would settle in in no time.

It wasn't her adaptability that was in question at the moment, however. It was the community's willingness to accept her. Since she tended to accept people pretty much as they were, it hadn't occurred to her that the citizens of Leesburg would regard her as being any different from them. But there was no doubt they did. After spending ten minutes listening to Bud Meiers, who was the owner of the town's only market and also its mayor, remind her it would take a while for folks to get used to what he called her "sophistication and big-city way of thinking," and after encountering the skeptical, assessing and curious glances from the seventy or so people wandering about the room, she was beginning to get a better picture of how she was perceived by the local citizenry.

They didn't see her as a woman who had come here wanting to be part of the community. They saw her only as someone who had been hired to do a specific job. Someone who was, first and foremost, an outsider.

She owed her children an extra hug tonight, certain they must have felt much the same way facing a jury of their own peers at their new schools this morning. Burdened with that thought, Sam unconsciously reached to twirl the ring on her left hand. It was an old habit. One she found herself doing when she was deep in thought, or nervous. It was also a habit that no longer provided the comfort it had for so long.

The gold band she'd worn for seventeen years was no longer there. She'd taken it off the night before they'd left Los Angeles.

"...just what we need," she overheard someone say as the mayor moved off to pump the hand of a man wearing a white T-shirt and a farmer's tan. "There's too many young people moving out. It's gotten so when a business owner dies, there's no one to take over, and another building gets boarded up."

"...over at the store today," someone else was saying, talking above the other conversations taking place around her, "...said Logan didn't look too happy about it at all."

"Don't imagine Farley is, either," came a deeper voice. "But the ranchers and the farmers have a way to make a living. We need something here in town, too."

"...seems nice enough," the quieter voice commented as Sam made her way over to look at the children's drawings papering one of the sickly mint green walls. "But she is a bit overdressed, don't you think?"

"Don't look now," came a voice from directly behind Sam's left ear. "But you're being discussed. Don't worry. I won't tell them you're older than I am. Coffee?" A plastic cup, holding what looked like steaming crude oil, materialized on Sam's right. The voice lowered. "Or would you rather I fill it with something stronger?"

Sam's smile softened with relief. "Definitely stronger," she whispered, carefully taking the cup as she turned to face the striking and statuesque young woman she'd spent the past half hour waiting for. Sam was older than Lindsey by eight years. But Lindsey had the height both Sam and their sister Annie lacked. Not that five foot four was short. It was just that five foot eight was so elegant. At least Annie and Sam had always thought so. "I thought you were going to pick me up."

Lindsey, wearing the slightly frazzled expression of the perpetually disorganized, offered an apologetic smile, then shoved back her thick, wheat-colored hair. "I tried to get out earlier. Honest," she added, as if she needed to convince her sister she hadn't simply forgotten her. "I'm just backed up at the shop. Time sort of tends to get away from me sometimes."

Windblown as Lindsey appeared, Sam figured she had probably run in from the parking lot. Her little sister always seemed to be going in three directions at once. That she actually seemed to *like* being harried was something Sam was hard-pressed to understand.

"If you're behind, why did you insist on coming over yesterday to help me finish unpacking? Not that I didn't love the company, Lindsey, but I told you the kids and I could do it."

"You'd have been up all night putting things away if I hadn't," Lindsey cut in. "You've been positively compulsive about getting that place to look like home. I'm always behind," she added, waving off her sister's concern before Sam could start feeling bad about having kept her from her work. "I just have a few more orders than I can handle right now, but that's not why I'm late. Amelia needed a ride because her car is at the mechanic's. You remember Amelia, don't you? She works in the ice cream parlor. Anyway," she continued before Sam could decide if she remembered Amelia or not, "by the time I drove her home, then got to your place, you'd already left. The kids said I'd just missed you."

The focus of Sam's concern immediately changed. Zeroing in on deep brown eyes very much like her own, she mentally held her breath. "Was everything all right at the house?"

"It was still standing," her sister replied, shrugging off the import of the question as only a woman without children could do. "Erin came out when I pulled up, and she didn't say anything, so I assume everything was fine."

As she spoke, her glance made a pass from Sam's honey-colored hair and the sedate little bow at her nape, to her navy pumps and the matching linen sheath in between. After a moment of hesitation she leaned closer.

Apology shifted to chagrin and her voice lowered. "I probably should have told you people aren't very formal here. We don't dress up for much. But don't worry about it," she hurried to say because she knew Sam would. "You look very...competent. Very 'in control.' But, then," she added, meaning it sincerely, "you always are."

It wasn't her sister's belated advice that had Sam feeling self-conscious when Babs from the Beauty Barn interrupted them to say hello. Considering the amount of denim in the room, Sam had already concluded that her attire was all wrong and resigned herself to the slightly askance glances she'd caught coming her way. What caused her uneasiness was her sister's well-intentioned compliment. She didn't deserve it any more than she deserved the hint of admiration that had been in Lindsey's voice.

Sam knew how to present a cool, calm front in just about any situation. It was a skill acquired as a child because, as the oldest, she'd been told it was up to her to set the best example. Over the past year, she'd honed that skill to perfection. She'd actually become quite adept at acting as if she had everything under control while, inside, she felt about as capable as her six-year-old.

Sam lifted her cup, scarcely tasting the stout brew. She might look competent, but she didn't feel it. She'd just moved her children a thousand miles from everything familiar and sunk nearly every dollar she had into a rundown old house she could afford only if she made this new job work. On top of that, her six-year-old had taken to crawling into bed with her in the middle of the night because she was afraid to be alone in her new bedroom, her nine-year old son had entered a stage that could only be described as obnoxious, and Erin, her sixteen-year-old, had declared Leesburg "a pit" and hadn't cracked a smile in the week since they'd arrived. If anything, the feeling knotting her stomach felt like panic.

The beautician, who sported a gravity-defying beehive in a shade of pinkish blond that Sam felt certain was unknown in nature, had just waved someone named Verna over to join them when Sam felt a tug on her arm.

Essie Fullbright, owner of the bakery three doors down from Lindsey's Country Boutique, offered a polite smile. Silver curls bobbing, and smelling faintly of vanilla, she nodded to a folding table at the front of the room.

"Bud wants you to sit up here with us, Samantha. He's going to introduce you first." Two dimples dented her pink cheeks, and her hazel eyes twinkled. The woman looked like Cinderella's fairy godmother. "Except for putting in a cattle guard out by the Yoder place, you're the only item on the agenda tonight."

Which meant she was the only reason most of these people had shown up.

The knot in Sam's stomach grew. Making a mental note to ask Lindsey how she'd made it into the inner circle of the town she'd stumbled upon a couple of years ago and never left, Sam excused herself from the relative safety of her sister and made her way through what the librarian had referred to as "the green room." Since all the walls in the crumbling old building were the same shade of washed-out mint, it seemed odd to Sam to single out its only meeting room with such a label. But Sam was learning in a hurry that one thing small towns had in abundance were eccentricities.

"Well, would you look at that."

The head table was centered between a faded map of Texas and a poster proclaiming Reading is *Fun*damental. Taking a chair at the end, Sam looked up when Essie spoke. The woman's pleasant features had crumpled in a contemplative frown.

"I wonder what he's doing here," the older woman muttered.

The owner of the gas station, a rather laid-back middle-aged gentleman, who'd been introduced to Sam earlier simply as Glen, was already seated at the middle of the table. Occupying himself by scraping the burnt tobacco in the bowl of his pipe into a small tin ashtray, he didn't bother to look up. "Who?"

"Logan Whitaker," Essie told him.

"Whitaker's here?" Looking over the top of his glasses, the man glanced toward the door. "Well, I'll be. I never figured to see him at one of these meetings."

With both council members looking so puzzled, Sam quietly asked "Why?"

"Just not like him," the man replied, as his attention returned to his pipe. Holding up the detached pipe stem, he squinted through it, more concerned with getting a good smoke than with his neighbor's apparently odd behavior. "About the only time he leaves the RW is when he comes in to get supplies. Of course he leaves when he's got business in Houston or Austin or some such place," he added, apparently satisfied that the stem was clean. "But I don't know much about those comings and goings since he had a tank and pump installed out at his place a few years back. Once he started fueling his own vehicles, he didn't have to gas up at my place anymore. Darn near quartered my profits when he did that."

"None of the Whitakers were ever what you'd call social," Essie felt compelled to add. "Especially the boys."

The ranch Glen had mentioned was familiar to Sam only because Bud's verbal tour of the area had included mention of an RW Ranch outside of town. She'd heard it was the largest cattle operation in the area. Nearly a million acres. But she hadn't heard the Whitaker name until now. And she hadn't a clue who this enigmatic Logan person was—other than that he was not a man a person could ignore. He'd no sooner entered the room than the buzz of conversation had hushed to whispers, heads turning as his powerful, self-assured strides carried him past the collection of farmers, business owners and interested citizens seating themselves in the rows of folding chairs. Big and brooding, the fluid strength in his muscles reminding Sam vaguely of a wolf stalking prey, he spoke to no one. He merely nodded to some of the men in the group, ignored the interest and speculation in the women's eyes and turned to lean against the wall at the back of the room.

It was apparent that Essie wasn't the only person surprised to see him. Judging from the others' reactions—everything from timid smiles to uncertain glances—it was apparent that just about everyone in the room knew him. Or, at least, knew who he was. There was no opportunity for Sam to learn anything more about him, though. The mayor was at the table. Smoothing his sparse hair over the bald spot on his head, he picked up his gavel. With a whack on the makeshift podium, he bestowed his ready smile on his constituents. Everyone other than the dark-haired man at the back of the room. Him he seemed to deliberately avoid.

Sam tried to pretend he wasn't there, too. But seated as she was, facing everyone else in the room, she didn't have much luck. He stood alone. Solitary. And that made his presence all the more notable. That he kept himself separate was clearly his choice, and that made as much of an impression on Sam as the way he stood so eerily still, as if his control over himself was absolute.

The thought made her shiver. He was a compelling man. Commanding. And handsome in a raw, decidedly rugged sort of way. At least, Sam would have thought him so had it not been for the hardness around his chiseled mouth and in his wintery blue eyes. Lean-hipped and wide-shouldered, he stood with his arms crossed over a chambray shirt as faded as his worn denims, a fist curled around the brim of a dark gray cowboy hat and his jaw locked tight enough to do serious damage to his back teeth. That he was displeased with something seemed obvious to Sam. What wasn't so obvious was why he was staring straight at her.

"Before we get into committee reports and such," Sam heard the mayor say as she dragged her glance away, "there's someone here I want y'all to meet. It's no secret that Leesburg is looking like an opry star way past her prime. Right now, we're patching the holes on Main best we can, using gravel and Homer Schmidt's tar pot, but we all know what that street really needs is a good chip seal from County Road 3 all the way through town. We could use a new roof on the bandstand in the square, and the grade school needs repairs, if we want to keep from closing it and sending our kids over to Dry Creek for schooling."

There were nods all around the room, underscored by grumbles from those whose vehicles' front ends had been knocked out of alignment by the aforementioned potholes. The man supporting the back wall remained as still as stone.

"Last election," the portly politician continued, his chest now puffing a bit, "I proposed a solution to our little cash flow problem, and most of you agreed by voting me into office. The best way to get the funds we need is by making this community grow.'' Raising a beefy hand toward Sam, he settled his affable smile on her. "Well, this is the lady who's going to make that happen, and she's come all the way from Los Angeles to help us out."

There were a few points Bud left out of his enthusiastic introduction, as he went on to recite Sam's qualifications, recounting her experience in community development gained over the twelve years she'd spent working for L.A.'s chamber of commerce. What he didn't mention was that her position in Los Angeles had been eliminated due to budget cutbacks. What *she* didn't mention, when she rose to acknowledge the polite applause, was that the loss of her job had only hastened the change she'd had to make anyway.

Leesburg's growth was hardly her first priority. She'd come to this beautiful little Hill Country town not because she felt any burning desire to boost its economy. She'd come here because for a year and a half she'd tried to maintain a sense of normalcy for her children by keeping everything as it had been before they'd lost their father. She hadn't been able to do it. Their lives had changed and there was no way to keep what had been. She'd come here, too, because she'd wanted to get her children away from the influences and dangers rife in a city where every headline, every newscast brought yet another reminder of just how close they were to gangs and drugs and guns. As if she'd needed a reminder of the violence wrought by that combination.

She'd come here because she'd wanted to raise her children where they were safe, where they might once again be happy. And she'd needed a job so she could support them. She'd have worked expanding fish factories in Alaska if she'd had to, just to accomplish those goals.

She would do a good job for Leesburg, though. Watching the various degrees of acceptance register on faces that didn't seem quite so unfamiliar as they had only a short while ago, Sam silently promised herself she'd do everything in her power to meet the goals these people set for her. She needed this job and this community far more than they needed her.

Because that need was so important, Sam felt herself stiffen when she once again encountered Logan Whitaker's eyes. It was as clear as the creek at the end of Jay Street that he wasn't impressed with her in the least, and that he wanted her to know it.

For a meeting that wasn't supposed to take very long, this one seemed to last forever—especially once Sam realized that Bud looked as if he were holding his breath when he asked if anyone had any questions for her. It seemed that, like the others, the mayor didn't quite know what to make of Logan's presence. Logan said nothing, though. He merely stuffed his hands in his pockets and settled himself more comfortably against the wall. Rather than looking as if he'd come to cause a problem, he looked very much like a man prepared to bide his time.

The image of the wolf returned. With it came an uneasiness that Sam didn't understand at all. She knew nothing about this man, other than that he made her feel terribly, disturbingly, vulnerable. But she suddenly felt an unnerving certainty that this Logan was not a man to cause a scene. He was a more dangerous type. The kind who, like the cunning predator of which he reminded her, watched and waited for the most vulnerable moment to strike.

* * *

He found that moment not long after Sam said good-night to her sister outside the library.

The night was balmy, the stars closer than Sam had ever realized stars could be. It was because she was looking up that she didn't notice him at first. And by the time she'd reminded herself that she had no business wasting time staring at stars, she was too involved with digging her keys out of her purse to notice who was watching her from across the street. She knew someone was, though. As she headed down the cracked sidewalk to her boringly mom-like beige sedan, seed pods crunching beneath her heels, she became aware of two men talking to each other near one of the pickup trucks parked along the opposite curb.

Having secured what she was looking for, she finally glanced up. The smile she'd been prepared to offer immediately faltered.

She recognized the shorter of the two men as Murry from the tack and saddle shop. She'd met him a couple of days ago when she'd made her rounds of the merchants with Bud. It was Logan Whitaker who had her attention, though. He was leaning against the black pickup's front fender, his booted feet crossed at the ankles and his arms crossed over his impossibly broad chest. The moment he saw her, he slowly unfolded his arms, pulled the curled brim of his dark hat a little lower over his eyes and pushed himself upright. Seconds later, having said something to Murry that had the saddle maker nodding before he headed for his own truck, Logan moved toward her.

There were still a few other people around the library building. Most of them seemed to be concentrated in two small knots in the tree-lined parking area at the end of the block. Just knowing there were still people around helped. Helped what, Sam wasn't sure, since she doubted that this

Logan person had mayhem in mind. Nonetheless, hearing the ominous thud of his boots on the pavement as he crossed the street, she decided she was grateful for the street lamp, too.

At least, she was until she found herself staring up at a jaw and mouth that looked even harder up close than they had from the safety of the other end of a room. She hadn't realized how big he actually was.

If she stood on her toes, the top of her head just might reach the point of his open collar.

He kept his own silent once-over blessedly brief.

"The name's Whitaker," he said in a voice as deep and as smooth as aged whiskey. The sound was rich. A little smoky. Definitely unnerving. "If you wouldn't mind, I'd like to ask you something."

Determined not to be uneasy, or at least not to let him know it, Sam held out her hand. "I don't mind at all," she responded, hoping her graciousness would make up for the lie. "I thought you might have had something on your mind when I saw you inside."

She wasn't sure which he hadn't expected; her willingness, or her insight. He didn't move. He simply stood towering over her, his eyes glittering over her face in the diffuse light of the street lamp, Finally, having reached some conclusion to which only he was privy, his glance moved to her hand. When he finally reached out to accept it, the gesture seemed more the acceptance of a challenge than an attempt at civility.

Small and soft, she slipped her palm into his and momentarily tightened her grip. Though her hand was completely engulfed, the gesture was every bit as businesslike as she intended. There was nothing at all businesslike, however, about the sensations of heat and strength she felt when his grip tightened a heartbeat later than it should have—or in the quick slash of displeasure that darkened his eyes just before he released her fingers and drew his hand back to push into his pocket.

Wondering how something as simple as a handshake could leave a person feeling as if she'd just been swallowed whole, Sam cleared her throat.

"You said you wanted to ask me something."

The muscle in his jaw jerked. "I just wondered how long you plan on being here."

"I'm afraid I don't understand..."

"I'd just like to know how long you plan to give the mayor's little project before you head back to Los Angeles."

Sam felt her back stiffen. Still, she kept her tone even, her manner as cooperative as she could make it. "I'm not planning on going back, Mr. Whitaker. My children and I are making our home here."

His glance darted to her left hand, his eyebrows snapping together. Noting the absence of a ring, perhaps noting, too, that she hadn't mentioned a husband, his brow lowered further. "How many do you have?"

Matching his expression, she told him, then added, "Why do you ask?" which he proceeded to ignore.

"And you've moved them here," he muttered, his tone utterly, disapprovingly, flat. "That's really too bad."

With his back to the pale light of the street lamp, his eyes were shadowed. As unnerving as it was not to fully see their expression, Sam had the feeling it would have been more unsettling to encounter the full extent of his thoughts.

"Why do you say that?" she ventured.

"Because it's just going to cost you to move back again. In the meantime, the money the town will pay you could be used for some of the repairs the mayor was talking about. Seems like a waste of funds all the way around to me."

"I believe they're looking at my salary as seed money, Mr. Whitaker," she responded, overlooking for the moment both his conclusion and his assumption that she was going anyplace, much less back to the city she'd just moved from. "I'll bring in far more than they'll pay me, once the mayor's plans for development are under way."

With deceptive casualness, his glance moved from the no-nonsense style of her hair and down the dress she would put away when she got home and not drag out again until she went to either a wedding or a funeral. She was attired perfectly for a meeting in the city, but the classic navy silk was definitely too sophisticated for a place where the best restaurant in town was a steak house a mile out on the highway.

"It's apparent I have a lot to learn about this town before I represent it to anyone else," she admitted, seeing no point in avoiding what he was probably already thinking. "And I fully intend to do my homework."

The line of his jaw was strong, the shape one a sculptor or painter might use to epitomize masculine beauty. Even in the shadows she could see that jaw grow harder. Remarkably, his voice remained quite even.

"I'm sure you're very good at what you do. But you're wasting your time here. This town has been trying to make something of itself for the last hundred years and this is as far as it's ever got. They might complain about it, and every few years someone might get an idea about how to make it something it's not, but people like things just the way they are. That's why it's stayed this way for so long. If I were you, I wouldn't go unpacking my bags just yet."

There was no threat in his tone. Nor was there any in his actions when he touched the brim of his hat and gave her a nod just before he turned to his truck. She felt threatened just the same. Not to mention intimidated. He knew it, too. She was as sure of that as she was of the knot in the pit of her stomach when she watched him toss his hat through the open window of his truck and climb inside.

Intimidating her had been the entire point of the conversation. Maybe, she thought, dismayed to find her hands shaking when she turned to unlock her car, intimidating her had been the entire point to everything he'd done that evening. The irritating part was that he'd succeeded. He'd rattled her so that she'd forgotten to wonder why he'd looked so displeased to learn she had children.

Chapter Two

"That was all he said?" From behind her pastry-filled display case, the silver-haired Essie raised a curious eyebrow. "That people like things the way they are?"

Drawing in a breath of air that smelled as fattening as some of Essie's nut-filled creations looked, Sam started to reply—only to find herself sighing as the bell over the door of the little German-style bakery announced yet another customer. Lindsey hadn't been able to tell her a thing about Logan when Sam had stopped by to see her this morning. But Lindsey had said that Essie knew everyone, and if anyone could tell Sam whether or not she needed to worry about Logan Whitaker, the owner of the bakery could.

The only problem was finding two uninterrupted minutes to talk to the woman. The arrival of the talking magpie in the white-and-pink waitress uniform was their third interruption in the last five minutes.

Louella Perkins worked the morning shift at the café over on the next block.

"Back again, Essie. Morning, Samantha," she added, managing to get in a nod and a smile for the woman she'd only met once, before she turned a thoughtful frown to the racks of baked goods on the wall. "We need another half dozen each of blueberry and bran. We've already gone through the dozen I picked up before we opened. Oh, and toss in a half dozen bear claws, too, will you? The boys from the mill stopped by this morning and cleaned us out."

"Busy morning over there?" Essie inquired, reaching under the counter.

"Was for a while. Virgil was in with Dryfus. And Lester said Wren's going to sell him his old tractor after all. Oh, and I heard Logan Whitaker showed up at the council meeting last night. If I'd known that, I'd have stopped by there myself. That's one boy I'd love to get my hands on. Course, I'd have better luck trying to catch a greased pig," she added, her tone utterly matter-of-fact. "No fella around here's slipperier than he is. And that's if you can even catch *sight* of the man."

"Seems that way," Essie muttered, unable to do anything more than confirm the consensus since she had nothing else to add. Yet.

"So," the waitress continued, turning her pleasant smile to Sam, while Essie turned a piece of flat pink cardboard into a box. "I hear Mildred Gunther's going to be watching your children for you in the afternoons."

Sam, feeling like a sparrow next to a peacock, blinked at the woman's bright coral lipstick. "You did?"

Louella nodded, the rhinestones across the top of her eyeglass frames flashing as brightly as the frosted streaks in her bouffant hairdo. "You can't have a better neigh-

bor than Mrs. G. Salt of the earth, that lady." Her carefully drawn eyebrows threatened to merge. "But I thought
you had a girl old enough to baby-sit after school."

"I do," Sam replied, amazed at the speed of the local
grapevine. Not just about Logan's appearance last night.
But about her conversation with her neighbor. She'd only
talked to Mildred this morning about watching Michael
and Amy. And then only because Erin had refused to get
involved in anything at her new school—including volleyball, which she'd always loved—and Sam hadn't
wanted to give her daughter any excuse to hibernate.
"Erin's going to help my sister at her store a couple of
afternoons a week, so she won't be available to watch her
brother and sister."

"She'll like that. Being at Lindsey's store and working
with all those clothes and accessories, I mean."

"I sure hope so," was Sam's quiet and heartfelt reply.

Erin didn't know she was working for Lindsey. Not yet.
But Sam doubted Erin would turn her aunt down when
Lindsey called her tonight about the prospect. Erin adored
clothes. She also adored her aunt. Which made the combination perfect. What Lindsey didn't know, though, was
that there had been far more to Sam's suggestion this
morning than the fact that Lindsey could use the help and
Erin would enjoy the work. Sam was desperate to get Erin
involved in something productive before her daughter
sank any deeper into the blue funk she was wallowing in.
Erin hadn't left the house unless she'd had to since the day
they'd arrived, and when Sam had asked her yesterday
how school had gone, her once-always-agreeable daughter had declared the kids at school "snobs," the town
"backward," and announced that she wanted to go back
to Los Angeles. She hated Leesburg.

Sam knew how hard it was to be the new kid on the block. With a father in the military, she and her sisters had found themselves in that unenviable position more times than Sam could remember. She also remembered exactly how it felt to not belong. And how hard it was to be the one trying to fit in. Since she'd arrived in Leesburg, she'd been feeling a lot of those old insecurities herself.

A good waitress, like a good bartender, learned to pick up on subtleties. From the speculation in Louella's eyes, she had clearly caught the insecurity in Sam's reply. But Essie had her order ready and Louella had customers waiting. After asking Essie to "add it to the bill," which wasn't necessary because Essie was already doing just that, and telling Sam not to be a stranger at the café, she scooted out the door with her pink boxes and another tidbit to add to the morning bulletin.

"Well, if that was all he said," Essie continued, as if there hadn't just been a two-minute lag in their conversation, "Claire was wrong. We were trying to figure out what you two were talking about after the meeting," she explained, apparently feeling no contrition over openly speculating about the reclusive rancher and the new woman in town. "But it was obviously nothing personal." A benign smile erased the disappointment in the grandmotherly woman's face. "The ranchers and the town's business folk don't always see eye-to-eye when it comes to progress around here, Samantha. Sounds to me like Logan was just putting in his two cents worth."

"There's a problem with *all* the ranchers?"

Essie's ample shoulders lifted in a shrug. "Some of them are more vocal about their opinions than others, but I'd say they were pretty much of the same mind. They all live outside the town limits, so they don't have much say as to what goes on here in town. Not that we don't value their input," she added, to make sure Sam understood the finer workings of the community. "They bring their business in, and their children go to school here, so it's their town, too. The only time there's any real disagreement is when talk turns to development."

Resting the backs of her hands on her hips, Essie cocked her head to one side. "You sure you're not forgetting something he said?" she coaxed. "What you're talking about isn't anything but plain old town business as usual. Nothing at all for you to be looking so concerned about. Not unless you're forgetting something, that is."

Sam hadn't been aware that her agitation showed so much. Or perhaps what she hadn't realized was how astute the older woman was. There were indeed a few details she had omitted from her comments to Essie that would explain why she'd shown up so early asking questions about the man. But Sam hadn't even told her sister how disturbing her encounter with Logan had been—or that she hadn't been able to shake the thought of him even as she'd fixed breakfast this morning and chased down socks and missing homework. The image that had impressed itself in her brain wouldn't go away. The image of a man with the hardest eyes she'd ever seen towering over her as he'd stood with his back to the street lamp.

"He did mention this isn't the first time the subject has come up," she offered, wondering if he had positioned himself that way deliberately, the light coming from behind him allowing him to see clearly, while protecting himself in shadow. "He also said people have been talking about making changes around here for years," she added, immediately dismissing her speculation. She knew precious little about Logan Whitaker, but she doubted he was a man who hid behind anything at all.

Essie's curls were restrained by a gray hairnet and not a single lock moved when the older woman shook her head. "People talk all the time." She waved her hand, the gesture seeming to indicate that a person would be well advised to dismiss fifty percent of what she heard and seriously question the other half. "Doesn't mean they get it right. I just don't recall ever hearing about Logan commenting on anything before. Not that I'm surprised at his position. He's what you might call real conservative. Rather like most of the folks around here," she had to admit. "But Logan... well, he's what I suppose a body might even call old-fashioned."

The feeling that she might have inadvertently landed in the middle of a tug-of-war didn't really bother Sam. There were always holdouts when it came to getting any group of people to agree on something. What caused her frown was the older woman's remark about Logan's conservative nature. Coming from someone who hadn't changed her hairstyle since 1955, such a comment could only mean that his mind-set lurked somewhere around the turn of the last century.

"What do you mean by old-fashioned?" she had to ask, not at all convinced the word had anything to do with the man she'd met last night—unless that was what they called the macho mentality out here.

You are in the heart of good-old-boy country, her sister had concluded, though and she had somehow managed to make the antiquated attitude sound like part of the place's charm.

"What I mean is that he's like the men who first settled this place," Essie said after thinking about it for a moment. "My Forrest was like that. God rest his soul. Hardworking. Responsible.

"That's what I supposed I'd have to say about Logan," Essie went on to conclude after another thoughtful pause. "Not much else you could say about him, what with the way he had to come back from school and take over that ranch after his pa died. And him bringing that boy back with him and having to raise him all by himself to boot.

"Of course, I suspect his ranch foreman's wife did most of the raising, up until she died some years back," she continued, more concerned at the moment with giving credit where it was due than with the way Sam's eyebrows rose. "But I don't believe Logan looked to anyone to help him out with any of it. Not even his brothers. He has two of them, you know. Neither of them has been around for years, though."

It didn't occur to Sam to wonder what had happened to his siblings. Essie's words had brought to mind the picture Sam already had of the hard, mountain of a man who'd all but silenced a room merely by walking into it. The image of that man caring for a small child refused to form. More accurately, she refused to let it. The thought was far too intriguing, far too provocative.

"A child?" she repeated, intrigued anyway. "His child?"

"Spitting image of him. The boy's name is Trevor. He comes in once in a while for my strudel."

"What happened to his mother?"

"From what I understand, she divorced Logan. Or maybe he divorced her. I'm not sure anybody really knows." She offered an amazingly sympathetic smile. "I really don't think you need to worry any more about him showing up last night. Logan strikes me as the kind of man who says his piece once and leaves it at that. As much as he keeps to himself, I doubt you'll be hearing anything more from him."

"I just don't want to make enemies, Essie. And I'm afraid I already have."

The kindly smile faded. The twinkling eyes turned thoughtful. Watching Sam through eyes that had seen the better part of six decades, it almost seemed as if she were trying to decide if Sam was worthy of her advice.

Apparently she'd decided she was.

"You're not going to make any enemies around here as long as you're honest with folks, Samantha. The business community is behind the mayor's plan, and we're the people you have to work with. Don't go selling goods you can't deliver and you'll be fine with us."

The tinkle of the bell over the door announced yet another customer. This time it was the postperson, who swore he'd never get through the rest of his rounds without a couple of Essie's doughnuts. Moments after his departure, an oven timer went off in the back of the shop. Not wanting to take any more of Essie's time, Sam thanked her for her help and then left as Essie hustled off to silence the nerve-racking buzz.

The aroma of freshly baked bread followed Sam outside. That tantalizing scent mingled with the delightful fragrance of clean air and the sweet perfume of the red petunias trailing from the window boxes on the quaint buildings surrounding the town square. It was as clear as the brilliant autumn sky that Essie felt Sam had nothing to worry about where Logan was concerned. He'd just wanted to get his opinion on the record. Therefore, she shouldn't take what had transpired personally.

Under any other circumstances, Sam wouldn't have. She would simply chalk the incident up to differing opinions on a business issue and relegate it to a mental file labeled Work. But it wasn't that simple. Despite what Essie had said, it was personal. Logan had made it that way when he'd threatened her sense of security—what little of it she had—by threatening her job. Granted, that threat had been ever so subtle, and Sam didn't know what he could do to back it up, but it had been there all the same.

Had that threat come from anyone else, Sam might have been able to take Essie's advice to ignore it. Coming from Logan, she could not. Never in her life had she met a man so unshakably confident. Or so overwhelmingly, unnervingly... male.

The simple fact of the matter was that Logan scared her.

The admission wasn't a revelation by any means. As Sam crossed the grassy square toward the small gray building that was her new office, she acknowledged that she'd been wary of him from the moment she'd found him watching her from the back of the library meeting room. But it was another kind of wariness she admitted to now. He scared her not only because he was opposed to what she was hired to do. He frightened her because of the jarring heat she'd felt when his hand had engulfed hers.

He'd felt that heat, too. She was sure of it. She'd sensed it in the way he'd hesitated when her hand had slipped into his. In the moments before he increased the pressure of his fingers, it had almost felt as if he'd been absorbed with the texture of her skin—or perhaps with the feel of it against his own—before he'd caught himself and let her go. He hadn't appeared as startled by that heat as she'd felt. He hadn't even seemed to find it unusual. He'd merely looked displeased.

Since displeasure was easier to cope with than fear, by the end of the week, having heard nothing from or about the man, Sam almost had herself convinced that displeasure was all she felt over the incident, too. What helped the most, though, was knowing that her chances of running into him were roughly equivalent to finding a snowball in the Sahara.

He had to go into town. There was no way around it.

Logan's frown was firmly in place when he reached the back door of the sprawling old ranch house and snatched his hat from its peg. Slapping it on his head as he bounded down the back stairs, he let the screen door slam behind him. He hadn't planned on going into town until tomorrow, but the feed he'd ordered hadn't been delivered and he wasn't going to risk the orphaned calves he was weaning by trusting that the delivery would be made tomorrow. As long as he was going, he figured he might as well run the rest of his errands. No sense making the trip twice.

Thinking he'd swing by the tack shop first and check on the new saddle he'd ordered, Logan headed across the yard and out toward the collection of carefully maintained outbuildings in search of his son. If he'd thought about it sooner, he could have called the school and left a message for Trevor to pick up the feed on his way home after classes. But Logan wasn't a man who wasted energy on what he hadn't done, or what could have been. He hadn't thought of it, so now he'd do the chore himself. He just needed to tell Trev where he was going and make sure there wasn't anything else he needed to pick up.

Seventeen-year-old Trev Whitaker was exactly where he always was at four o'clock in the afternoon. With the horses. Logan's son was as capable and dependable as any of his men and rapidly becoming better with the more skittish animals than even some of the most seasoned hands.

None of those hands were around at the moment. From his office in the house, Logan had seen Hank, his foreman, and Archie, one of the wranglers, ride off toward the north range while he'd been trying to track down his load of feed. The others currently in his employ were all out with the herds or over at the breeding barns.

Yet, it didn't sound as if Trevor was alone. What Logan heard as he breathed in the familiar perfume of wood shavings, horse, leather and liniment, wasn't the usual murmurings of a man to a horse. When he entered the wide, open passageway separating two long rows of stalls, he could hear the hushed sounds of voices. One was nearly as deep as his own. The other, distinctly feminine. Those feminine tones sounded rather foreign in a place that seldom saw anything female that wasn't wandering around on four legs.

"...sister and brother and I would have been fine if she'd let us stay where we were," he heard that girlish voice confide. "I mean, we never even lived anywhere else except in that house, and she just sold everything like none of it mattered and moved us here so she could take this stupid job. So what if she's the director and gets to name her own hours." The unfamiliar voice lowered, the hint of insolence fading as it became more disheartened. "Now, everything's changed and she says *I'm* the one who has to try harder."

"There's no chance of going back?" Logan heard his son ask.

"Not unless I go by myself."

"You'd do that?"

A thoughtful silence preceded a quiet, "I don't know."

"If you don't go back and you don't want to stay here, what do you want?"

In the silence, the soft whinny of a horse joined the thump of horseflesh against the side of a stall. When the girl spoke again, her voice sounded incredibly sad.

"If I could have anything?"

"Sure."

"If I could have anything," she repeated, "I'd want everything to be like it was." She paused, a horse's gentle snuffling filling the lapse. "I guess more than anything, I just want my dad back. I'd give anything to see him again. Even if it was just once. Just to say goodbye. I never got a chance to do that," the girl concluded in a way that made it sound as if she knew she was asking for the impossible. "She wouldn't let me."

Logan's stride hadn't slowed since he'd entered the barn. Not even when he'd first heard the young voices. Now, the sound of his boots muffled by the wood shavings covering the cement floor, he rounded the corner to the section where the mares were kept—and saw a slender young girl in jeans and a short pink tank top leaning over the top of a stall gate. Hair the color of wheat shot with sunshine cascaded down her back and she rested her chin on her crossed arms. Inside the stall, Trev slipped a hackamore over the docile chestnut's head.

Catching Logan's scent, the horse showed more interest in Logan's arrival than did Trevor. She lifted her great head, snuffling and dancing at the sight of the man who'd sat up with her the first three nights after she'd been born, rubbing her because she kept forgetting to breathe.

Looking up to see what Firelight was getting so excited about, the young man shoved his dark hair back from his eyes and muttered, "Hi, Dad." With an expert flick of his fingers, he slipped a leather strap through a metal loop. "The way she's dancing around, I thought that might be you."

Trevor had his father's angular features and the same firm mouth. He had his mother's eyes, though; their clear, pewter gray color the only physical reminder he had of the woman who'd given him birth. In every other respect he was a Whitaker. From the stubborn jaw to the quiet reserve that usually kept him an arm's length from anyone he didn't already know. He was even nearly as big as his father. Already six feet tall, his physique was honed hard from working at his dad's side—something he'd been doing since he was old enough to pick up a hay fork.

"This is Erin," he added with a nod toward the girl who'd just lowered her sneaker-clad feet to the ground and disengaged herself from the stall's four-foot-high gate. "She's never seen a horse up close, so I brought her out to watch while I exercise them."

Erin had turned around when Trevor had first spoken. From where Logan had stopped to rub Firelight's velvety nose, it looked to him as if the girl's eyes were a bit red around the rims. As if the hay might have gotten to her. Or as if she'd been crying. What he noticed mostly, though, was how those hazel eyes widened as they traveled the six feet three inches from the toes of his scarred boots to his battered hat.

Pushing her sunshine-streaked hair back from a face that probably had half the boys in town sighing when they saw her, she managed a smile Logan could only think of as shy.

"There aren't any ranches where we're from," she said to him, sounding as if she was apologizing for that oversight. "I hope you don't mind, Mr. Whitaker. My coming out here, I mean."

She took a step back, seeming embarrassed to have been overheard and maybe a little rattled by the fact that she had to look so far up to see him. He doubted she was more than an inch or two over five feet.

"Her family moved here from Los Angeles a couple of weeks ago." Metal clicked when Trevor clipped the lunge line onto the ring at the base of the hackamore. In his eyes flicked a hint of warning. "Her mom's the lady you were talking to Hank about the other night."

The warning hadn't been necessary. Though Trev had apparently considered it a possibility, given his dad's less-than-complimentary comments during the conversation he'd mentioned, Logan wasn't going to say anything to embarrass the girl. And he'd already figured out who she was. Even if what he'd overheard her saying to his son hadn't brought him to that conclusion, studying the fragile lines of her face would have done it. He'd bet Samantha Gray had looked just like her fifteen or so years ago. Freckles on her nose and all. Though, until now, he honestly hadn't considered that the woman he'd met in town last week could have a daughter old enough to fill out a tank top and jeans the way this young lady did.

Clearing his throat, Logan gave the girl a quick nod to acknowledge the introduction and opened the gate wide so his son could lead out the chestnut.

"Hank and Archie went out to help with strays in the north quarter. I'll help Wes take care of the barn stock when I get back." The rhythmic clop of horse hooves came to a halt when Logan glanced at his watch. The Feed & Hardware didn't close for another hour. "Can you think of anything we need from town?"

"You're going in?"

"Have to. Sharkey's didn't deliver today."

Trevor couldn't think of anything his dad didn't already have on his list. At least, that was what he said after he'd looked over the scrap of paper Logan handed him. With a sort of ambivalent amusement, Logan doubted the boy even noticed what was on the list to begin with, much less considered what wasn't on it. Not with a pretty young thing like Erin watching his every move.

She was the first girl his son had ever brought to the ranch. As Logan considered the significance of that event, he had to admit she could well be the first female to set foot on it in ten years.

A feeling Logan couldn't begin to identify accompanied him out of the stables and across the open compound to where he'd parked his pickup. He'd seen the way his son's glance had strayed over Erin Gray's coltish, but definitely feminine, form. He knew exactly what his son had been thinking, too, and it hadn't been about how she'd never seen a horse up close before—or how unfair it had been of her mother to upend their lives as she had. Just because Logan tended to suppress his need for a woman didn't mean he could expect a healthy seventeen-year-old to pretend the opposite sex didn't exist.

Logan slammed the door of the pickup with more force than was necessary. Until a week ago, he had been doing fine suppressing that need. Eighteen-hour days of working himself until he damn near dropped did a fair job of dampening the restlessness he sometimes felt. That restlessness had no real direction, anyway. At last it hadn't. Now when he felt it, he found his thoughts straying to the memory of eyes the color of rich coffee and of a mouth that looked so soft and full a man could drive himself crazy thinking how it would feel on his skin.

Logan jammed the truck into gear. Samantha Gray was like a burr under a saddle as far as he was concerned. He didn't like what she was doing to the town and he didn't like the way she made him feel. He liked even less that she'd sold her house out from under her children and taken them so far away from their father, apparently without allowing them the opportunity to say goodbye.

"...moved us here so she could take this stupid job..."

Logan didn't bother to consider why the girl's words caused his stomach to churn. He wasn't a man who believed in analyzing when it came to gut reactions. Too often, flipping something over to see what lay beneath it revealed all manner of ugliness, and there were some things best left right where they lay. He knew only that he hadn't liked what he'd heard—and that he had little use for a woman who put her own needs ahead of her children's.

By the time Logan turned off the two-lane highway at the Y and had followed the curve in the road to where it became Leesburg's Main Street, he'd pretty much decided there wasn't too much about Samantha Gray that he did appreciate. That went double for her presence when he walked into the hardware store and found himself slowing his stride to a stop.

The cultured tones of a melodious, feminine voice rode softly over the twang of country music and static coming from the radio behind Leesburg Feed & Hardware's cluttered counter. "You mean this, Phil?"

From where Logan stopped by the irrigation supplies, he saw her glance at the label on a roll of white tape and hold it up.

"Or would this be better?" In her other hand, she had a can of plumbers' putty.

When he'd first come in, Logan had headed to the far side of the cluttered store to get a box of nails. Now, walking toward the front, he nudged up the brim of his hat to dispassionately study the slim figure bent over a low rack of plumbing materials. She was dressed a little more practically today in trim slacks and some sort of oversize blue shirt that hid every curve he suspected she possessed. Practical or not, she still didn't look to him like she had any business being in the town.

"You might have better luck with the tape, ma'am," he heard Phil call back over the aisles. "And the wrench you're going to need is over on the wall by the saw blades and hammers and such. You'll probably need new washers, too. Let me finish ringing up this order and I'll get 'em for you."

In the bright fluorescent lights, her pale hair shimmered with hints of gold and silver as she shook her head. "That's okay. I'll manage." Her voice lost its volume. "I think," she muttered.

Listening to the clunk and ring of Gil Webster's coveted old-fashioned cash register, a garishly ornate thing that had sat in that same spot for as long as he could remember, Logan watched Samantha rise. In one hand she held the roll of tape and an eight-inch section of plastic pipe. Pressed under her opposite arm was a magazine-size book. Even encumbered as she was, she still managed to look graceful as she dipped her head to one side and tucked her hair behind one ear.

The look on her face was one of concentration and maybe a little frustration. Until she looked up. The moment she saw him, she went stock-still.

Twenty feet of worn plank flooring separated them. Even from that distance, Logan could see the uncertainty flicker in her eyes, her hesitation as marked as that of a stunned doe. Yet, she didn't back away. She couldn't. Not with a wall full of gaskets and hoses and pipes behind her. The thought had occurred to her, though. Logan would have sworn to it in the moments before his glance slipped to the cautious smile forming on her very appealing mouth. Even when it was as clear as the small stones in her ears that she found his presence disconcerting, she refused to be anything but friendly.

Since he'd never been a man to play games, he had no time for people who did. "The wrenches are that way." Hitching his thumb over his shoulder, he glanced toward hands that looked far too feminine to be familiar with the items she held. He had no trouble at all remembering how small her hand had felt in his callused grip. How incredibly, impossibly soft. He was not particularly appreciative of the fact that something so brief should have made such an impression. "On the back wall."

Samantha opened her mouth just as the noisy cash register went silent. But it was the lazy drawl of the proprietor he heard. "Is that you, Logan?"

"Yeah, Gil," he called back, his position behind a rack of electrical supplies blocking the store owner's view of him. "It's me."

Something heavy scraped across the counter. "Didn't see you come in. What brings you into town this time of the week?"

"I need a few bags of grain. And some ground soy if you've got any."

"Oh, yeah," Gil muttered, as if he'd just remembered something critical. "I heard Sharkey's truck broke down." The noise started up again, only this time he talked right over it. "Their driver didn't get out to the Circle J, either. You want your regular order as long as you're here?"

"I'd appreciate it."

"I'll get it together soon as I finish this and help Mrs. Gray. Unless you want to help her for me. This here's going to take me a minute."

For a moment Logan didn't reply. He just stood weighing his options. Not finding either one terribly pleasing, he finally muttered, "Sure," in a tone that must have been considerably less than enthusiastic, judging from the quickness of her response.

"That's really not necessary," she told him, looking very much as if she wished he'd move since he was blocking the aisle. "I don't want to take up your time."

"You'll be saving me time. The sooner Gil gets to my order, the sooner I can get out of here." Without waiting for her to tempt him with another excuse, he turned on his heel, heading back the way he'd come. "What size wrench do you need? A ten-inch?" he suggested, assuming she needed it for the pipe in her hand.

He'd reached the end of the aisle before he heard the light tap of her shoes behind him. Another few seconds passed before he heard her say quietly, "I'm not sure."

A half dozen steps later, he came to a halt by the display of hand tools. Hands on his hips, he turned to ask exactly what she needed the wrench for and saw that she'd opened the book she'd had tucked under her arm.

Concentrating on what she was reading, she came up beside him and stopped an arm's length away. Out of curiosity he took a step closer, his glance swinging toward the pages upon which she seemed so intent. His focus had scarcely shifted to the elementary-looking plumbing diagram before his thoughts short-circuited.

She stood near his elbow, the top of her head barely reaching his shoulder. With her head bent as it was, her face was concealed from him. He could see only her hair, thick, shiny and looking as soft as corn silk, and the back of her neck where her hair had parted over it. That faint strip of exposed skin looked like cream-colored velvet. But it wasn't just how impossibly soft she looked that made him feel as if one of his bulls had just rammed into his gut. It was the scent of spring clinging to her, something light and feminine and as gentle as the sound of her voice when she looked up at him a moment later.

"I guess a ten-inch is right," she offered, deferring to his judgment. "Aren't they adjustable?"

The bull backed up, charged and hit again. The feathery fringe of her lashes swept up, her eyes meeting his to reveal an apologetic smile and a healthy hint of doubt about what she was trying to do. It was the vulnerability underscoring it all that hit him hardest, though. He hadn't expected it. And it didn't fit at all with the image of her that had been shaping in his mind.

That the image might not be accurate—or that it was at all self-protective—was not a thought he allowed himself to consider.

The muscle in his jaw working, he tipped the book up with one finger so he could read the title.

The words *Plumbing Made Easy* were emblazoned over the silhouette of a drainpipe. The book didn't look like anything Gil would have carried in the rack of do-it-yourself and gardening books over by the seed display.

"Where did you get that?"

"At the library."

A faint frown flashed across his forehead. "What are you trying to fix?"

"My kitchen sink. My son forgot we don't have a garbage disposal in this house. I got the sink unclogged. But now it leaks more than before."

Logan's eyes narrowed on her face. He wasn't going to ask what she'd done unclogging it that would have made a leak worse. Or why it was leaking in the first place. He also wasn't going to ask himself why he was standing there wondering why she'd decided to check a book out of the library and tackle the plumbing herself instead of asking around for a handyman to do it.

"Here." He snagged one of the wrenches from the hooks and held it out to her. "This ought to do it. What else do you need?"

It was with no small amount of trepidation that Samantha took the tool he held out to her. The cool gray-blue eyes studying her from beneath the brim of a dusty gray hat held what looked suspiciously like curiosity. She couldn't be certain, though. That hat shadowed his eyes, making it hard to discern his expression—which was probably exactly why he wore it so low to begin with.

He wasn't hiding from anyone by concealing his thoughts, she finally realized. He was simply keeping them at a disadvantage.

Wishing she'd thought to keep a few of Jim's tools out when she'd had her two-days-before-moving-day garage sale, she jerked her attention back to the diagram. "I need a...slip joint washer and compression nuts and sleeves."

Logan said nothing. He simply turned on his heel and walked back over to where she'd first turned to find him watching her.

He was obviously a man of few words. Wondering if he was always so reserved, or if it was only her presence that made him so reticent, she took the items he handed her. A moment later, having confirmed that she had everything, she offered him a quiet "Thank you" and left him to deposit her purchases on the counter. She didn't know which bothered her more. That he intimidated the daylights out of her, or the irritation she felt with herself for feeling that way.

"That do it for you?" Gil asked.

"I hope so." She eyed her purchases, wondering how men could possibly enjoy shopping for this sort of thing.

"I'm beginning to think I should take out stock in this place. This is my third trip this week."

The older man didn't return her slightly strained smile. Switching his wad of chew to his other cheek, Gil's expression grew thoughtful. "You know, Mrs. Gray, putting new weather stripping on your back door and replacing a few missing drawer handles is one thing, but what you're planning on tackling here requires some expertise. There's a plumber over in Fredricksburg. Might take a day or two for him to get over this way, but it might be cheaper in the long run for you to call him."

From the skeptical look in his eyes when he added her book to the bag, she knew he was thinking she'd probably just wind up calling in a professional, anyway. Truth be known, she'd have loved to call a plumber. But a plumber wasn't in the budget at the moment, and a leaking kitchen sink wasn't something she could let go until her next paycheck. There were a lot of little things she'd had to learn to do herself in the past year.

"I'll manage," she told Gil, because she really had no choice.

With a faint shrug, the burly gentleman glanced toward Logan as if to say it was her time to waste if she wanted and muttered, "Suit yourself."

Since she was a little iffy on the project herself, she didn't mind Gil's skepticism. It was Logan's she wished she didn't have to contend with. Not that she minded him looking so sure she hadn't a clue what she was doing. What unnerved her was the dispassionate scrutiny beneath the doubt. It was almost as if he were comparing her to someone. Or, perhaps, as if he were measuring her somehow.

It was the latter impression that stuck when his eyes moved up to hers a few moments later. From the steadiness of his gaze it was apparent that, whatever his criteria had been, she had definitely come up lacking.

It's nothing personal, Essie had said. But Essie hadn't seen the way Logan looked at her.

Wanting nothing more than to escape to the haven of her new home, imperfect though it was, she picked up her bag and thanked Gil for his help. Logan undoubtedly didn't want to be bothered with her thanks again, so she simply did what he did when he didn't feel like talking and gave him a nod before she headed out the door.

She hadn't realized she was holding her breath until she stepped out onto the sidewalk and the door clattered to a close behind her.

Because Sam hadn't had that much to do at her office this afternoon, she'd brought Amy and Michael with her while she finished up her errands. At the moment, they were sitting on the wooden bench facing the street, ruining their dinner with ice-cream cones from the Sweet Shoppe.

Until a few minutes ago, Sam thought, it had definitely been one of her better days. Her work was going slowly, but well. Michael had made 100 percent on his first math test, and Amy had slept all night last night in her own bed. Granted, Amy had managed to stay put only because she'd wanted to be near the orphaned bird she'd brought home so she could give it its 4:00 a.m. feeding, which Sam had been stuck with, of course. But Sam didn't get too picky about how a milestone was met when it came to progress with one of her children.

Even Erin had made a stab at coming around. Though she worried Sam with how quiet she had become. Erin was spending two afternoons a week at Lindsey's boutique. By some miracle, she'd also changed her mind and gone out for the volleyball team. She was at practice right now.

That meant, at that very moment, all was well with her children. So Sam took heart in that fact and, refusing to look behind her, she smiled at the little girl who'd just caught sight of her.

There was something about seeing Amy flip back her long, blond ponytail and grin at her with her ice cream mustache that went a long way to ease the tension that had crept into Sam's shoulders. A little more of that uneasiness dissipated when she spotted Michael crawling around the end of the bench trying to catch the disgusting-looking bug with which he no doubt planned to terrorize his sisters. At the moment, things were almost...normal.

Checking to make sure that Michael's quarry wasn't something poisonous, seeing that it was only something brown with a zillion fuzzy legs, Sam ignored the dirt he was grinding into the knees of his jeans and knelt down in front of Amy. Michael, incredibly, had used his napkins. The little girl had obviously forgotten what the ones wadded in her fist were for.

Sam had the double chocolate moustache reduced to a faint brown smear and had deposited a quick kiss on Amy's turned-up nose when she finally rose. As she did, she glanced to the side and felt herself go still.

Logan stood by the loading platform at the far end of the building, his booted feet planted apart and a huge bag slung over one shoulder. He was quite pointedly watching her.

Seeing her mother's smile fade, or perhaps seeing the man watching them, Amy reached for her hand.

A few scrambled heartbeats later, Logan turned away.

Chapter Three

The first time the high school principal called Sam, she was sure there had been some mistake. Erin had never skipped a class in her life. Sam was therefore absolutely positive that the man had confused her daughter with some other child the morning he'd called to check on Erin's absence. Sam had even dropped Erin off herself that day because it had been raining, so she knew her daughter had arrived there safely.

It hadn't been a mistake, though. Erin wasn't in school. And by the time she arrived home that afternoon—dropped off by a boy in what Michael described as an "awesome red pickup," Sam had practically paced a trench in the living room carpet waiting for her.

As if Sam wasn't upset enough, Erin immediately compounded the problem by acting as if she had no idea what her mother was talking about.

"Of course I went to school," she muttered, hugging her brown knapsack after she pulled it from her shoulder. "You took me, remember?"

"I know you went to school, Erin. The point is that you didn't *stay* there. What I want to know is where you were and who that boy was."

Seeing that her mother wasn't backing down, and too new at deception to be any good at it, Erin sent her mother a militant glare. "I was with Trev. Trev Whitaker," she added, saying the name as if she was sure her mother hadn't a clue who she was talking about.

The fact that her mother knew exactly who she was talking about was completely lost on Erin. The name didn't jar Sam as it might have, though. The principal, who had struck Sam as being more concerned with Erin's influence on the other students than with the girl's need to fit in, had mentioned to Sam that Erin's only friend appeared to be "the Whitaker boy," whom he'd described as a bit of a loner. He'd also added that he was a smart young man who was very mature for his age and very much like his father.

The latter two traits had done little to put Sam's mind at ease. She tried very hard, however, to keep her ambivalence about Logan from influencing the situation. As insecure as she felt about what was happening with Erin, she didn't know if she was succeeding or not.

She did know that she didn't want her daughter spending time with someone who encouraged her to skip school.

"He didn't encourage me." Erin's reaction was immediate. "He only has classes half days sometimes, and I told him it was okay."

"Told him what was okay?" Shaking her head in a need to understand, Sam reached for her daughter. "That you could skip school?"

Erin moved back, forcing Sam's hands to slide from her shoulders.

"Can I go to my room now?"

"Erin, we need to talk about this."

"Come on, Mom. I didn't do anything you need to worry about."

Sam wanted desperately to believe her. She was also desperate to keep her daughter from shutting her out. That was why she didn't ground her—which would have totally defeated her efforts to keep Erin involved with her new school. She did tell Erin, however, that she wasn't to spend any more time with Trevor until after she brought the boy in to meet her.

The second time the principal called, three days later, was a repeat of the first, minus Sam's insistence that he must have made a mistake. Erin hadn't skipped a whole day this time. Only her last two classes. Still, when Sam confronted Erin late that particular afternoon, she wasn't quite so lenient. She was also convinced that spending so much time with just one person—namely Trevor—was not a good idea and told Erin, very patiently, she'd thought, that Erin was not to accept any more rides from him. She was to walk straight home after school on the days she didn't have volleyball practice and stay with her brother and sister, or help at Lindsey's shop.

That had been a week ago. And for a solid week, Erin had gone about her chores at home in grudging silence. Not looking forward to another evening playing a silent game of battle of the wills, Sam called Lindsey to invite her over for dinner. The kids adored their aunt, and Lindsey's company would be a great buffer.

"It's only hot dogs and beans, but at least you won't have to heat it yourself. You could probably use the break," Sam told her sister, hoping she wasn't sounding as desperate for the company as she felt. "You've been working on that department store order every night for two weeks. Just come with Erin when you two finish up at the shop tonight."

"I'd really like to," Sam heard Lindsey say, missing the confusion in her voice as she motioned for Michael to turn down the volume of the beeps on his electronic game. "But I've got a meeting tonight. And Erin's not here, Sam. She called a few minutes ago and said she had volleyball practice. Didn't you know that?"

Puzzled, Sam glanced at the calendar beside the kitchen wall phone to be sure she had the right day. She was entirely capable of scrambling the days of the week. Or of forgetting who was to be where on any given day. That's why she had notes for everything. Even now she was staring at a neon pink reminder that 4-H orientation for Amy was on Thursday night. Half-covered under that one was a brilliant blue square reminding her to bake cupcakes for Michael's Cub Scout meeting tomorrow.

Even before Sam realized she hadn't lost track of which child was supposed to be where, puzzlement turned to foreboding. Erin had skipped school twice last week. Was she now skipping work?

"Are you going to be there for a while, Lindsey?"

"Until six," came her sister's now curious voice. "What's going on?"

"I don't know. Nothing, I hope. I'll call you back in a while."

Within seconds Sam had hung up the phone, peeled the electric blue note from the calendar and slapped it on the front of the oven so she wouldn't forget Michael's cupcakes, and hollered for Amy and Michael to get in the car. They were going for a quick run over to the high school.

"Do I hafta go?" Michael wanted to know.

"Yes," she said without hesitation. "And no, you may not take your sister's bird. Put it back in its shoe box before she finds out you're pestering it and stop trying to feed it that poor bug."

"Aw, Mom."

"Aw, Michael," she mimicked, and shooed him out the door.

It took two minutes to get from the house to the grade school. One more minute to continue to the end of Summer Street, turn left at the football field and drive the long block to the two-story, red brick high school. Five minutes after that, Sam didn't know whether she was supposed to explode or panic.

Erin didn't have volleyball practice. There was a practice all right, but according to the coach, who also happened to be Erin's math teacher, Erin hadn't gone out for the team. As far as he knew, she'd never even expressed any interest in it. What made the situation worse was that, according to one of the chattier girls Sam spoke with in the gym, Erin had been seen driving off with Trevor.

"I heard him ask if she wanted to work the horses with him," the girl said, sounding a little envious of the newcomer's friendship with the senior boy. "They left right after the last bell."

"For where?" was Sam's perfectly logical, and admirably calm, response.

The teenager's slow blink seemed to imply she couldn't believe Sam had to ask such a question. Since Sam was from the city, though, the girl apparently decided she was operating with a handicap and very politely replied, "To the RW. The Whitakers' ranch," she expanded. "That's where their horses are, ma'am."

It didn't occur to Sam to go home and wait for Erin. Nor did she bother to figure out what compelled her to do what she did. Maternal protectiveness. Disappointment. Anger. Or some combination of the three. Not only had Erin lied to both her mother and her aunt, she had deliberately defied Sam's instructions about cooling it with Trevor.

By the time Sam left Amy and Michael with Mrs. Gunther and was turning off the narrow highway onto the entrance road of Logan's ranch, every ounce of indecision she'd ever felt about doing what was best for her children had wadded itself into a knot in her stomach. As hard as it had been for them to adjust to life without their father, it had only been since the move that Erin had turned into someone Sam no longer recognized. Sam understood the girl's upheaval. At least she hoped she did. What Sam didn't know was how to get Erin to understand that the move had been necessary for a number of reasons. What bothered her even more was that she wasn't at all sure how to deal with her daughter. That scared the daylights out of her.

The thought of having to deal with Logan didn't help matters much, either.

As Sam crested yet another of the rolling hills, a house came into view a half mile down the road. The land outside Leesburg was far from the flat, arid stretches she'd always envisioned at the mention of Texas. Here, in Hill Country, the land undulated with the gentle swells of green and gold grasses and lush, verdant trees. In the spring, there were wildflowers. Millions of them, turning the land purple and red, yellow, blue and pink. Sam had seen postcards of those flowers, and already envisioned pictures of those vibrant blooms on the promotional materials she was designing. But her job was the last thing on her mind at the moment, and the only colors she noticed now were the reddish browns and whites of the horned steers watching her pass from where they lay in the field with their legs tucked beneath them.

Logan's ranch was situated around and through a valley that seemed to stretch on forever. From her vantage point, Sam could easily see the huge complex of outbuildings forming the heart of the operation. A wide and winding river meandered to the north, miles of fencing locked in the south and east, and rises of granite blocked her view of the west. It was the modest house situated in front of what looked like a huge barn that had her attention, however. Logan's black truck was parked next to it. So was the red one Trevor drove.

There was no answer at the front door of the white wood and red brick house. Nor were any signs of life visible through the door's window. Or in any of the four, white-framed windows lining the long porch when she peered into them. Her glance through the door's window, however, revealed an interior that appeared as spare in appointments as the porch itself. Only a grandfather clock sat in the wide hallway. The bare wood floor gleamed in the late-afternoon sun.

Sam turned back to the porch. There were hooks for a porch swing, but nothing hanging on them. No mat welcomed visitors. Even the terra-cotta pots, looking as if they might have once held some sort of bloom, sat empty by each of the three columns supporting the porch roof. It was almost as if the pots themselves now sufficed as decoration.

Not allowing herself to wonder why she'd been struck more by what wasn't there instead of what was, concerning herself only with what she would say to Erin when she found her, Sam ducked beneath the sweeping branches of a sprawling live oak and followed the low white fence that separated the house's grassy yard from the rest of the enormous property.

The outbuildings were farther away than they had appeared from the top of the hill. The nearest, an open garage in which were parked a tractor, a fork lift and, incongruously, an old, antiquated sportscar, was nearly a city block away. Across the huge expanse of hard-packed dirt sat an enormous barn and metal-fenced bull pens. Beyond that were corrals and a stable.

It was from the direction of the pens, one of which contained an enormously stocky, decidedly ill-tempered-looking white-faced bull, that a wiry cowhand wearing a hat the color of dirt sauntered toward her. Intent on his destination, he didn't notice her until she called out to him.

"Excuse me." She moved closer, lifting her hand against the glare of the setting sun bouncing off a silver horse trailer. "I'm looking for my daughter."

At first the man simply stopped in the tractor tracks criss-crossing the heavily traveled area, looking at her as if she'd spoken in a language he didn't understand. About six seconds later, he snatched his crumpled hat from his head.

"Beg your pardon, ma'am?"

"I'm looking for... Trevor," she told him, thinking it would be easier to find Erin by finding who she was with, rather than by explaining who Erin was. "Or Mr. Whitaker," she added, when she saw the man frowning. "Can you tell me where I might find either one of them?"

There were streaks of dirt on the man's freckled and sunburned face. He ran two of those streaks together when he rubbed his chin with the back of his hand.

"I'm sorry, ma'am," he drawled, slapping his hat back over the coppery hair that had been flattened beneath it.

"Don't know for sure that either one of them's around at the moment. The boss is out with one of the herds. Least he was a while ago. Got a steer stuck in some brambles," he added, looking as if he'd been doing some steer wrestling himself, dusty and disheveled as he was. "As for Trev, you might find him down at the stables. Or in one of the corrals behind it. That's that long white building down there."

"Thank you..."

"Archie," he supplied when he realized she was waiting for his name. "Archie Oakes, ma'am." The hat came off again, the gesture accompanied this time with a nod and what would have been a handshake, had he not realized that his hand was dirty and he couldn't offer a dirty hand to a lady.

He wiped his hand off, anyway, using the side of his denims, which were just as badly in need of washing. "If you can't find him, come back up to the workshop." He lifted his hat toward what looked to be some sort of mechanic's shop in the opposite direction. "I'll be in there working on chutes."

The man was being as polite as he knew how to be. Touched by his almost old-fashioned manners, Sam smiled. "Thank you, Mr. Oakes," she said, her gratitude seeming to deepen the color of the man's sunburn. "I'll do that."

The thought that the fates might spare her an encounter with Logan and let her find Trevor and Erin before she ran into him, lasted just long enough for Sam to reach the first of the fenced circles the very helpful Archie had indicated. It was empty. Of people, anyway. The half dozen horses that had been turned out into the enclosures, most of them the color of dark cinnamon and all of them magnificent, eyed her briefly then went back to swatting at flies with their tails or wandering the perimeter of the metal pipe fencing.

"Looking for someone?"

With the warm breeze shifting directions, Sam couldn't quite tell where that dark and disturbing rumble had come from. There was no doubt in her mind, however, who that deep-timbred voice belonged to. It sang along her nerve endings, taunting her with its richness, and its displeasure.

No more anxious for the encounter than Logan sounded, Sam slowly turned, marveling at how swiftly the knot in her stomach had doubled.

The muffled thud of horse hooves now came from the direction of the voice—which had come from inside the stables. The long, wide building was open on both ends, but because she was several yards from the structure and because the sun was so bright behind it, she couldn't really do much more than discern shapes inside. There were two shapes in the middle of the passageway—a horse and a man holding its reins.

The man moved to one side, opened a gate, then patted the rump of the horse. A moment later, the huge animal having disappeared from her view, the gate closed and the shadow of the man loomed toward her—only to stop at what looked to be a protrusion of some sort sticking out from a wall.

The hat came off and Logan bent over. A moment later, she heard the sound of water splashing on concrete and saw him lift a hose to the back of his neck. He turned off the water, pushed his hair straight back, and the hat went back on.

Sam started toward the building. Dragging in a lungful of air that smelled of earth and hay and animals, she stopped a few feet from the wide, rolled-back doors and steeled herself to face him.

"I'm looking for my daughter."

It had been on the tip of her tongue to add that she thought Erin was with his son, and that she'd appreciate it if he'd just tell her where they were so she could get Erin and leave. She would have said precisely that, too, had shadow not turned to substance when Logan walked to a halt six feet in front of her.

His proximity wasn't what made her go so suddenly still. It was the way he stood with his feet planted apart and his worn chambray shirt hanging open over his very solid—and very naked— chest. He'd pulled that shirt out of his jeans, rather recently she would guess from the sharpness of the creases and wrinkles in its tails. It was damp under the arms from sweat, and wet around the collar from perspiration and being doused by the hose. Droplets of water glittered in the wood brown hair flaring over skin only a shade or two lighter than his tanned and weathered face. There were droplets, too, where he'd splashed the cooling liquid on himself. They clung to his unshaven jaw, glistening against the raw, angry red scratches on his cheek and ran in rivulets over the scratches along the side of his strong throat.

As if he knew what had her attention, he raised his arm and wiped those droplets off with his torn shirtsleeve.

It wasn't propriety that made Sam's glance fall to the toes of his Western boots—boots that clearly served utility over style and looked as beaten and battered as the man himself. What caused her glance to jerk down felt more like self-preservation. He'd obviously done battle with the brambles that had caught the steer, and possibly with the steer itself. Yet, even sweaty, dirty and scratched up—or maybe because of it—her first reaction had been to reach toward those fiery-looking scrapes and ask if he was all right. For some reason she couldn't begin to explain, she had the feeling no one ever showed much concern for him, and her own had been there before she could even question it.

Disconcerting as that had been, even more so was the sharp, unmistakable tug of heat low in her stomach.

Self-preservation had forced her glance down. That same survival instinct now coaxed her eyes up to the granitelike set of his jaw. That her glance had to pass the rippled muscles of his abdomen and the dark whorl of hair arrowing behind his scarred brown leather belt couldn't be helped. She simply couldn't let him know how easily he rattled her.

She had the feeling he knew anyway.

"Your daughter isn't here."

Sam's eyes jerked to his. His gaze hadn't wavered. Steady and shadowed beneath the curled brim of his hat, his eyes held hers with the faint hint of antagonism that had been there since the moment they'd met.

"I'm sorry. I was under—"

"Trev took her riding," he said, graciously relieving her of misunderstanding what he meant. "I don't imagine they'll be much longer. He has chores to do."

Confusion swept Sam's features. "Riding? Erin doesn't ride."

"Sure she does."

"My daughter's never been on a horse in her life, Mr. Whitaker. Not even a pony," she added, as visions of plaster and broken bones, or worse, elicited a totally new kind of fear. "She doesn't know the first thing about handling an animal that size."

"I hate to contradict you," he told her, not sounding contrite at all, "but your daughter has been on a horse. I wouldn't say she's ready to go entering any rodeos, but she can ride." From his back pocket, he pulled out a red handkerchief. Gingerly, he touched it to one of the angrier scratches on his cheek, his jaw hardening against the sting of salty perspiration. "You might know that yourself if you'd stay home with your kids."

It was warm outside. Somewhere near eighty, Sam had heard someone comment today. With the heat moving into her cheeks, it suddenly felt much warmer.

She took a step closer. "What did you say?"

"You heard me," he muttered, and started to turn away.

Without thinking, she caught his forearm to stop him.

The impression of having just grabbed solid stone registered on the periphery of Sam's thoughts. It also occurred to her, vaguely, that like stone, Logan was probably just about as yielding. He made no effort to pull away. He merely glanced pointedly at her hand, making it clear that he expected her to make the move that would give him back his space.

With her fingers clutching his forearm, her palm hot from the heat and dampness radiating through the cotton sleeve, her small, slender hand looked almost like a child's. For one panicky moment, she felt overpowered and her courage faltered. Logan was not a man to be pushed, and he clearly didn't like being crowded. But she couldn't let his terse conclusion go.

"Explain what you mean by that remark," she insisted, though, for her own sake, she did drop her hand and take a step away. "Are you implying that I'm neglecting my children?"

"Lady, look. This is your problem."

"You're the one who made the insinuation."

That was true enough. And he looked very much as if he wished he'd just kept his mouth shut. "I just call 'em like I see 'em. Like I said, Trev and Erin should be along anytime now. You're welcome to wait here, if you want. I have work to do."

Turning on the heel of his battered boot, he started for the shadows.

"Is it all women, or is it just me you dislike so much?"

The abruptness of her question, or perhaps the quiet way she posed it, stopped Logan in his tracks. He was not a man often given to explaining himself. Or to offering his opinion unless it was something he felt strongly about. Even then, he didn't always share his thoughts. When he did, he saw no point in beating around the bush. Especially when someone kept pushing.

"I have nothing against a woman...so long as she's someone else's problem. As for you, I just don't much care for what you're doing. Not with the town and not with your kids. At least not with your oldest," he was forced to qualify because he really couldn't fault what he'd seen of her with her younger ones outside the feed and hardware store. "I already told you how I feel about that job you took, but that's nothing compared to how I feel about a mother who's so preoccupied with her life that she doesn't know what's going on with her own kids. You didn't even know your daughter had been coming out here, did you?"

Sam didn't get a chance to answer. Taken aback by his quiet vehemence, she started to tell him the situation was not at all what it seemed. But trying to figure out how to do that without admitting that her daughter was hardly talking to her anymore caused her to hesitate.

That hesitation seemed to be all the answer he needed.

"I didn't think so." His voice grew tighter. "If you had, I imagine she'd have told you she's been learning to ride the past couple of weeks. There are probably a couple of other things she'd have told you, too. Or maybe she has," he added, jamming the handkerchief back in his pocket again, "and you just aren't listening."

"Told me what?" Too amazed at his audacity to consider how deep his anger ran—or why it was even there—she could only look up in bewilderment. And hope. "Has she talked to you?"

"Not to me," he muttered in a way that made her think he'd expected her to look a little less encouraged and a lot more guilty. "I've heard her talking to my son."

"What has she said?"

His eyes narrowed. "Ask her."

Hating the position he was putting her in, Sam's chin edged up ever so slightly. "I'm asking you. You seem to think there's something I should know, so tell me what it is."

"Look, lady..."

"I need to know." She saw no way around the admission. "She's not talking to me the way she used to."

"Maybe she would if you'd spend a little more time on her... and a little less trying to turn Leesburg into a metropolis."

For a man who tended to keep his opinions to himself, once a person got the knack of prying out answers, he was actually quite generous with his conclusions. At least that was what Sam thought, as she stared at the implacable blue eyes boring into hers. As upset as she already was with her daughter, to have this arrogant, insensitive... cowboy... stand there in judgment of her, made maintaining her composure an act of sheer will.

"Mr. Whitaker," she began, refusing to rise to his bate. "I would dearly love to stay home with my children and be homeroom mom and Cub Scout leader and all the other things I could do if I didn't have to work. But the fact of the matter is that I have to support my children somehow. Whether or not you approve of how I choose to do that is your problem. All I care about right now is whatever you've heard Erin say."

Logan didn't seem at all impressed with her calm but brutally honest response. For several seconds, he stood watching her, seeming to weigh whether or not he cared to share the information she wanted. Or, perhaps, what he wrestled with was whether or not he wanted to be bothered with her at all.

As if he wanted to be truly perverse about it, he waited a full thirty seconds before he answered.

"She wants to go back to Los Angeles."

Disappointment leaked out with her sigh. "I know that," she told him, thinking she should have known better than to hope for a break with Erin. She was on her own with her. Just like she was on her own with everything else.

"She knows we can't go back. Even if I could afford it...which I can't," she added, because the insurance money was gone and all she had left was her salary, "the choice to move from the city was deliberate. It's hard enough on children to have only one parent, but a single parent in a city has twice as much to worry about. You're raising a child alone," she said, daring to hope he might understand her concerns, even if he'd never had to face them. "Would you have wanted to raise your son in a place where you had to worry about his safety every time he set foot out the door by himself?"

Her appeal gained her nothing. Not only did he ignore the question, it only added to the edge in his voice. "She's also upset because you didn't let her say goodbye to her father."

Logan didn't expect the pain he saw slice through Sam's eyes in the moments before she closed them. He'd expected defensiveness. Or, possibly, more of the unflappable calm she seemed to possess in abundance. But the pain caught him totally unprepared. So did her too-quiet response.

"I didn't know she was still upset about that." Defeat entered her voice, puzzling him even more. "I explained every way I knew how that it was best that she didn't."

"Maybe it wasn't best for her."

At his suggestion, Sam hesitated.

"Do you know what happened to her father?" she finally asked, it never occurring to her that Logan didn't know her husband was dead, only that he might not have been privy to the circumstances. "Did Erin tell you . . . or Trevor," she amended, because Logan had said he'd only overheard her daughter talking with his son, "how her father died? Kids of cops know there's a chance they'll lose their dad every time he goes to work, but my kids never thought it would happen to them. To them their dad was invincible. He just didn't happen to be invincible when it came to a gang and a sawed-off shotgun."

Expecting nothing from Logan but the tense silence she got, Sam missed the way his eyes closed when she shoved her fingers through her hair. The gesture spoke of nerves stretched to their limits. "I explained that they needed to remember him the way they'd last seen him," she continued, because, even as frustrated with Logan as she felt, she wanted him to understand why she'd denied her daughter such a reasonable-sounding request. "The little one's accepted that. But Erin needed more.

"The children were told that their father had been shot in the line of duty," she explained, fighting the memory of Jim's partner appearing at her door. He hadn't had to say a word for her to know that something had gone horribly wrong. He'd just stood there, looking at her with his eyes filled with tears. "The department psychologist thought it would be best to tell them only what I thought they could handle. So I only told them that he'd taken a shot in his chest. That seemed to be enough, until Erin wanted to see him.

"To say goodbye," she added, too busy holding back the ache in her voice to wonder why Logan winced. "That was when I told her what they hadn't even told me until after Jim's partner took me to the morgue. That there wasn't anything left to see. Her father's face was gone because that was where he'd taken the other hit."

She couldn't hold Logan's glance. Something that bore a suspicious resemblance to sympathy had slipped over the hard angles of his face. No more comfortable with that emotion than he looked with it himself, she concentrated on the scraggly clumps of grass stubbornly growing at the end of the stable. There was no water there and the hard dirt would make them fight for every millimeter their roots gained, but they were determined to survive.

It was pretty pathetic, she thought, that she could identify so strongly with crabgrass.

"Erin wanted to go anyway," she heard him quietly conclude.

"And I wouldn't let her. So now she blames me for not letting her see him that one last time, and I have no idea what to do about it. All I know is that, as hard as it was for her to lose him, it would have been even harder for her to deal with seeing him.''

Sam was shaking. From the memories. And, surprisingly, from anger. But she wasn't sure if her anger was with the man now taking off his hat to shove his fingers through his hair, or with the Fates that had so capriciously altered the lives of what had once been a relatively happy family. The only thing she knew for certain was that she needed to be away from Logan. He was making her remember things she didn't want to think about. What was worse was that he was making her remember how awfully, horribly alone she sometimes felt—and that was the worst feeling of all.

It also didn't help that his broad chest and muscled arms looked as strong as they undoubtedly were. Wrapped in such arms, a woman would feel protected. Safe. If only for a little while.

"By the way," she added, thinking it monumentally unfair that, on top of everything else, he was now reminding her of how very long it had been since she'd been held. "I do not neglect my children. They are the reason I took the job you seem to have such a problem with. But even if I'd wanted to be president of a Fortune Five Hundred company and have my children raised by nannies in Gstaad, it wouldn't be anyone's business but mine." She started past him then, her legs not much steadier than her voice. She'd never told off anyone in her life. Unless she was mistaken, she might have just achieved a personal first. "I'll wait for Erin in the car."

She made it to the corner of the building before the syncopated beat of horse hooves on hard ground had her turning around. From where he'd remained in the shadow of the stable, Logan watched her lift her hand to shade her eyes. Her slender body was as stiff as bailing wire, and the breeze ruffled the pale strands of her hair much as her own fingers had done moments ago. With her attention on the riders, she didn't so much as glance in his direction.

He wouldn't blame her if she walked off without saying another word. As he started toward her, he wasn't even sure what he was going to say himself. He knew only that he'd been completely off base about her. He also knew he'd never seen anyone look so desperately in need of a pair of arms as she had in the moments before she'd told him why she hadn't allowed Erin to see her father.

Given that she'd just done a commendable job of putting him in his place, he figured he was the last person from whom she'd accept comfort. It was just as well. He didn't know a thing about offering solace to a distressed woman.

Trev and Erin had cleared the farthest corral and were on the wide path leading to the stables when Logan came up beside Sam. Trev's mount was one of the more spirited bays. Erin was on Firelight. It wasn't the horse who balked. It was Erin. Seeing her mother, she pulled back on the reins to slow the chestnut down. Knowing she was nearing her stall and her feed, Firelight shook her head, whinnying her displeasure at being held back.

Had Logan been paying closer attention to the girl, he'd have felt a bit of admiration for the way Erin kept the headstrong animal from charging ahead. But his attention was on her mother. Sam seemed far calmer than he would have expected. But her hands clasped in a death grip told him she was nowhere near as together as she looked.

"We need to leave now, Erin," he heard her tell her daughter.

Erin's long hair hung in a single braid over her shoulder. Looking somewhere between apprehensive and guilty as sin itself, she reached up to roll the end of it through her fingers. "I need to hose the horse off first." Her glance darted toward Trevor, as if seeking confirmation. Or protection. "She's pretty lathered."

Logan stepped forward. Rubbing the horse's nose with one hand, he reached for Erin's reins with the other. "We'll take care of it," he said and glanced toward his son.

There didn't seem to be any need for Trev to ask what was going on. Given how closely the two females resembled each other and considering that the tension between them was as thick as mosquitoes in summer, Logan figured the boy had already come to the obvious conclusions.

Trev dismounted. With a quick and wary glance toward the woman openly studying him, he walked over to Erin and stopped beside her. Without a moment's hesitation, he settled his hands on her waist and murmured something neither adult could hear. A moment later, Erin's hands settled on his shoulders and he lifted her effortlessly to the ground.

Sam said nothing. Despite her silence, Logan knew she'd missed nothing of the intimate exchange between his son and her daughter. He had a feeling she wasn't at all sure how she felt about what she'd seen, either.

That bothered him. A lot. Not because he had any problem with their kids being friends, or however it was they thought of themselves. What bothered him was his acute awareness of her, and how easily he could sense her distress. Even as Erin walked reluctantly toward them, he could sense how disappointed and upset Sam was with her daughter.

Erin's chin jutted up. "I'm not late."

"This isn't about being late getting home, Erin." Sam's voice sounded subdued, as if all the energy had been drained from it. "But I really don't think you want to discuss this here."

There was too much of a little-girl-lost quality in Erin's expression for the defiance she attempted to work. She was a child lashing out because she didn't know what else to do. Still, she managed a definite glare in Sam's direction just before she headed for the car parked near the house. Sam didn't react to the expression. She merely took a deep breath of air that smelled like earth and sunshine and animals and glanced toward the man whose presence seemed determined to haunt her life. Trevor was already walking off with both horses.

The wind picked up for a moment, swirling bits of wood chips and hay over the hard-packed ground. The bark of a dog came from somewhere behind the barn. As Sam met the guarded speculation in Logan's eyes, she heard the baleful bawling of a calf.

As incongruous as it seemed, for that one, fleeting moment, it occurred to Sam that it was almost peaceful here. The impression didn't last long, but for the few seconds that it did, she simply stood there, wondering at it—and looking far too vulnerable for her own good.

"I'm sorry," Logan said, not quite sure what all he was apologizing for, but knowing it was a start.

She lowered her head, her disquiet returning. "Me, too."

There was apparently nothing more she wanted to say. Unable to think of anything himself, Logan watched the lovely, shaken woman turn and follow her daughter to the car parked up near the house.

Sam closed the car door with a solid thud. "Why did you do this?"

Slunk down on the beige vinyl seat, her eyes on the beige dashboard, Erin muttered, "Because I wanted to be with Trevor."

"You didn't have to lie to be with him, Erin. All you had to do was introduce him to me. That was all I wanted. When you first started pulling this stuff, I told you I just wanted to meet him before you went anywhere else with him. That's not an unreasonable request for a parent to make. But you chose not to bring him over."

"Why should you care who I spend my time with?"

The question was as unexpected as the anger so suddenly visible in Erin's red-rimmed eyes.

"I care because I love you," Sam said fiercely, amazed that Erin should have asked such a thing. "I care because you've never acted the way you've been acting the past month. You've *never* lied about anything before, and now you've lied to me. And to Aunt Lindsey."

"If you cared about me," Erin accused, tears welling, "you'd never have moved us here. Why can't we go home?"

"This *is* home, Erin. Honey, we've talked..."

"This will *never* be home." Her voice lowered partly in plea, partly in pout. "I hate it here. But you don't care about that. And you don't care that the only thing I do like is coming out here with Trevor. Now you probably won't let me do that, either."

Sam's patience had run out. So had her ability to reason with someone who refused to be reasonable herself. Later, she would bring up the subject of her father. Talk to her again. Or try to. Right now she had a more immediate matter to contend with.

"You're right," Sam said, her tone as flat as the tire on the antique car in the garage. "I won't. Not for two weeks. And if I catch you sneaking out here, or if you lie to me or anyone else again, you might just find yourself grounded until you graduate.''

Erin's mouth was open, either in astonishment or in protest. Sam wasn't sure. At that particular moment, she didn't care to figure it out, either. As she added that she wanted Erin to bake a batch of cupcakes for her brother's scout meeting when they got home, she was thinking only that she'd give just about anything for Erin to be ten years old again.

Sam wasn't ready to deal with boy trouble. Not this kind, anyway. She thought she'd handled the kids occasional, at times uncomfortable, and always unpredictable questions about sex pretty well. So far. And so far she had assumed that all of Erin's inquiries over the last few years had been—she hoped—theoretical in nature.

Theory, however, suddenly looked in danger of being put into practice. A person would have had to be blind to miss the way Erin had looked at Logan's son when he'd helped her off that huge beast of an animal. But what made her truly nervous was the familiarity in the way he had touched her. Trev Whitaker was nothing like the young and gangly boys Erin had counted among her friends at the small private school she'd attended in Los Angeles. Those boys scarcely had peach fuzz growing on their faces, much less sported a five o'clock shadow. Not one of them had had the neck and shoulders of a football player, either. Or the quiet, self-assured manner that was apparently genetic with the Whitaker men.

Sam's consternation about the son did little to alleviate her ambivalence about his father. She had little time to indulge the odd restlessness filling her, however. After she and Erin returned home, there was dinner to prepare and cupcakes to bake—which meant that Erin slammed cooking utensils around until Amy, concerned about the frown on her sister's face, asked why she was mad at the cookie racks. Her seriousness, miraculously, made Erin smile. That had led to Amy giving her big sister a hug—which had caused Michael to start making gagging sounds from where he'd hidden under the kitchen table with his tape recorder. His latest twist on the bug-thing was to deposit the insect *du jour* on a surface near one, or, preferably, both, of his sisters and record their shrieks—which he then used later, at full volume, to send them out of their skin a second time.

The concept was actually rather creative, Sam had thought, though she did side with the girls on this one. Especially since he was bringing the bugs into the house and not always catching them to return to the great outdoors after he'd aged his sisters a bit.

All in all, the evening was almost typical. And, as the early part of the evening tended to do, the time sped by. Because Erin insisted she had a headache and went to her room right after dinner, Sam didn't get a chance to talk to her as she'd wanted to do. Still, it had been after eleven o'clock before Sam gave Amy's bird its last feeding of the day and fell into bed herself, only to lie in the dark watching the shadows move across her ceiling. But the evening had passed without any more trauma—and Sam had learned how to be grateful for the little things.

She would have been a little more grateful, however, if she hadn't lain there half the night trying to not think about the man who had somehow elicited sympathy from her over scratches he'd acquired wrestling a steer, while at the same time making her want to slug him for being so ill-tempered and judgmental.

To her dismay, she was still toying with that dichotomy when he walked into the Leesburg Chamber of Commerce Office the next day.

Chapter Four

The bell over the entrance of the small gray building sandwiched between Doc Weiger's office and the Leesburg News wasn't really necessary. The groan of old hinges and the rattle of questionably secure glass announced callers as effectively as the more musical sound. At least, that was Logan's opinion when he opened the door next to a hand-lettered sign proclaiming the premises to be the Leesburg Chamber of Commerce.

Lowering his head, he pulled off his hat and crossed the threshold. It looked to him as if the twenty-by-thirty foot area had pretty much been gutted, painted white, then turned over to its new directress—who was nowhere to be seen.

The door rattled to a close behind him. There wasn't much in sight anywhere, actually. Across the elbow-high counter separating the open office from the tiled area where he stood, the only furniture visible was a desk and a couple of folding chairs. Against another wall sat a large worktable and a filing cabinet. All were either beige or white. The colors brightening the room were supplied by a small but healthy-looking fern on the counter beside him and from the snapshots, maps and advertisements tacked to the large cork board above the cluttered worktable. In the far corner, a flag of the United States stood above the red, white and blue flag of Texas with its lone, white star.

Logan's attention focused on the desk. More specifically on a folded square of white paper on which was scrawled "I LOVE U, MOM" inside what looked to be a heart—or maybe it was a butterfly—and signed "LOVE, AMY." It was propped next to a picture of Erin and two younger kids who, when he looked closer, appeared smaller than anyone he'd been around in a long time.

He'd noticed the smell of coffee when he'd first walked in. Now, hearing what sounded like the slam of a cupboard, he glanced toward the open door at the back of the room.

Samantha materialized in that doorway, her eyes on the steaming hot pink mug of coffee in her right hand. It was obvious she hadn't heard him come in. The moment she glanced up and realized she wasn't alone, her left palm flattened at the base of her throat. An instant later, her eyes jerked back to the cup as if to be sure she hadn't dripped on her newly laid, gray carpet.

It wasn't the start he'd given her that made Logan wish he were just about anywhere else at that moment. It was the dismay she couldn't keep from creeping over her lovely features.

Ever so carefully, she set the colorful mug on the edge of the worktable. "I can't hear a thing in the storage room," she said, as if she needed to explain her less-than-welcoming reaction. "It's amazing how thick these old

walls are. It's fresh," she added, with a nod toward the
steaming mug. "If you'd like a cup."

"I won't be staying that long. But, thank you," he
added, finding her graciousness disconcerting. Certainly
it was unexpected—considering how uncomfortable she
found his presence. "I just want to apologize. I didn't
know you were a widow, Mrs. Gray. I knew it was just you
and your children here, but I somehow figured you were
divorced." Had he come into town more often, or paid
any attention to the gossip when he was here, he might
have known more about her situation. He supposed he
could have asked his son about her, too, but he hadn't
wanted to admit being that curious about her. "I'm sorry
about what happened to your husband. For you and for
your children."

Her wariness remained. "I appreciate your sympathy,
Mr. Whitaker. But what, exactly, do you want to apologize for?"

"The way I was with you yesterday."

"You're always like that with me."

Her tone was that of simple fact. Yet, Logan's denial
was immediate. To himself, anyway. When he opened his
mouth, his conscience all but kicked him in the teeth.

She spoke the truth, and there was no denying it. He'd
found himself annoyed by her in one way or another since
the moment they met. At first, he'd been put off by her
goals and by her nerve, simply because she was a stranger
intent on changing something she knew little or nothing
about. Then, he'd overheard Erin and made his judgment without giving her mother the slightest benefit of a
doubt. He was still opposed to what Samantha had been
hired to do, and he didn't agree at all with how she'd chosen to handle the situation between their children, but he
had promised himself to be reasonable—and a whole lot

more careful around her. He was usually quite good at keeping his thoughts and feelings to himself—something more than one woman had pointed out in less than complimentary terms. This particular one just seemed to push a few buttons he didn't know he had.

"Then, I'm sorry for that, too," he finally said.

Logan had set his hat on the counter's glossy white surface, his left hand splayed next to it as if he never let the beat up old thing get too far from his reach. It seemed odd to Sam to see him without his eyes shadowed by its brim. Yet, its absence revealed nothing. Not by so much as the twitch of a muscle did his chiseled features reveal anything other than the absolute control he maintained over himself—and quite possibly, everything around him.

Not sure if she admired that control, or simply felt intimidated by it, she stuffed her hands into the pockets of her corduroy slacks. "You didn't come all the way into town to apologize to me, did you?"

"Not entirely," he admitted, seeing no point in mentioning how he'd fought the idea to begin with. "I want to see what you're doing about this development you and the council are talking about. I'd like you to show me your plans. That is part of what you were hired to do," he continued, when her skepticism kept her quiet a moment too long. "Isn't it? Let people know just how you're going to make Leesburg grow?"

"Yes. Of course, it is. I— It's just—"

Quite deliberately, Sam cut herself off. She was not in the habit of stumbling about whatever it was she needed to say. She was also not in the habit of having her palms sweat just because a man tended to let his eyes drift to her mouth while she spoke—not that she'd had the experience often.

"Why?" she concluded.

"Because I'm interested."

"In any particular aspect?" she inquired, not believing for an instant that he was softening his stance.

"Whatever you're willing to show me."

He appeared sincere enough. If a face that looked carved of granite could possess such a quality. Considering him as entitled to an explanation as anyone else who might ask, doing her best to keep from looking too closely at the pink scratches on his cleanly shaven jaw to make sure they were healing properly, she reached for the new town map she was creating and laid it on the three-foot-wide counter.

She'd just picked up a pencil to indicate their location on the stylized drawing when the stub slipped from her fingers.

Wanting to catch it before it rolled off the other side, Sam immediately grabbed for it.

So did Logan.

Her hand came down flat on the pencil.

Logan's hand came down flat on hers.

It was the weight she noticed first, and the heat from his palm searing into her skin. His hand was broad, his fingers long, the nails blunt and well trimmed. There was no denying that he had a working man's hands, scarred and callused as they were. They were capable hands. And strong. The kind that could take on anything, and probably had.

As big as it was, his hand completely obliterated hers. Yet, it wasn't his strength holding her so still. Watching his fingers curve to slip beneath her palm, lifting her hand to cradle it in his own, she was aware only of something she never would have expected of him. Extraordinary... gentleness.

Only seconds passed, scattered though they were. His thumb brushed her knuckles, then skimmed over the fragile bones leading to her wrist. The motion seemed either unwilling or unconscious, but the very restraint of that mesmerizing touch made Sam aware of how easily he could have hurt her had his hand slapped down any harder.

Apparently that was what he was thinking, too.

"Are you okay?" he asked, his eyes seeking hers.

She glanced up, her head inches from his. Feeling the jolt of heat when their eyes met, the best she could give him was a nod.

He was a man who knew his strength. It was the gentleness he didn't seem at all familiar with. Possibly it was something he didn't even know he possessed. She couldn't deny it was there, though. She felt it in the way he slowly lifted his thumb, as if abruptness might cause her to break, then slipped his hand out from beneath hers.

A moment later, he'd drawn back and cleared his throat.

"So what is this?" he asked as if nothing at all had happened.

Telling herself that nothing had, but shaken nonetheless, Sam fought for the same distance Logan so easily managed and reached for the pencil. More carefully, this time. She couldn't quite achieve that distance, though. As she attempted to explain the publicity material she was creating, a faint tension seemed to permeate the room. That vaguely electric sensation made her edgy and caused the muscle in his jaw to work. But at least, for once, he wasn't looking as if he were about to swallow her whole. If anything, the look in his eyes when she glanced up again to find him watching her was pure speculation.

It made no sense at all to Sam, but she actually preferred his coolness. Without it, he seemed far too dangerous.

Needing desperately to focus on what she was doing, she pulled a mock-up of a merchant's brochure between them and kept her attention on the papers spread over the counter.

Logan's attention remained on Sam.

He'd seen the look in her eyes—that unmistakable curiosity that spoke of awareness. What he'd felt himself was the tug of pure, sensual heat low in his gut.

Shoving his hands into his pockets, he tried to concentrate on what she was saying. That was why he'd come here, after all. To find out what she planned to do. Instead, he found himself drawn to the sound of her voice as she spoke. To its softness. He was drawn, too, to the shape of her hands. The gracefulness of their movements. Her skin was every bit as soft as he'd remembered, and her bones so incredibly small. There was a delicacy about her that reminded him of china cups his mother had once kept on a shelf in the kitchen, a fineness that bordered on fragility. His mother had been gone for years now, and the cups had disappeared not too long after her death. Odd, he thought, that he should remember them now. Stranger still that he should look at this woman and think of the only beautiful things his mother had ever possessed.

"... and we plan to solicit light industry," she added, jolting his attention back to what she was saying rather than how she sounded saying it.

It didn't take long for Logan to catch enough of what Sam added about having convinced the mayor to go for growth in phases rather than all at once to make him believe she was as good as he'd feared she might be. Anyone who could talk Bud Meiers into modifying *his* idea of how something should be done could probably accomplish anything she set her mind to.

Her approach, however, did not change Logan's mind. He still saw no redeeming merit whatsoever in what she had been hired to do. The very fact that Sam was capable of causing it to happen was precisely why he took her presence seriously.

Which was why he asked how much she knew about this part of Texas and how much of it she'd actually seen.

"I've read a lot. And I have seen quite a bit," she added, thinking of the hours she'd spent in her car listening to her children whine about how bored they were while she'd noted landmarks and buildings on her Points of Interest list. "Probably just about everything accessible to the public by road within fifty miles."

"Did you go off any of those roads?"

"Not really," she admitted, not trusting the innocent sounding question. "Why?"

"Because there's something you need to see. I want...I mean," he amended, softening what had started out sounding suspiciously like an order, "I think it might be a good idea for you to come back out to the ranch." Mindful of her sudden caution, not at all pleased with how the distrust sweeping her expression made him feel, he reached for his hat. "I'd like to show you something."

"What?"

"I can't explain it. It's just something you should see before you get in too much deeper here."

"You want to show me your side of the argument?"

"Something like that."

She hadn't missed his reference to her questionable permanency in the area. She also realized that he hadn't made a single comment about the plans she and the mayor had finally worked out. Thinking he'd probably just done her a favor by exercising that restraint, Sam considered only that his request was fair. The more she learned about the area, the better able she would be to serve it. The fact that he might hold some influence with the other ranchers was also something she needed to keep in mind.

Hoping she sounded more enthusiastic than she felt, she quietly ventured, "When?"

"Anytime after Sunday. I won't have time before then."

"Tuesday?"

His wide shoulders lifted in a shrug. "Suits me."

"What time should I be there?"

"Sun up."

She would see what he wanted her to see. She would not do it before she was fully conscious. "I'm afraid nine o'clock is the best I can do. Will that be a problem?"

"Yeah. Half the day will be gone."

"Well, mine will only be a couple of hours old. I have to get my kids off to school before I go anywhere."

At the mention of her children, he settled his hat on his head, which added another six inches to his already imposing height, and his glance swung to the photograph on her desk.

"Nine-thirty's fine." Quite deliberately, he pulled his glance back to her. Seconds later, his quietly assessing glance was traveling from the top of her head to where the counter cut her off at the waist. "Wear something you won't mind getting dirty. And boots, if you've got them."

His last words were met by the jarring ring of the telephone. It wasn't necessary for Sam to excuse herself to answer it. He had already turned to the door, his mission complete. A moment later, with the rattle of glass panes and the tinkle of the bell, he'd walked out into the brilliant September sunshine. Yet, even as she picked up the telephone, Sam was still wondering at the way he had looked at her pictures, and why the sight of three beautiful, smiling children should have made him look so solemn.

The sunshine was missing Tuesday morning. Huge, billowing clouds in varying shades of gray obliterated it. The temperature had plunged, too. According to the locals, autumn in this part of Texas was "usually warm, but sometimes cold," which told Sam nothing—other than that she should be prepared for anything.

That was exactly what she was doing, too, when she arrived at the RW ranch's main house. Preparing herself for anything—and hoping to get through the day with as little disagreement as possible.

Logan must have seen her coming. No sooner had Sam stepped out of her car and zipped her denim jacket against the damp chill, than she noticed him walking toward her from the barn.

His hat, as always, sat low on his brow, and his long, brown oilcloth coat flapped open with each stride. His boots, the only boots he seemed to own since she'd never seen him wearing any others, were caked with mud. There were spatters of mud, too, around the bottoms of his worn and faded jeans.

It had finally stopped raining. But it was apparent that Logan had been working in the downpour that had kept her windshield wipers busy most of the half hour it had taken her to get here. Watching him step around one of the puddles scattered about the yard, Sam saw him whip off his hat. Water flew as he slapped it against his thigh. A moment later, still moving toward her, he shoved his dark hair straight back and resettled his hat on his head.

A shiver that felt more like nerves than chill shuddered through her when he met her eyes. Without breaking stride, his glance jerked from the clip securing her hair at her nape to her lavender-and-tan hiking boots. She'd bought the boots for a camping trip three years ago and hadn't worn them since.

"Am I okay for wherever it is we're going?" she asked, doing double-time to keep up with him, since he hadn't slowed down when he passed her.

With one hand unfastening the top button of his coat, he gave her a quick, no nonsense once-over. "Probably."

"Where *are* we going, anyway?"

With a shrug, the coat came off. A half a dozen steps later, he turned into the long, open garage and threw the wet garment into the back of a canvas-topped Jeep. "To the top of a hill."

"Any particular hill?"

"Yeah," he muttered, his less-than-informative response making her wonder if he was upset or merely rushed.

Logan was neither. As he held the door for her to get in, then asked her to hang on while he made a quick call down to the breeding barn to tell his foreman where he'd be, he was simply going at his usual pace. Aside from the constant maintenance of buildings, holding pens, fencing, chutes, mechanical equipment and horses, he was constantly monitoring the condition and nutritional content of the pastures, fields and meadows on which his range cattle fed. All that was *after* he devoted whatever time was needed to his breeding program: the most complex and most essential factor in the entire operation. He had both spring and fall calving seasons and because his stock came from his own line of prizewinning bulls, he'd achieved an operation that was highly profitable, highly controlled and took every waking hour of his day.

Yet, it wasn't the ranch occupying his thoughts as he drove past the stable and corrals and the horses huddled beneath the ramudas. It was how to make the woman beside him understand what she was about to help destroy.

There was something else he needed to know first.

"How's Erin?"

Though his focus remained on the dirt and gravel road, he was aware of Sam turning toward him. And of her brief hesitation.

"She's fine. Thank you for asking."

"I didn't do it to be polite. I asked because I want to know."

"I answered you," she said defensively, not at all sure why he was scowling.

"Well, try answering again. With the truth this time. You're not very good at pretending things are all right when they're not, anyway."

Even more confused, she scowled right back.

With his eyes on the road, her effort was wasted.

"You said she was having problems because of what happened to her dad," he continued. "How much difficulty are you talking about?"

Despite the fact that he could apparently see right through her, Sam's first instinct was to tell him that everything *was* under control. It was a knee-jerk sort of response with her, one she would have given anyone who'd expressed concern. But Logan was perfectly within his rights to want answers. Because of his son. Heaven knew if her daughter was interested in a "troubled child," she'd want to know just how troubled that child was.

"It's been worse since we moved," she admitted, disconcerted to know he could read her so easily. "Losing their dad was hard on all the kids. They were crazy about Jim, but he and Erin were especially close. He..."

She started to say he was a great dad, but an image of Jim, grinning while he and Erin helped Amy with her first steps, flashed through her mind and the words died before they could form. He'd been more than a great dad. He'd been a good husband.

Aware that Logan was looking toward her, Sam lowered her glance from the hills rolling before them. Head bent, she concentrated on the whitened threads at the knee of her jeans.

Logan deserved answers to his questions. He had no right to bits of memory from a life that no longer existed.

Clearing her throat, she willed that memory and the ache that had come with it back to the private place that held all the other memories lying in wait for the most unsuspecting moment to strike. Someday, when she was stronger—and old—she would take those memories out and linger over them like old photographs. Right now, though some of them had, mercifully, faded, there were still those that could too easily bring back all the pain of what she'd lost.

"I thought she was dealing with the loss of her dad," Sam finally said, aware that he was waiting for her to continue and oddly grateful for the time he allowed her to collect her thoughts. "She was doing okay before we moved. She was even doing things with her friends again." Working at the threads at her knee, she made a tiny hole. "Leaving them was what was so hard, I think. Her 'best' friend had flaked out on her not too long after her dad died. But she was really close to Mindy and Shawna. I think she's written a letter a day to them since we got here."

"Her friend ran out on her?"

"The girls were all barely fifteen at the time." Sam had tried very hard not hold the other child's behavior against her. Unfortunately, since her little girl had been hurt, she hadn't been terribly successful. "Her friend had never lost anyone close to her, and she just didn't know how to handle it when Erin got down or didn't feel like being her old fun self anymore.

"We used to talk about how hard it was when friends didn't know what to say or do," she added, missing the closeness she and Erin had once shared. "And I always knew what was going on with her, because she'd tell me everything. That's why I knew it was so hard for her to lose her friends. But as sweet as she was, I kept thinking she wouldn't have any trouble making new ones here...if she'd just give herself and the other kids a chance. Once she gets *involved* again, she won't have so much time to dwell on what she doesn't have anymore."

A sigh of frustration, or maybe it was fatigue, leaked out before Sam could stop it. "That's one of the reasons I thought it was a good idea for her to spend less time with your son. She was spending so much time with him, she wasn't letting herself get to know anyone else." The hole at her knee grew a little larger. "I told her she can only see Trevor at school. At least, for a while."

Logan's grip tightened on the wheel. "Trev mentioned that."

Sam abandoned the destruction of her jeans. Logan's tone had gone absolutely flat.

They were on a gentle upward grade, the compound a good mile or so behind them. Because Logan kept his focus on the road—or, more accurately, the condition of the fencing running just to the left of it—Sam could discern little beyond disapproval in his expression.

"She needs to get involved with school and develop some interests she can share with other kids," she explained, wanting Logan to see she wasn't being unreasonable about this. "She can't do that if she's spending so much time with Trevor."

"He was teaching her how to ride. That *takes* time."

"I'm not talking about riding."

Something that hinted at exasperation flashed through his expression. "You said you wanted her to get involved with something. Right?"

"What's . . . ?"

"Right?" he prompted, refusing to let her go any further until they'd clarified this particular point.

Feeling as if she were tightening the spring on her own trap, seeing no way out of whatever it was she'd backed into, she quietly muttered, "That's what I said."

"That's what I thought. So what's wrong with her being interested in horses? There probably isn't a kid within fifty miles of here who doesn't ride. It'll give her something in common with the kids you want her to get to know."

Sam opened her mouth, then closed it again. There was nothing wrong with horses. If Erin wanted to learn how to ride, that was great. But riding wasn't what she was talking about.

"Well?" he demanded, waiting for her to deny his logic. "Wouldn't it make more sense to let her be around Trev and the horses than to take away the only interest she does seem to have here?"

"If we were just talking about riding, then, yes," she agreed. "It would make sense." What didn't make sense was Logan himself and why he was taking Erin's side. Or was it Trevor's? "Why are you doing this?"

Logan felt himself hesitate. He wasn't sure he could answer that question. Or, if he would want to answer it even if he could. Maybe he was doing it because he couldn't see any logic at all to her argument, and anything that wasn't logical baffled him. He was a pragmatic and realistic man, one who saw things as either fitting or not. Everything and everyone had a purpose and a place and an order, and anything that tested the basic tenets of sensibility was simply beyond his comprehension.

Or maybe it had to do with the way Trevor had left the table right after supper the past several nights, no longer willing to take Hank and Dusty's good-natured ribbing about where "his little gal" had been lately.

Those were certainly possibilities. But as Logan swung the Jeep around the top of the knob and cut the vehicle's engine, he had the uneasy feeling that what he was doing had more to do with the ache he'd heard in Erin's voice the day he'd first met her, and the sadness he'd seen in Samantha's eyes just before her spirit had surfaced and she'd all but told him to go to hell the day she'd come for her daughter.

He remembered that feeling. And he'd hated it. That feeling of being completely... lost.

Far more comfortable with the idea that it wasn't empathy he felt so much as guilt over the way he'd treated Samantha the past couple of weeks, he muttered, "Beats me," and opened his door. "It just seems you're saying one thing and doing another."

"It's not the riding," she repeated, scrambling out herself to meet him in front of the tan and slightly dented Jeep. "It's Trevor. Not that I disapprove of him," she hurried to add when Logan's brows pressed together. "I mean, it's not him personally. Exactly. I don't know your son at all,'' she rushed on, wondering how much deeper she could go before she buried herself. "I'm sure he's..."

"He's a good kid, Samantha."

"I'm sure he is," she returned, conceding to the dangerous glint in his eyes. "But that's just it. He's *not* a kid. At least, he doesn't... look like one."

At the slow arch of Logan's eyebrows, Sam's glance gradually slid down the front of his flannel shirt. She had the feeling he was getting her point, even if she did think he was being deliberately obtuse about it.

"If the time they spend riding isn't the problem, exactly what are you worried about?"

With her attention on his pocket, she quietly said, "What they do when they're not on the horses."

It was a moment before Logan spoke. When he did, there was a heavy dose of caution in his voice. "If you're already having trouble with your daughter, it seems to me the surest way to make something more appealing is to make it forbidden. What are you going to do? Lock her up until she's twenty-one?"

"Of course not." The oldest she'd threatened was eighteen. "I'm only trying to put a little distance between her and a situation that might be more than she can handle. Even if I weren't concerned about their relationship," she continued, growing less comfortable with this subject by the second, "Erin still has to listen when I tell her she can't do something. Part of the reason she can't come out here is because she disobeyed me about being with your son, she lied to her aunt about where she was going, and she'd been lying to me for weeks about being at volleyball practice."

Sam hadn't meant to be quite so blunt. Or quite so informative. She also didn't expect the quiet, almost thoughtful way Logan was studying her.

"Has she ever given you any reason to worry before? About sex, I mean?"

"No," Sam replied truthfully.

"Then let's not borrow trouble. My son has a good head on his shoulders, and I trust him. You'll just have to trust your daughter, too. Let her come back out. From what I've seen, they're more interested in the horses than each other, anyway."

Sam blinked up at him in disbelief. First because he seemed to regard this situation as one they faced together. But mostly because she couldn't believe he didn't see a potential problem brewing. She'd seen the way Trevor had looked at her daughter. It was very much the way Logan was looking at her right now. As if he were imagining how her mouth would feel beneath his; as if, once he tasted her, he knew he wouldn't want to settle for only the feel of her lips.

A ball of heat gathered low in Sam's stomach. As unsettling—and intriguing—as Sam found the Whitaker appeal, that appeal could leave an inexperienced and vulnerable sixteen-year old as helpless as a lamb facing a wolf.

"I don't think it's just the horses they're thinking about."

"Maybe not," he agreed with an ease that made her wonder if he'd only meant to make her feel better by suggesting nothing was going on between their children. "Either way," he went on, "there's nothing you can do about how either one of them thinks, or feels. You can let Erin look forward to riding again, though.

"If it makes you feel any better," he added, his voice sounding quieter with the rush of wind through the tall grass, "Whitaker men aren't in the habit of taking advantage of unwilling or unsuspecting women." With the tip of his finger he reached out and touched the brass zipper pull near the neck of her denim jacket. "You're a perfect example."

His eyes roamed her face, then skimmed down her throat, his glance coming to rest on the pull he absently rubbed between his forefinger and thumb.

He looked back to meet her eyes. "You'd be amazed at the control I'm exercising with you right now."

Chapter Five

The sky was clearing. Streaks of sunlight fanned between the heavy clouds, warming the damp earth and taking the grayness from the day. In the trees, birds that had sought shelter among their branches began their exuberant chatter. Sam scarcely noticed. Rooted as firmly as a scrub oak clinging to rocky ground, she was aware of little beyond the man who became more of a mystery to her with each passing moment.

Logan remained motionless, his eyes intent on hers. As near as he stood, it was necessary for her to tilt her head back to see his face. Not for a moment did it occur to her to look away. He was being as open and honest with her as he could without actually verbalizing the images in his mind. Images that darkened his eyes when they touched her mouth, lingering there before moving on to caress her throat, then drift down her body. Sam had never realized how disconcerting such honesty could be.

He still held the pull of her zipper between his forefinger and thumb, his knuckles lightly brushing the denim just above her breasts. It wasn't his touch holding her. He held her there with little more than the intensity in his eyes. And the heat.

She could easily have stepped back.

He could just as easily tug to bring her forward.

Her heart had just slammed against her ribs when Logan's hand fell.

With the arch of his eyebrow, he quietly murmured, "See?"

Sam felt her breath leak out, slowly, like air from an old tire. What escaped with it felt much like the numbness that had settled so deeply inside her that she hadn't even realized it existed. There had been no mistaking the sort of control he was talking about, and the thought that she tempted this man made her feel things she hadn't felt in a very long time. Vital. Feminine. Alive. But she needed the numbness he seemed to be destroying. It protected her from everything she didn't have the strength to face, or to ever hope for again, and she scrambled desperately for its cover.

He must have caught that desperation.

"You can trust me, Samantha." There was assurance in his voice, along with an edge she didn't understand at all. "I meant what I said. I've never made a move on a lady who wasn't willing, and I have no intention of starting now. You don't need to be afraid of me."

"I'm not."

The denial had barely formed before he saw her fingers close over the pull on her jacket.

An unfamiliar satisfaction filled him at her unconscious reaction. "I think we've already established that you don't lie very well. At least, not to me."

He really didn't want her to be afraid of him. More than that, he wanted her to believe him. Why, he couldn't really say. Nor did it matter at the moment.

What *he* wanted to believe was that he could keep his hands off her.

Muttering a terse "Come on," that made it sound as if she were the one holding them up, he turned and left her standing by the Jeep.

Shivering against the breeze, Sam stuffed her hands into her jacket pockets and followed. She wasn't afraid of Logan. What she felt at the moment rested more between distrust and confusion. Logan had just quite deliberately turned her insides to jelly with little more than the touch of his fingers, then proceeded to shrug off that circumstance as little more than a phenomenon he fully intended to ignore. More confusing still was that, only moments before, he had actually sounded as if he'd been trying to help with Erin.

Had the thought not seemed so absurd, she might almost have felt relieved by it. As it was, she had no idea why he would want to do such a thing. Nor did she want to consider why she found the thought so appealing. All she knew for certain when she saw what it was he wanted her to see, was that there was no sense in trying to second guess Logan Whitaker. She would have bet her brand-new power screwdriver that he had brought her to this rise overlooking the valley to show her his land. What he wanted her to see was Leesburg much as it had been for the past one hundred years.

Sam hadn't realized how far they'd driven until she saw the town off in the distance. On a clear day, the sweeping vista below them would have been impressive enough. With the sky painted by rays of golden sunlight streaking through pearl gray clouds and with great swaths of azure growing off to the east, the view took on a slightly surrealistic quality.

From where Sam stood with the breeze ruffling the grass around her ankles, the town itself looked to her like a miniature village for a toy train set. Beyond the town, to the south, was a patchwork quilt of farmland and a scattering of houses. To the west was more of the same, along with miles of open, rolling space that stretched from the town limits and seemed to continue on forever. Sam knew from the maps she'd studied of the area that most of the land belonged to the RW and some to the Circle J. But it was the open space to the east of town that had Sam's attention. Like Logan's land, it was all so amazingly, beautifully untouched. There were no roads to speak of, other than the one she'd taken to get here; but with the addition of a few more, she could easily envision the town's new master plan.

That was Sam's initial thought as Logan turned to her. "Imagine this view filled with buildings and highways and signs."

"That's what I am doing," she returned.

"So are you seeing what you came here to find?" he asked, his tone deceptively mild. "Or what you just left?"

His question brought her up short. He didn't seem to expect an answer, though. All he wanted her to do was hear him out.

"I'm not going to waste your time going on about how what you're going to do will pollute what my cattle breathe and eat, and how your development will encroach on the best range land in the state. The folks down there have determined there's a need for capital and they've come up with a way to raise it."

"Hold it," she interjected, willing to listen, but wanting to get the facts straight. "Why do you always refer to it as what *I'm* going to do? It's their plan."

"Because they can't do it without you. It's not just their plan anymore, either. Or the mayor's, just because he thought of it. Even if some of the ideas weren't yours, it's your town now. You chose it, remember? You chose it because you want your children to grow up in a safe place. That is what you said, isn't it?"

With the uncomfortable feeling that her own words were about to haunt her, Sam gave him a confirming nod.

Logan stepped closer, the certainty in his eyes clearly visible. "How safe will it be when strangers start moving in and the place gets too big to notice that someone doesn't belong? I don't fault you for what you want for your kids," he told her, sounding as if he might actually admire what she was attempting to do for her children had she been attempting to do it anywhere else. "I just don't see how you can expect to keep what you came here for, when you're paving the way for the very problems you moved from in the city. I'm not saying Leesburg's going to turn into Dallas, but even if you only doubled the number of people living down there, you'll be taking something away that can't ever be put back."

The man was ruthless. Reasonable, but definitely ruthless. His own agenda had to do with his land, his livelihood, which came as no surprise at all to Sam. She had expected that. But he hadn't attempted to sway her by pleading his cause. Instead, he'd homed in on her Achilles' heel with frightening accuracy—and jerked her squarely into the middle of a situation she had, until that moment, regarded only as her job.

The fact that it was her job made it necessary to defend it. "I told you the other day that Bud agreed we should proceed more slowly than he'd first thought. Even if everything goes on schedule, it will be a couple of years before..."

"Before you have to face the consequences of your actions?"

"Before any real results will be seen," she corrected, the sinking feeling in her stomach telling her it was much the same thing. "Maybe the plans will have changed by then."

"Maybe they won't."

Her chin came up. "Look. I'm not going to quit, if that's what you have in mind."

A month ago, that was exactly what he would have hoped she'd do. "I know you need the job," he conceded, as irritated as he was impressed by her stubbornness. The welfare of three children depended on her. "Maybe you could just figure out a different way to do it."

"To do my job?"

"Why not? You're smart. Come up with an alternative plan."

Just like that? "Such as?" she inquired, too baffled by his suggestion to feel flattered by his grudging compliment.

His wide shoulders lifted in a careless shrug. "I'm just a rancher. You're the expert at community development, or whatever it is you call it."

His self-deprecation was as unbelievable as his suggestion. Come up with an alternative, he'd said, as if she had a magic hat full of ways to attract more money to the town coffers. The only magic she could think of was winning a multi-state lottery, and she saw those chances as somewhere between zip and nil. Logan had made her see one thing, though. Not only did they not see eye-to-eye on much of anything, but they could both look at exactly the same thing and see something completely different.

Pushing back her breeze-blown hair, she turned to look toward the town. She had seen the view surrounding them and noticed only what preoccupied her, looking right past what was actually there. He'd looked and seen the fields, meadows and trees. The enormous granite balds rising from the valley floor. The lush peacefulness of the Pedernales as it wound its way toward the Colorado River.

Disconcerted to find that it was only when she looked at it as he did that she could see its peacefulness, she focused on a narrow ribbon of road heading off in the distance.

"Where does that road go?" she asked, needing to consider something, anything, other than the disturbing effect this man had on her thoughts.

"Over to Dry Creek." A clump of wheatgrass brushed the knee of his jeans. Snapping off one of the long blades, he absently drew it through his fingers. "That was the road that brought the settlers here some hundred and fifty years ago. The only difference is that now it's asphalt instead of dirt."

"In other words," she ventured, "it hasn't really changed that much and it's still serving its purpose?"

"You could say that."

"If it had been up to you, would you have paved it?"

The look he slanted her was surprisingly tolerant. "I'm not opposed to improvement, Samantha. Contrary to what you might think, I even believe in electric lights, indoor plumbing and allowing women to vote."

He'd meant to put her in her place. What he'd done was answer her question, in spades. The man probably only bowed to progress when it met his own needs. "So what else has changed around here?'' she asked, refusing to let him get his back up.

The entire point of bringing her here had been to show her that nothing much *had* changed. But as Logan jammed his hands into his pockets to keep from brushing back the hair the breeze tugged across her cheek, he started a slow loop around the top of their overlook, he found his purpose becoming confused. What he'd intended to tell her was how nearly every building in town had been built within twenty years of the town's founding and how the lands surrounding the town had been in the same families for generations. And he did. But the questions she asked as she walked beside him had him going far deeper than he'd intended.

''Doesn't property ever change hands?''

''Not around here,'' he answered easily, certain he was proving his point. ''There's been a Farley heading the Circle J for the last ninety years. The Murdocks have held their land longer than that.''

''What about the RW?''

''Same thing. The original land has had a Whitaker on it from the minute it was staked. Where we are now was once Rutlidge property, but it merged with the ranch about forty years ago.''

''Rutlidge?'' she repeated, the name unfamiliar.

''My mother. The land was hers when she married my father.''

They had reached the far side of the hill. Below them, a herd of young, healthy Herefords grazed in the sporadic morning sun. As Logan's eyes narrowed in the herd's direction, it looked to Sam as if his attention had turned completely to his cattle. But from the way his jaw tightened, she doubted he noticed them at all.

Until that moment, he had said nothing about his family, or who had passed on to him the history he had related to her. Yet, someone or something had instilled his deep-seated need to keep this place as it was. That need was definitely there. She'd realized that when his voice lost its edge as he'd spoken of the land. That need had to do with far more than the impact change would make on his business. It had to do with preserving something that he couldn't find anywhere else.

Two hours ago, she wouldn't have considered such a thought. Now, she couldn't help it. She couldn't help watching him, either, fascinated by his quiet transformation when he looked up to watch an eagle soaring above them in that huge expanse of sky.

The sight was truly remarkable. Not the eagle, majestic though it was. What was remarkable to Sam was how different Logan looked just then. As he followed the eagle's flight, the hardness slipped from his rugged features, his broad shoulders lowering as if somehow relieved of an invisible weight. More remarkable still was that she could almost feel the tension within him ease.

She didn't understand the reasons it was so, and Logan might not have even understood them himself, but this land was his reason for being ... and what made his being possible. He was a part of the ebb and flow of nature surrounding them, and as long as nothing interrupted or countered that flow, he was content to do his part.

Content. But never truly at peace.

Wanting very much to understand what created the tie that kept him isolated in this wild and beautiful place, she wondered what robbed him of that peace. His father was gone. That she knew from Essie. "Your parents are both gone now?"

His head snapped toward her. "Yeah," he muttered, flicking away the piece of grass he'd toyed with as they'd walked.

"Did you inherit this land from your mother, then?"

"From my father. She died long before he did. It was left to me and one of my brothers."

"Did something happen to the other one?"

Puzzlement shifted beneath the brim of Logan's hat. "What do mean?"

"You said one of your brothers. I understood you had two."

"I do," he told her, the edge slipping back into his voice. "Nothing has happened to either one of them, as far as I know. We don't speak all that often."

"I'm sorry," she whispered, her sympathy unexpected. "That must be hard. Does Trevor hear from them? Like at Thanksgiving or Christmas?" she expanded when he didn't seem to know why she would ask such a thing. "Kids need to keep in touch with their families."

Logan's glance flicked over her. "Those days don't mean much around here. They just sort of come and go." The open space before them drew his attention, saving him from the concern in her eyes. "Jett and Cal are welcome home anytime they want to come. They both know that. But my middle brother hasn't set foot on this place in almost seventeen years. Jett isn't much fonder of it. Unless Trev wants to look Cal up, or Jett is passing through Austin or Houston, I doubt he'll be seeing either of them anytime soon."

That he accepted the lack of communication that existed between the three brothers made Sam feel even worse for him than she'd been prepared to feel a few moments ago. That he thought of holidays with ambivalence instead of anticipation only compounded the feeling. But feeling bad for Logan felt dangerous, too, so she concentrated on her curiosity. It seemed odd that his siblings would have feelings about this place that were so strongly the opposite of his own.

"You were the only one who wanted to ranch, then," she concluded, still searching for what held him to this place.

It wasn't the observation that had Logan frowning at her. It was her assumption that he'd had a choice.

"It wasn't a question of wanting to do it. There wasn't anyone else to do it. My youngest brother had already run off, and Cal was only seventeen. There wasn't anyone else. Look." He checked his watch. Starting to swear, he caught himself and settled for letting his jaw tense instead. "We have to get back. I didn't realize how long we'd been gone."

Wishing he wouldn't take such huge steps, much preferring the pace he'd set before, Sam hurried after him. He hadn't wasted an instant once he'd decided he'd said all he was going to say, and she practically had to do double-time to keep up with him. A feat not easily managed on rocky ground while dodging large clumps of grass and bushes.

Catching up with him by a scraggly juniper, she grabbed his arm to slow him down. His stride covered half again the ground hers did. "If you don't want to talk about your brothers, just say so. You don't have to leave me in the dust."

He immediately slowed. "Thank you," she muttered, letting her hand fall. "You might be used to this ground, but I'm not."

The look he slanted her was amazingly droll. But he said nothing. He merely caught her hand in his, his fin-

gers folding around hers as if he didn't care to waste time
waiting for her to find her way over the uneven land-
scape, and picked up speed again. He didn't go quite as
fast as a moment ago, but they definitely moved more
quickly than they had when they'd covered that same
ground a couple of hours earlier.

Sam didn't realize they'd been gone so long, either.

It only took them a few minutes to get back to the Jeep.
But they didn't head straight for the compound. Logan
had seen something from the top of the hill that he wanted
to check out, so they bumped their way down the hill and
over what was quite literally a cow path to where the herd
they'd watched was grazing. He didn't go into the herd,
which was fine with Sam because, while the steers looked
docile enough from a distance, up close, with their long,
curving horns, they looked awfully...big. He followed a
fence-line road out to where he could drive into the
meadow, then got out to pull up a clump of grass, roots
and all, and drop it into a plastic bag from the metal box
in the bed of the truck.

"What's that for?" she asked, curious.

"Analysis. I need to check the nutrient content."

"Do you send it to a lab?"

"I have my own."

He ran the tests himself, just as he did all the tests necessary in his breeding program. He could trust the results
that way.

Sam wasn't surprised so much as she was daunted by
the sheer number of tasks involved in running such an
operation. The knowledge required impressed her even
more. She told him so, too, not caring if he thought her
naive. But he didn't seem to mind her questions at all this
time, and talking was easier than enduring the decidedly
tense silences. That was why it seemed only natural that

she should ask if ranching management was what he'd been studying when he'd had to come back home.

They were back in the Jeep headed for the compound when she posed her question. Turned slightly in the passenger seat, she saw his dark eyebrows form a single slash.

"How did you know I'd had to leave school?"

"Essie at the bakery told me. I asked her about you the morning after the meeting."

He couldn't fault her inquiry. And the way she held his glance dared him to try.

"I was in graduate school," he told her. "Studying to be a vet. What else did Essie have to say?"

She studied his profile, looking for some trace of resentment over the sacrifice he'd made. There was none. "She said that you were a decent, responsible man. And that you brought your son with you, but not your wife." She hesitated, wondering if she should ask. "She said she didn't know why, though."

It had been so long ago that he'd all but forgotten the reasons himself. Certainly they had ceased to matter. Logan almost said so, too, until he remembered what he'd all but forced Sam to tell him a few days ago. Considering what he'd made her recall, the least he could do was be honest with her.

"Karen didn't want to come. She'd decided a career was more important."

Logan's words echoed in Sam's head: *I already told you how I feel about that job you took, but that's nothing compared to how I feel about a mother who's so preoccupied with her life that she doesn't know what's going on with her kids.*

It was no wonder he'd disliked her so much, she thought, absently rubbing her bare ring finger. On top of opposing what she'd been hired to do and thinking she

was neglecting her daughter, she'd brought back the feelings of anger, betrayal and abandonment he had suffered
because of his wife. It was a miracle the man had been as
civil as he had.

"How old was Trevor?"

"Six months."

"Does he ever see her?"

"We've never heard a word from her. She dropped her
little bomb the night Hank called to tell me Pop was dead,
and Trevor and I left the next morning."

It wasn't as if he hadn't known of Karen's ambitions,
he told her, his eyes straight ahead and his voice as flat as
the horizon. It was just that those ambitions had developed after they'd been married and she'd switched her
major from education to media. She'd decided she wanted
to be in newscasting, so it came as no great surprise when
she'd jumped at the chance to work at a station in Houston. He supposed he shouldn't have been surprised, either, when she'd calmly informed him she wasn't going to
be held back by having to take care of a child. He just
shouldn't have believed her the year before when she'd
gone on about how she wanted nothing more than to settle down on the ranch and work horses and raise a garden and babies and be there with him.

That was what he told Samantha. What he didn't tell
her was that he shouldn't have wanted the picture Karen
had painted that year before so badly; the one he remembered from his early youth when his mom had been alive
and his father... happy.

The Jeep tended to rev when it idled for more than a
minute, which was the only reason Logan noticed that
he'd stopped beside the garage. Sam was looking at him
with more concern than he'd seen in a woman's eyes in a
very long time.

Logan killed the engine and was out of the vehicle before that concern could find a voice. He hadn't thought about his ex-wife in years. It had been years, too, since he'd considered why he so seldom saw his brothers and why they willingly left him to tend the land that rightfully belonged to all of them. He didn't particularly appreciate that Sam had caused him to acknowledge those memories now. He appreciated even less that she wouldn't allow him to let them go.

"You wanted a family, didn't you?"

"I have a family," he told her and slammed the door of the Jeep a little harder than necessary.

Sam flinched at the angry sound. But she knew it wasn't anger causing him to shut her out. It was self-protection. Watching Logan, listening to him, she had too easily recognized the lost dreams when he'd spoken of his wife and of his child. Though hers and Logan's circumstances were very different, those were the dreams she had lost, too: that ideal of someone to share home and family with. She knew how a person could deny that dream when the hope of having it was gone.

"Hey, boss!" a rusty voice hollered from across the yard. Hank, his foreman, cupped his hands around his mouth, making a megaphone to carry his already booming baritone. "The vet's here checking over Durham. Want me to have him look at that new mustang while he's here?"

Logan swore to himself. He'd forgotten about the vet coming out this morning.

Calling back to the bow-legged, barrel of a man in coveralls that he'd be right there, thinking his foreman looked far too speculative for his liking—Logan did his best to curb his impatience. He wasn't precisely sure who that impatience was with, anyway. Samantha. Or himself.

She was already out of the Jeep. Stopping near the front fender, she smiled at the old coot in the coveralls.

Pulling his unlit cigar from his mouth, Hank exposed a minimum of teeth, self-consciously tipped his ancient hat to scratch at his forehead. After giving what appeared to be a nod in Sam's direction, he stuffed the stub back under his moustache and hustled himself back inside the barn.

Logan pulled his own hat even lower. "I've got to go. Think about what I said about coming up with an alternative, will you? About Erin, too."

"I will. But I can't promise anything."

"That's fair enough."

She thanked him then for what he'd shown her and turned to head for her car. As she did, Logan found himself wondering if she was only being as gracious as she always seemed to be, or if she actually did intend to consider what he'd said.

He wouldn't blame her if she didn't. Not after the way he'd treated her. But he told himself he'd done what he could to make up for that and let himself consider only the relief he felt now that she was gone. Every time he'd met her eyes, he experienced that unmistakable clenching low in his abdomen. A man could only take so much of that before he had to either get away or do something about it.

Something about her had gotten to him; her scent, her smile, her guts. He wasn't sure. Nor did it matter. He knew only that if she weren't putting down roots in Leesburg, he'd definitely be interested in taking her to his bed. But Leesburg was too small a place for ex-lovers, and she came with too many entanglements—three of them to be exact. Samantha wasn't the kind of woman with whom a man could have an easy affair. Therefore, he'd just ignore the undeniable physical effect she had on him. Or so he was telling himself an hour later when Hank told him he'd just seen Samantha heading back up the road to the ranch. On foot.

Logan met her at the top of the hill. Bringing his truck to a stop, he leaned across the seat of his pickup and pushed open the passenger door. "What's wrong?"

"My car has a flat tire."

"Where is it?"

"About a mile down the road. Maybe two." She shrugged, looking partly chagrined, but mostly annoyed. "I'm not very good at judging distances."

"I'll change it."

"You can't. I mean, I'm sure you know how. I just don't have a spare. I took it out to make room for Michael's science experiment," she explained when his only response had been to take a deep breath. "I forgot to put it back in."

Logan glanced at his watch. Then, back at her. It had been his idea for her to come to the ranch in the first place. "Get in," he told her, feeling responsible and none to happy about it. "I'll take you back to town."

It was obvious from the strain beneath her quiet, 'Thank you," and the soft smile accompanying it, that she hated having to impose. She even asked if one of his men could drive her since she knew he was busy, but Logan needed them doing their jobs. He told her that, too. Then, noticing how she kept glancing at her watch, he asked if she had an appointment somewhere.

Not an appointment. She just needed to get home. School would be out soon, and the neighbor who watched her younger ones could only stay until four o'clock today. She didn't want them alone in an empty house.

Logan didn't like the thought of that either, though he kept his opinion to himself. In fact, he said very little after that, preoccupied as he was with the task at hand and those he'd left behind. Coming upon her car near milepost 56, a little over two miles away, he had her wait in the truck while he jacked up her car and removed the flat. After tossing the tire in the bed of the truck, he drove the twenty miles to the gas station at the Y in the road just inside the town limits and dropped the tire off to be patched.

"I'll be back in half an hour to pick it up," he told the mechanic who'd wandered out of the service bay.

"You don't have to do that," Sam told him as soon as he'd climbed back into the truck. "I'll ask my sister to help me with it after she closes up her shop tonight."

To her surprise he didn't ask if she'd ever changed a tire before. Being his unpredictable self, his concerns went in an entirely different direction. "What time will that be?"

"About six."

"It's dark by then. The two of you don't need to be on the road in the dark changing a tire. Especially with your car sitting at the bottom of a rise. Someone could come over the top and not even see you until you were coming through their windshield."

It wasn't until they were halfway down Main that Sam said anything else. Then, it was only to tell him that her house was the last one on Lockemore. The white one, next to the open field.

Logan pulled up in front of the old Victorian-style house. Painted white with blue shutters, it was spared much of the architectural gingerbread that adorned the other residences visible beyond the expanses of shrubs and lawn. A boy's blue bicycle lay half-hidden in some of that shrubbery. Another, this one a vivid pink with purple flowers and training wheels, sat parked by the steps leading up to the narrow porch.

It was the house directly across the street that had Logan's attention, however. Specifically, the two elderly women sitting on its porch. The moment he pulled up in front of Samantha's house, their speculation began, their white heads drawn together as if by some strange magnetic force and their mouths moving a mile a minute.

Magpies, he thought, reaching for the keys to turn off the ignition. They reminded him of magpies.

"Mind if I use your phone?"

Chapter Six

Sam had just closed the front door behind Logan when she heard Mrs. Gunther shriek.

The startling sound came from the kitchen. Right on top of it came Amy's higher-pitched screech, along with the commotion of scrambling feet, chairs scraping over linoleum and the annoyed squeal of a kitten. A split second of silence was interrupted by the frantic chirping of a bird.

Sam's purse and jacket landed on the narrow table beneath the wall mirror in the entry. "Excuse me," she muttered to Logan, and disappeared through a door near the polished staircase.

Logan, thinking it odd that Sam looked more resigned than alarmed, left his hat next to Sam's purse and followed. The air smelled of starched curtains, lemon oil and the flowers on the dining room table. When he followed

Sam into the short hall leading to the kitchen, he thought he also smelled fresh paint.

"It went under the stove," Logan heard a shaking female voice announce. "Oh, dear. Michael, can you— Samantha." When the woman saw Sam she all but sighed in relief. "I'm so sorry. I didn't mean to scream like that. It just startled me so. Dreadful awful, thing." A shudder scurried through her tone. "I'd say it was a mouse. But it *rattled* when it moved." The shudder became visible when she wiggled her finger toward the stove. "It hasn't come out yet."

Logan reached the doorway of the bright and airy kitchen in time to see a woman in her mid-sixties nod in the direction of the stove. The woman, whose steel gray hair was coiled in a bun, was holding the shoulders of a little girl with pale blond pigtails. From the way she had the child's back pressed to the front of her yellow floral dress, it was hard to tell if she was safeguarding the child or hiding behind her. The child's grip on a small orange kitten was definitely protective, however. And probably painful for the cat. The wriggling ball of fur was doing its level best to struggle free of those well-meaning little hands.

Sam had come to a halt by the refrigerator, the top quarter of which was covered with snapshots, magnets shaped like vegetables and several small squares of brightly covered notes. From where Logan remained in the doorway, he saw her glance fall on the fair-haired young boy sitting ever so innocently at the table, his eyes glued to the small electronic game he was busily playing.

"I don't think it's a mouse, Mrs. Gunther. I think it might be something we were looking for last night." The epitome of calm, Sam's eyebrow arched ever so slowly. "What do you think, Michael?"

The boy didn't look up. He kept playing his game, his thumbs rotating rapidly. "Maybe," he mumbled, his innocence suddenly in question.

"Did you see it?"

"Sort of."

"Is it a mouse?"

"No."

"Isn't there something you should be doing, then?"

With a sigh that made it apparent he was being greatly put upon, Michael laid down the game next to the homework he was supposed to be doing and slid from his chair. His blue eyes looked a little red around the rims, as if he might be coming down with a cold. He sneezed, only adding to the suspicion. Taking a jar from a cupboard, he snatched a dish towel from the counter and sprawled on the floor in front of the stove.

Sam looked as if she were about to protest the use of her good towel. Instead, apparently deciding the admonishment wasn't worth it, she turned to the woman she'd called Mrs. Gunther.

"Are you all right?" Her eyes swept the woman's face, then her arms opened to the little girl moving in for a hug. "Maybe you should sit down. You look a little pale."

"It scared us, Mommy."

"I know it did," Sam murmured to her daughter, wrapping the wide-eyed child in her arms. "I could hear you clear by the front door. Mrs. Gunther?" she asked, her concerns equally divided.

"I'm fine. Fine," the woman repeated, seeming more embarrassed than anything else. "I was just cleaning up from the children's snack and this...this...*thing*...raced across the drainboard and down the front of the cabinet. Why, I never in my life saw anything move so fast."

With her hand over her heart, she again pointed her less-than-steady finger toward the stove. It was clearly her intention to show Sam the exact path the monster had taken, when she turned enough to realize Sam wasn't the only adult interested in her story.

"Oh, my," she said, staring up at the big man filling the doorway. "You have company." Her finger fell, along with her eyebrows as she contemplated Logan. "You're one of the Whitaker boys, aren't you?"

"Yes, ma'am," came the quiet reply.

"I thought so. You must be Logan, then. You've had the RW for quite a while now."

Why Mrs. Gunther felt it necessary to tell him who he was and what he did was beyond Sam—unless she did it to check the credibility of her memory. Sam had noticed that many of the older women in town did the same thing: recited people's backgrounds as if there was going to be a test they simply couldn't allow themselves to fail.

Logan didn't seem to think the tendency unusual, though. Having reverted to reticence, he merely nodded again.

"I'm Mildred Gunther. Harriet Gunther is my sister-in-law." When Harriet's name elicited no acknowledging spark of interest, she added, "Harriet owns the flower shop."

Logan's interest in anything floral was about equal with his interest in small talk. Seeing that she couldn't coax him into a conversation, Mrs. Gunther turned the speculation in her expression on Samantha.

"I do wish you'd called to tell me you were going to be late." She cast a sideways glance at Logan, the look loaded with interest. Catching herself, she smiled at Sam. "I wouldn't mind staying, ordinarily, but I have cards this afternoon."

"I know, Mrs. G., and I'm sorry. I didn't know I was going to run behind schedule."

"She had a flat," Logan added, thinking she might as well get to the point so the older woman's mental wheels could stop spinning.

"Flat tire? Yes. Well, I suppose that does happen."

Mrs. Gunther was not allowed to indulge her speculation about Sam and her rescuer any further. Michael had stuck the long handle of a wooden spoon under the stove. He was now scrambling to his knees. "I see it! It's right in the— Uh-oh."

Sam didn't like the sound of that at all. "Michael. You get that thing and get it out of here."

"I'm trying, Mom. It's hiding back there."

Knowing Amy would scream again if she even thought she saw what her brother was now diligently searching for, Sam smoothed her hand over her little girl's shoulder and told her to go on upstairs to her room. All Amy did was shake her head and wrap her free arm around her mother's leg.

In lieu of barring her view of the bug with walls, Sam moved Amy behind her. "I swear, Michael, if you bring another bug into this house..."

Amy tugged on Sam's pants. "You said we're not supposed to swear, Mommy."

The little girl's voice held admonishment. Even if that hadn't made Sam go silent, the unexpected flash of amusement in Logan's eyes would have done it.

As attractive as he was, the man would be positively devastating if he ever smiled.

"It won't come out," Michael decided from his prone position. "I've gotta move the stove."

Sam was about to inform her four-foot, not-quite-seventy-pound son that he wasn't moving anything anywhere, when Mrs. Gunther stepped forward. "I really must go, Samantha. My friend is due to pick me up in just a few a minutes." A yellow sweater lay over the back of a chair. Clutching it to her chest while dubiously eyeing first Michael, then Logan, she practically backed toward the door. "I'll see you tomorrow."

Sam felt awful. She told the dear woman so, adding how sorry she was that she'd received such a fright. Mrs. G. waved it off, seeming much more interested in Logan as she glanced back toward him, than she was in the creature lurking under the stove. Now that she was out of harm's way.

Still, Sam didn't give her neighbor's interest in the rancher all that much thought. Even before she turned back inside, Sam had been conscious of a scraping sound and the murmur of voices behind her. Her son's voice cautious but respectful. Logan's quiet and sure. Now those voices had her complete attention.

"Can you see it?" Logan asked.

Michael, who knew better, was now on the counter. Logan stood in front of the stove. He had it pulled halfway out.

"Yeah. It's right down there in the corner."

"You want to catch it in that jar?"

Michael said he did. So Logan told him to get down from the counter and he would pull the stove all the way out. Michael needed to be ready with the jar, though, and to be prepared in case the beetle changed direction. Logan would turn the stove to let the bug through on the right.

"It could come from underneath," he warned the boy. "But we'll hope it reacts like cattle and heads for the most apparent escape."

"Is that what cows do?"

"When they're spooked it is."

"What's spooked?"

"Frightened. Scared."

Michael, Sam's budding skeptic, eyed Logan warily. "A cow can get scared?"

"Sure can. Doesn't take much to frighten one, either. Especially at night when they can't see. Sometimes all it takes is the flick of a cigarette lighter to spook one and start a stampede."

"Really?"

Wide shoulders lifted in a that's-the-way-it-is shrug.

"Do you think the beetle's spooked?"

"Don't know. I've never herded beetles."

Accepting his pragmatism, Michael, who was also more logical than he sometimes pretended to be, returned to the matter at hand. "What if it comes up the side of the cabinet?"

A white dish rack sat next to the sink. It still held the breakfast dishes Erin had washed that morning.

Logan picked up a blue plastic bowl. "I'll get it."

The little operation went far smoother than Sam would have expected. But then she'd never expected what she was seeing, anyway. As Logan gripped the sides of the stove and slid it all the way out, she didn't know which was the more remarkable—the deference and cooperation Michael showed a man who was an absolute stranger to him, or the patience Logan had just exhibited with a young boy's insatiable curiosity.

"Ready?" she heard Logan ask.

"Ready," Michael returned, crouched like a kid anticipating a fast ball over home plate.

Muscles bunched, Logan swung the side of the stove out a few inches farther. With the encouragement of the wooden spoon, the beetle darted straight for the opening. The dishcloth came down over the beetle, the jar came down over the mobile lump under the towel and with the expert flick of the cloth and the quick slap of a lid, Michael had the cause of Mrs. Gunther's panic enclosed in glass.

A moment later Logan had the stove back in place. It would have taken Sam forever to wrestle that thing in and out of there.

When he turned, he eyed the three-inch-long black beetle in the canning jar. Sam, he noticed, was keeping her distance.

"It's no wonder you almost gave that lady a heart attack."

Michael smiled, the expression bringing out the dimple in his cheek. "I've never seen one this size. Isn't it great?"

Logan smiled back. The expression looked rusty. Almost unfamiliar. But it was enough to prove to Sam that she'd been right about *devastating*—and to widen Michael's grin. At least until he looked over to where his mom stood with his little sister at the end of the table. The moment Michael saw the pinch of his mom's mouth, his smile faded.

It was the replusive-looking bug clinging to the side of the jar that made Sam look so disgusted. She wasn't particularly happy with Michael for bringing it in, either. But the thought that she'd just robbed her son of his animation made Sam feel miserable. She couldn't remember how long it had been since she'd seen him smile broadly enough to see his dimple.

"Please take that outside," she asked, just as Michael sneezed again. "Blow your nose, first. You know where the tissues are.

"And you, missy," she said, her voice softening as she turned to the wide-eyed little girl clinging to her leg, "you have to keep that kitten out of here. I told you we can't have it in the house."

"But it's lonesome on the back porch."

Sam felt a too-familiar catch in her heart. Lowering herself so she was even with her little girl's eyes, she smoothed the baby-fine strands of hair back from the impish little face. It wasn't the kitten who was lonely. "I've explained to you that we can't keep the kitten, honey. Your brother is allergic to cats. We're going to have to find another home for it," she explained, feeling more like Scrooge by the minute. "In the meantime, it has to stay on the porch. If you want to hold him, go outside with him. Okay? And while you're out there, put your bike away. Mike's too. His is in the bushes."

"'Kay," Amy replied dejectedly. "But if we can't find a home, can we keep it?"

"We'll find it a home. Oh, geeze," she muttered, suddenly remembering the other sound she'd heard a while ago. "The bird. Where's the bird?"

"He's in the corner." Amy, still clutching the hapless kitten, pointed to the stack of paint cans and drop cloths that formed the "house" she'd built for her kitten. "You want me to get it?"

"Not when you're holding the kitten, honey. It traumatizes Tweety."

"'Kay," she muttered again, and headed toward the back door to the rambling backyard that Amy had, at first, thought was their own personal, private park. Amy didn't have to ask what traumatize meant. It was a word she'd heard and had had explained by the police department psychologist when they'd gone through the survivors' counseling the department had provided. She'd be far more apt to ask who Logan was. Surprisingly she said nothing about the man. She merely eyed him as one might a huge, imposing statue, then wandered out the door.

"Thank you for helping Michael. We looked all over the house for that thing last night." Sam offered Logan a faint smile, then distractedly shook her head. "I'm sorry. You wanted to use the phone." She motioned toward the wall. "It's right there."

He should ignore the strain beneath her smile. He certainly wanted to. Instead, as Logan picked up the phone to let Hank know he'd be a while, he found himself wondering just how many of these little crises Sam faced in the course of her day. The little girl didn't appear to be any sort of trouble, other than for what appeared to be a penchant for collecting stray animals, but he'd bet the boy had given her one or two of the silver hairs he'd noticed when she wore her hair pulled back. Then there was Erin.

"But we can't keep it, honey," he heard Sam saying, when he stepped out onto the screened-in porch a minute later. She sat on the back step with her arm around her youngest daughter. The shy child had the kitten in her lap and her lower lip had a definite quiver to it. "It makes Michael sick."

"Erin says Michael makes her sick sometimes but you don't give him away."

"That's a different kind of sick," Sam returned patiently. "Even if it wasn't, we don't give family away."

"Even if we want to real bad?"

"Even then." Her smile was gentle and full of understanding. "We're stuck with each other no matter what."

"Kitty is family."

Weariness entered Sam's voice. "Amy..." she began, only to cut herself off when Logan pushed the screen door open with a groaning squeak. She'd meant to oil it. He knew that, because he'd seen it on her list of things to fix, along with the holes in the porch screens and the broken board on the bottom step. He hadn't been snooping. The bilious green note had been stuck right next to the telephone.

"Would you come in here for a minute?" he asked, when she turned to look up at him. "Alone?" he added, in case her daughter planned on gluing herself to her mother's hip.

He waited until they were back in the kitchen and out of earshot before he said anything else.

"Are you serious about getting rid of the kitten?"

She must have mistaken his frown for disapproval. "I don't have any choice. Michael's—"

"I'm not criticizing," he said, not particularly pleased with the way she'd automatically assumed he was. "I was just going to say I'll take it."

"You will? Why?"

"I'll use it for a barn cat."

"What's a barn cat, Mommy?"

Like a shadow, Amy had followed. She looked worried. She also appeared considerably more concerned about Logan's presence than she had only moments ago.

"Mr. Whitaker will have to explain that to you, honey. I'm not really sure."

The top of the kid's head barely reached the middle of his thigh. She was delicate, like her mother, and there was a sweetness about her that made a guy feel kind of, well...protective, he supposed, though he didn't know if he cared much for the feeling. As small as she was and with that worried look on her little face as she stared up at him, she also made Logan feel like some sort of giant ogre.

Not wanting to intimidate the child, and thinking it easier to talk to her if they could see more eye-to-eye, he moved to where she hovered in the doorway. Hitching at the knees of his jeans, leather boots and knees creaking, he lowered himself to his haunches.

A barn cat, he explained, was a cat who lived in one of the barns or stables on a ranch. Like everyone else on a ranch, it had a job to do. That job was to catch mice. Though Amy looked a bit skeptical at first, she was fascinated that cats could have a real job. What fascinated Sam was Logan.

She stood back, her glance on his dark head while she watched him tell her little girl that he had a couple of other cats who would "show the kitten the ropes," because Amy felt sure her kitten didn't know how to catch mice yet. There would be people around, too, and other animals, he assured her, when her worries shifted back to it being lonesome.

Sam couldn't help but wonder at his patience, the same patience he'd shown Michael. It seemed as natural to him as the reserve that made him look a little wary of the normally shy little girl. He didn't look completely comfortable hunkered down by her. Yet, he didn't appear as if he wanted to bolt and run, either. Recalling the way he'd looked at the pictures on her desk, and remembering how displeased he'd been to learn when they'd first met that she even had children, Sam would have thought he'd find kids as appealing as an encounter with a briar patch. But he didn't dislike children. As she considered him now, she realized that he was probably more drawn to them than he wanted to admit.

"I guess it's okay, then," she heard Amy say in her soft, shy voice. Her little mouth twisted. "But can I come see her? At her barn?"

Logan's wide shoulders lifted in a dismissing shrug. "If it's okay with your mom."

Big brown eyes turned to Sam.

It was the eyes of cool blue that had her protectively crossing her arms.

"We'll see," was all Sam could promise.

Logan didn't question why he'd offered to take the kitten. But he was wondering why he'd told the little girl she could visit the little orange fur ball when he heard the front door open.

He'd just straightened from his crouch in front of Amy when Erin walked in. Right behind her, nearly colliding with her because Erin stopped so abruptly when she saw him, was a tall, slender woman whose pretty smile faded with the lift of her eyebrow. "Hi," Lindsey said without hesitation, then jerked her glance toward Samantha. "What's going on?"

That same question was echoed in Erin's suddenly defensive expression.

Sam felt her own defenses slip into place the moment she encountered Erin's accusing expression. Tamping down the too-familiar combination of hurt and unwanted irritation that arose every time Erin adopted that particular look, she smiled at her sister and turned to her daughter.

"My car has a flat tire," she explained, certain Erin thought the senior Whitaker's presence had something to do with her and Trevor. "Logan brought me back into town and dropped the tire off at the garage to be repaired. That's all that's 'going on,'" she added, keeping her tone deliberately light in the hopes that Erin would lighten up herself.

Lindsey glanced toward her niece. "I told you it was nothing to worry about," she said, making it sound as if Erin had recognized the truck parked out front and started to panic.

Smiling now, because Logan's presence didn't appear to be causing a problem for her sister or her niece, Lindsey turned her attention back to the man studying all three women. "I'm Lindsey. Sam's sister. You're Trevor's father?"

Logan stepped forward. Feeling completely out of his element, he accepted Sam's sister's friendly handshake, then stepped back, feeling antsy. He didn't know if it was being surrounded by so many women, or just being closed off from the open sky, but he suddenly felt a profound and urgent need to be on his way.

"That tire should be ready by now. If you don't have time to come with me," he said to Sam, "maybe your sister can give you a ride out later to pick it up. I'll change the flat on my way back to the ranch."

Sam didn't want to impose on her sister. She wanted even less to impose on Logan. The man looked as if he were about to start pacing.

"I'll get the tire," she told him. "You've done more than enough by bringing me home."

"We've already discussed this." Impatience glinted in his eyes. "I'll change the tire."

"Really. I can do it. You have—"

"For heaven's sake, Sam," Lindsey cut in just as exasperation swept Logan's features. "Let him change it. You don't have to do everything yourself."

"Listen to your sister," he muttered. "You'll take her out to pick up her car?" he asked Lindsey.

"Sure," Sam's ever-so-helpful sibling returned with a shrug.

"Fine."

The fact that Sam preferred the arrangement Logan had just made had nothing to do with the frown she aimed at his broad back when he crouched back down in front of

Amy. The frown that matched the one he'd just given her was there solely because she did not appreciate being steamrollered. Even though she did very much appreciate not having to wrestle with a tire.

"I have to go now," she heard him tell her somber-looking little girl.

He wasn't being friendly by acknowledging the child. Not that his manner hadn't softened considerably. He just wanted to let Amy know it was time to hand over her kitten.

Amy knew exactly what he wanted.

"Now?"

"I'm afraid so."

The child's mouth twisted. Looking resigned, she blew out a deep breath that fluttered the wisps of baby-fine hair on her forehead and held her feline friend out with both hands.

Mewling in protest, the dangling kitten scrambled to find a foothold in the air. Before it could become totally panicked, Logan had its skinny little legs tucked beneath it in the palm of his large hand. By the time he rose, the kitten was tucked snugly at the crook of his elbow, its tiny head looking even smaller in the big man's arm.

Hearing it purr, Amy smiled. "It likes you."

Innocent. Shy. Sweet. The kid was going to be a heartbreaker, Logan thought, smiling back because, somehow, the fact that the kitten liked him seemed to mean it was okay for her to like him, too.

That thought had no sooner occurred than his defenses kicked in, flattening his smile and dulling the pleasure he'd felt at the child's acceptance. He had some making up to do for the way he'd treated her mother, so he'd take the kitten off Sam's hands if it would help. What he wouldn't do was risk the precarious peace he'd worked so hard to achieve, by getting involved in Sam's life any more than he had to. Once Samantha came up with an alternative to the mayor's plan, and Logan could be satisfied that she could support her children without interfering with anything that affected his life, everything would be back to normal.

It was Amy who stood in the door as Logan's truck pulled away from the curb. Sam stood a couple of feet behind her, just in case a hug was needed.

"He looked a little put out," Lindsey observed.

"I told him I'd take care of it."

"Not with changing the tire. With you. He just wanted to help, Sam. If he was frustrated with anything, I think it was with you for arguing with him about it."

Sam would buy the last half of her sister's rationale. People probably didn't question Logan very often, much less argue with him. It was the first part she was having trouble with. The part about him wanting to help.

She didn't get a chance to ask her sister why she felt so certain of that. When Sam turned to face her sister, it was Erin's eye she caught. Her teenager was standing at the foot of the stairs, her arms crossed defensively over the lace-appliqued T-shirt Lindsey had given her from her store.

"I want to live with Shawna."

The thought was totally incongruous, given her daughter's words and the predictable sinking sensation that came with them. But the picture of Amy's kitten nestled in the crook of Logan's arm suddenly materialized in Sam's head. It had looked so safe there, so secure.

She blinked the image away, actually feeling envious. Secure was one thing she hadn't felt in so long, she was beginning to suspect the feeling no longer existed. This wasn't the first time Erin had unsettled her by saying she wanted to go back to Los Angeles. It was, however, the first time she'd been this specific about where in Los Angeles she wanted to go.

"Have you talked to Shawna's mother about this?" Or your Aunt Lindsey? Sam wondered, looking at her sister to see if perhaps her daughter had confided in her.

If the frown Lindsey turned on Erin was any indication, the announcement was also news to her.

Tucking her lower lip between her teeth, Erin hesitated.

The lip popped out. "Not yet."

"Then you and I will talk about it first. Okay? Right after dinner..."

"You don't really want to leave here," Lindsey said, trying to help. "What about Trevor? Isn't there a dance coming up?"

"I'm grounded."

"You are? For how long?"

"Forever."

Concern replacing the frown, Lindsey turned back to her sister. "You're not going to make her miss the dance are you?"

"She's only grounded for another week," Sam corrected, mentally beseeching the ceiling. "And she never mentioned a dance. What dance, Erin?"

"The one the juniors put on for the harvest festival."

"It's all the girls talk about when they come into the shop," Lindsey offered. "It's not until the end of the month, but the kids are already buying their dresses."

Dances were important stuff. At least they had been when Sam was a girl. And they had been important to Erin, too. Until this year. "Why didn't you tell me about it, honey?"

"Because I'm grounded," Erin repeated, still sounding as if the condition were permanent.

"You won't be by the time it gets here," Sam reminded her, caught between the need to stick to her guns, because consistency was so important to a child's sense of security, and the possibility that Logan was right. Trevor was the one friend Erin had here, and Sam was keeping her from him. Erin needed reasons to want to stay. Obviously, her family wasn't enough. "You only have a week to go before you can go back out to the ranch... for your riding lessons."

"You'll let me do that?"

Sam nodded. "Logan says you're pretty good."

Erin didn't return her mother's smile and, at the compliment, she merely turned her glance to the floor. But at least she seemed to have forgotten about going to live with Shawna, when she said she was going to do her homework and headed up the stairs to her room.

Lindsey waited until she heard Erin's door close before she touched Sam's arm. "She's not going anywhere, Sam. She's too crazy about Trevor. Did you know he wants to be a vet?"

Like father like son, Sam thought, and told her sister she hadn't known. She told Lindsey, too, that she found his plans admirable, and tried to be encouraged by her sister's assurance. But Erin was making her nervous with her talk of wanting to leave. Even though it seemed logical to believe her daughter was just testing to see how far she could be pushed, Sam couldn't quite shake the uneasiness that had come with that particular conversation.

One good thing came of it, though—the seed of an idea for the alternative plan Logan wanted her to come up with. After talking to Lindsey about it all through supper

that evening, it had grown into a full-fledged plan—which
was why Sam called Logan first thing the next morning.

The only problem was that she needed his help. And he
wasn't at all anxious to give it.

Chapter Seven

S am didn't see Logan again until twenty minutes after he'd walked out on the meeting. He returned just as the three ranchers he'd called, at her request, were leaving his house with their wives.

She had wanted his support. What she had received had been his silence as he'd leaned against the back wall of his sparsely equipped country-style kitchen, as separate from the others gathered around the old pine table as he had kept himself the night she'd met him. Then, in the middle of the discussion, he'd walked out.

Not sure she could mask how she'd felt when she'd seen Logan's jaw harden just before he'd turned away and left the room, Sam kept her attention on the vehicles nosed up to the low rail fence and listened to the muffled thud of Logan's boots on the porch. From where she stood between the white posts, she could see the interior lights come on in Ty and Zoe Murdock's truck. Through the open door behind her came the steady bong of the grandfather clock striking eight.

"I don't know if they'll all agree to participate or not," she said, when she heard Logan stop beside her. She kept her eyes straight ahead, though she did hug her arms a little tighter against the damp night chill. "The Murdocks and the Muellers might, but that Farley..." Farley was the devil's advocate personified. "Anyway, they all said they'd get back to you on it by the end of the week."

Unable to avoid the inevitable any longer, Sam turned in the pale light to face Logan. When she'd arrived a little over an hour ago, he'd seemed uneasy and edgy. That edginess had escalated to agitation. Now, with his guests departing, he looked more haggard than anything else.

"I'll walk you to your car," he said over the roar and chug of heavy-duty truck engines and the crunch of gravel beneath deeply treaded tires.

He wanted to be rid of her, she knew. Just as he'd been so anxious to leave her house the other day, he was now impatient to get her away from his. She would leave. Under her own steam. But not until she had an answer.

"I'm going," she told him. "Just answer one question for me first. Since you don't like my idea," she went on before he could do anything more than frown, "what do you suggest I do?"

Incomprehension deepened his scowl. "I never said I had a problem with it."

"It was hardly necessary. Leaving the room was a pretty eloquent statement."

For about six seconds, Logan did nothing but stare at her, his eyes steady on her face. Then, muttering under his breath, he pushed his fingers through his hair.

Sam's chin edged up. "Excuse me?"

Had it not been for the vulnerability lurking in her eyes, the arch of her eyebrow might have almost been intimidating. Logan didn't doubt that she wanted it to be. It was the same expression he'd seen her use on her son when she'd asked if he was privy to what sort of life-form lurked beneath her stove.

"You don't want me to repeat it," Logan informed her, thinking her nowhere near as tough as she tried to be. He did have to hand one thing to her, though. She hadn't backed down when Farley and Mueller had started in about what was in this little deal for her. *A decent place to raise my kids and a job,* she'd told them and they'd both, finally, shut up. "But as long as we're answering questions," Logan continued, "why don't you tell me why you've been so sure I'm going to oppose whatever you come up with. You wouldn't tell me what you had in mind when you asked me to call some of the other ranchers, and now you're assuming—"

"I didn't tell you because you were in a hurry when I talked to you," she cut in, amazed he could think there was anything else she could assume. He'd sounded then as impatient as he looked now.

She obviously did not bring out the same qualities in him as did her children. "I didn't want to risk you shooting my idea down before I got a chance to really explain it."

His frown was swift and as dark as the night that had encroached over the hills. "What made you think I'd shoot it down?"

"Because we haven't managed to agree on much of anything else. As it is, when I did explain, you walked out."

She turned away, at a loss as to what he expected of her. She turned right back, refusing to concede. "You were the one who wanted me to come up with an alternative, Logan. This is all I can think of that will keep the town as it is and still bring in money. There's no reason it shouldn't work, either. If the ranchers will help with the expenses to expand the harvest festival, we could make enough by bringing in people from places like San Antonio and Austin to at least put a new sprinkler system in the school. If this works, there are other events the town can sponsor that would bring in money without bringing in permanent business. That's what you want, isn't it? Something that leaves everything around here basically the way it is?''

"I don't have a problem with what you proposed," he contradicted, wondering why it was only when she was yelling at him that she got so animated. Not that she actually was. But her eyes sure were. "The idea's great. I hope it works."

"Then why did you walk out like that?"

His fingers went through his hair again. When his hand came down, he looked very much as if he was about to start pacing the porch. "I just...needed air. It was too crowded in there."

At the defeat in his tone, Sam felt her defensiveness slowly leak from her body. With seven people sitting at a table that seated twelve and nothing in the spacious room other than the chairs they sat on and the appliances built into the L-shaped counter, it hadn't been crowded at all.

A little more of her disquiet faded as she watched him knead the muscles in his neck. She knew from some of the remarks Zoe and Mrs. Mueller had made that it had been years since they had been on the RW. Mrs. Mueller hadn't been there since Vi Whitaker's funeral nearly thirty years ago. Not only because she hadn't been invited, but because Ben Whitaker had apparently "taken to drink" not long after his wife's death. From what Zoe had intimated, Logan's father had become an unpredictable and violent man. Their husbands had even stopped associating with him, though once Logan took over and started his breeding program, they'd started doing business with the ranch again.

As unsettled as Sam had felt when he'd walked out, that disquiet hadn't blocked the swift sympathy she'd felt for the boy who had suffered such a childhood. But she hadn't considered how something that had happened so long ago could still be affecting him now. Thinking only about how unfair Logan was being when he left, she hadn't realized that it wasn't the topic that had sent him from the room.

Most of the years he'd grown up here, people had stayed away. When he'd come back, he'd had no time for anything but the responsibilities of taking over the ranch and raising his son—which meant there was never anyone around but the people who worked here.

Being alone was what he was accustomed to. And he wasn't comfortable with anything else. It was no wonder he'd hesitated on the phone the other day before he'd become so abrupt.

"You could have told me you didn't want to ask them here, Logan." She'd thought she hadn't had his support. She couldn't have been more wrong. By hosting the meeting, he'd told the people who'd come here everything they needed to know about where he stood. And he hadn't even known what she was going to say. "I just thought they would be more receptive to meeting at your ranch than in town."

"They were."

He wouldn't admit to having suffered so much as a hint of discomfort at having his space invaded. Nor would he admit to what had to be profound relief now that he had his space back. He was not the sort of man who could stand to be crowded or confined. Not for very long.

As badly as he seemed to need it, she wanted to give him back his privacy. And she needed to leave before she started feeling any worse than she already did for a man who worked so hard at keeping his fences in place.

"Thank you," she had to tell him. "I really appreciate what you did. Asking them here, I mean."

Her only acknowledgement from him was a faint shrug.

Not sure what else she'd expected, she added, "I'd better go."

Though she hesitated, Logan said nothing to stop her. He simply fell into step beside her after she turned away, walking with her, his hands stuffed in his pockets until they'd cleared the pool of light spilling from the porch.

He'd done what he had because it was important to him. And to her. He didn't question the matter any further than that. He was just relieved that she hadn't pressed him on why he'd walked out. He hadn't lied to her. He had needed some air. Not because he hadn't been all that comfortable having the gathering in his house. That hadn't been as bad as he'd thought it would be. He'd needed to get out of there because it was the only way he could keep from jumping to Sam's defense when everyone had started in. He hadn't made it very far, though. He'd simply paced outside the back door, listening to every word and knowing he'd bolt right back inside if it sounded as if they were getting too hard on her. As he had been when they'd first met.

He had no business feeling that protective about her.

He also had no business thinking how beautiful she looked in the moonlight.

"The stones are loose here. Be careful."

She would be, she told him, and gave him a quick smile that said, capable as she was, she appreciated not being out here alone in the dark.

It was only here, at the end of the house, where the sprawling trees cast shadows in the moonlight, that night encroached so heavily. The sounds of crickets seemed more insistent somehow, the howl of a lone coyote sounded so very close. Beyond those shadows the stables and barns were lit with floodlights. But here, where the pale yellow lights from the house didn't reach and where the land rolled away into open meadow, only outlines and shapes were visible.

All Logan noticed was the shape of her mouth when she turned to look up at him. It looked so soft. So inviting. Like the delicate outline of her face, her throat. The gentle shape of her breasts. He'd spent half the evening wishing she'd never set foot in his house, the other half wishing she was under him in his bed.

When they reached her car, she stopped, her keys jingling lightly as she pulled them from her purse. "You'll let me know when you hear from anyone?"

"You'll be the first."

"Do you think they'll take very long?"

"I have no idea. We'll just have to wait and see."

He'd said *we* and when he had, she'd looked up with a question in her eyes. But she didn't voice it. All she did was give him a soft, almost sad, smile. "I guess so."

He moved closer. Something he shouldn't have done because he was now close enough to catch the scent of her perfume. It was light, innocently seductive, and each breath he drew made the dull ache in his groin grow heavier.

"What will you do if they don't go for it?"

"Worry about it when the time comes." Moonlight shimmered in her hair as, tipping her head, she gave him a resigned smile. "I really don't want to think about that right now."

She couldn't. Not when she was so busy thinking about how dangerous it was standing in the dark with this man. His nearness was crowding out every other concern in her mind—even the thoughts of Erin that had been bothering her when she first arrived.

Troubling as that situation was, thinking about Erin felt infinitely safer. Especially when she found herself thinking about how good it would feel to be held against his very solid-looking chest. So she concentrated on her daughter.

"I told Erin she could come back out next week. For riding lessons," she added, in case he'd forgotten what he'd suggested. "You're probably right about riding giving her something in common with the other kids."

"But you still don't like the idea of her relationship with my son."

The pinch of her brow had been there for several reasons. That was one of them. "He's her friend." And everybody needs someone.

She couldn't bring herself to say that, though. Not to this man who had made it so clear he needed no one.

She was trying. Heaven help her, Sam truly was trying as best she could to face the fact that her daughter had needs she couldn't meet, and to keep from driving Erin away by protecting her too much. She didn't know if she could make this man understand that. Or if he could comprehend how hard it was for her to understand how he could defend something for his son that he wouldn't allow for himself.

Not sure why she was letting it matter, she opened the door with a quiet click.

The door had scarcely parted from its frame when, just as quietly, Logan reached past her and pushed it closed again.

Her eyes collided with his.

Wariness shifted into place. Logan saw it. Yet, she didn't move. And now that she was close enough to touch, he couldn't make himself back away.

"What is it?" she asked, her voice suddenly hushed.

For a moment Logan said nothing. He simply stood, blocking her way.

When he did speak, his voice held a deep rasp. "I should let you go."

"Yes," she whispered, thinking she should move, knowing she wouldn't. "You should."

But he didn't. He held her with nothing more than the intensity in his eyes as they moved over her face—and the touch of his fingers when he lifted his hand and slowly skimmed her cheek.

He smiled. A small quirk of his mouth that made her knees go weak. Or, maybe, what caused that betraying unsteadiness was the way he brushed his thumb over her bottom lip.

"That may be a first."

"What?"

"I think we just agreed on something."

"We did?"

"Didn't you just agree I was right about Erin?" His eyebrows slowly arched over the gleam in his eyes. "About riding," he reminded.

"We only partly agreed. She's still grounded until next week."

"Yeah." Distracted, he drew his thumb along her lower lip once more. With her slow intake of breath, the fullness trembled. "I guess it was just partly, then."

Sam felt that trembling move down, settling deep inside. She wasn't ready for this. For the yearning he awakened with only the touch of his hand. But that yearning was there. And she knew he could see it.

The gleam in his eyes turned feral. His jaw locked with his deeply drawn breath. She heard him swear, the sound short, succinct and as tight as his expression.

A moment later, his head lowered to block the light of the moon.

His lips touched hers softer than she could ever imagine something that looked so hard could be. Warm, firm, full, they settled over her mouth, their heat sweeping through her. But she had no sooner drawn in her breath than she heard a moan rumble deep in his chest and that heady pressure increased.

From the way he'd sworn, Sam knew he hadn't wanted to give in. It was entirely possible, too, that he would regret it when he realized that he'd actually lost a bit of his formidable control. Maybe she would, too. But it wasn't regret she tasted on his lips as he angled her face to deepen the kiss. It was desire and heat, and he was melting something inside her that had felt so very cold.

It had almost been easier when she'd been numbed by that chill.

It was her need for that life-giving heat that felt so threatening when he lifted her arms to loop around his neck. He pulled her against him, drawing her up on tiptoe because he was so much taller than she. Stunned by the flow of heat coursing through her, she went with embarrassing ease, flowing against the solid wall of his chest.

Logan would have been better off if she'd pulled away.

The thought registered vaguely, somewhere in that part of his mind that stored his little remaining common sense. He ignored it. Pulling her closer, he tangled his tongue with hers when she opened to him and felt his whole body tighten. She tasted like summer rain. Warm, sweet. And she felt like heaven in his arms. As slender as she was, he hadn't expected her breasts to feel so full, or for the curve of her hips to feel so lush when he trailed his hand over her bottom and coaxed her more intimately against him.

He heard her gasp against his mouth. Or maybe it was he who moaned. It didn't matter. Smoothing his hand up her spine, images danced through his mind. Images of them lying among tangled sheets; of himself cradled between her legs. He had to be crazy to be doing this to himself. And he was, indeed, going to call himself six kinds of fool for not letting her go when he'd had the chance.

It was torture to let her go now. But he had to. She had pulled her hands down between them, her small fists resting on his chest. He needed to pull back before she did, if only to prove to himself that he could.

Lifting his head, vaguely aware of an arc of light cutting across them, he let his hands slowly fall from her shoulders. He'd known he would regret touching her even before he'd done it. Simply imagining how she might respond to him had made his nights restless enough. Knowing how she tasted, how perfectly her body fit against his, would now make those nights pure torture.

Without a word, he reached for the door, aware now of the sound of a vehicle coming down the graveled road.

This time it was Sam who held it shut. "Why did you do that?"

Shaken, confused, she searched his shadowed features. They betrayed nothing.

"Do you want an apology?"

No! she started to say. But his quiet question served its purpose. He'd pulled back, closing her out because she had, somehow, gotten too close. He didn't want an answer, and, too shaken to know what she wanted or why, she didn't have a response.

Her hand fell from the door, moving to her throat to still the pulse pounding there. Or possibly to hide it.

"Tell Amy her kitten's okay." Gravel crunched beneath Logan's boot when he shifted. "I don't want her worrying about it."

The kitten. He'd just pulled the emotional rug out from under her and he was talking about a kitten.

He'd also remembered to consider a six-year-old's feelings. The man was hopeless.

With the dull click of metal, Logan pulled open her door. As he did, one of the trucks that had departed a short time ago pulled up and a door inside the house slammed.

Ty Murdock waved in their direction, his voice booming across the twenty yards separating them. "The wife forgot her scarf."

"Dad?" a young male voice called from inside the house. "You in here?"

"I've got to go." As if to avoid brushing against her, he stepped back, his hand tightening on the door as he held it for her to get in. "Forget that happened, will you?"

Sam said nothing. Slipping past his brooding frame, she unfolded her hand to release the keys biting into her palm. Not until she was safely inside did she look back up to see him walking away in the pale silver light.

She'd forget it all right. The day pigs flew.

* * *

Pigs had yet to grow wings when Sam heard from Logan two days later. The call came while she refereed an argument between Erin and Michael over how slowly Michael was drying the dishes Erin washed, so Sam missed what Amy had said to him when the little girl answered the phone.

His rumbled "Hi," sent a low hum skimming over her nerves. "What's a damnation?"

Puzzlement made her release her breath. "A damnation?" she repeated.

"Amy said she has one."

The pixie-faced child, who'd blithely informed Sam that "the kitten's new dad" was on the telephone, had already wandered back to the table to finish her job of clearing the supper dishes. Sam didn't need to ask Amy what Logan was talking about, however. Nor did she care to consider why the sound of Logan's voice had her heart beating like a teenager receiving a call from her first crush. Skimming a glance past where Erin stoically ignored the face her brother was making at her, Sam felt a smile form. Logan sounded completely confused.

"It's the kids' new puppy. It has spots so she thinks it's a Dalmation. Like in the Walt Disney movie."

She had no idea what to make of the pause on the other end of the line—or of the fact that she was holding the receiver tightly enough to snap the thing in half.

"Right," he finally said, his clipped tone that of a man who had no idea what she was talking about and was afraid to ask. "Look, Samantha. I'm running a little late here. I just wanted to let you know everyone but Farley went for your idea. He's going to wait and see how your plans shape up before committing himself, but I think he'll come around." She heard the rustle of paper and what sounded like a long, low snort. She'd heard that sound before. Out by Logan's bull pens. Apparently he was calling from one of the barns. "You don't need me involved in this anymore, do you?"

This time it was Sam who hesitated. "Not unless you want to be."

"I don't. I'll donate my share, but Zoe Murdock said she'd coordinate what you need with the ranchers."

"She will?"

"Apparently she's in town a couple days a week. You two can work it out when she's there."

His pulling back wasn't unexpected. As it was, everyone Sam had talked with about her idea was surprised that Logan, reclusive as they all perceived him to be, had gone as far as he had. Sam, therefore, told herself she wasn't surprised, either. What she hadn't counted on was the disappointment she felt at his bluntness. It was more than disappointment, actually. The feeling that was centered in her chest felt suspiciously like hurt.

She realized she must have been wearing that feeling on her face. Her silence had caused Erin to stop being subtle about eavesdropping on the conversation, and her daughter was now openly watching her. Her hands dripping soap suds, Erin wore an expression of uneasy curiosity.

"That's fine, Logan. Great," Sam added, trying for an enthusiasm she didn't feel. "Do you have her phone number handy?"

He didn't. But he told her it was listed, then paused to say something to someone near him. When he turned his attention back to her, the silence became heavy with the weight of whatever else he wanted to say to her. Or ask. But whatever it was that had him hesitating remained as private as he so obviously preferred his life to be. All he did say was that he had to go, then broke the connection within seconds of Sam's embarrassingly reluctant good-bye.

He wasn't the type to be involved. Not in the community. Not with her.

Forget that happened.

Apparently, Logan Whitaker always meant what he said.

Chapter Eight

Logan was, indeed, a man of his word. According to Zoe, who proved to be an absolute wonder when it came to coaxing materials and money out of her neighbors, Logan had been first to put up his cash. He'd done so even before Lindsey, who had worked on last year's harvest festival, had taken Sam's ideas and turned her creativity loose on them.

In a city it would have taken months to expand such an event. But in a small community, committees were made up of the people who actually did the work, not just people who sat around talking about who to get to do it. Within days the high school shop instructor had volunteered his shop classes to build whatever additional booths were needed, adding Alpine "gingerbread" in keeping with the newly adopted Oktoberfest theme that Lindsey had suggested. The home ec teacher had her students making *Apfelschnitzel* and *Aprikosen,* and canning peach preserves to be sold in jars with gingham ruffled lids under a banner claiming Old World Treats, which the art class was making. The quilting club went into overtime, stitching quilts to sell and to raffle.

Even the old men who sat around the barbershop analyzing, scrutinizing and criticizing, got into the spirit by turning their energies to debating the virtues of the various sorts of *wurst* that would be sold. Every organization, group and club was scrambling to stock an additional booth. The high school band was even learning an oom-pah number that was driving crazy everyone who could hear them practicing on the playing field—which was most of the town since the high school was only two blocks from the square.

The spirit of cooperation was truly alive, despite the rush to get so much additional work done by the end of October, and no one complained about how much work was involved. Not even Erin. She spent every available minute at the school working on the huge, arching signs Lindsey had designed for the town square and the football field where the majority of the festivities would take place. That Trevor was at the school with some of the men from the RW building fencing for a beer garden no doubt had much to do with her desire to help. Sam was just grateful to have her daughter so involved.

However, she wasn't sure how she felt, when, a week into the preparations, her daughter stopped by the Chamber office with a message from Logan.

The message had come through Trevor, who had just left for the RW to take care of his horses.

That was what Erin said, anyway, when she dropped her brown canvas backpack on the waist-high counter and idly glanced at the ad her mother was putting together for a San Antonio newspaper. After contemplating the layout while she chewed the bright pink lipstick off her bottom lip, Erin casually reached over and switched two sections of copy and nudged the top border down.

"I've been playing with that layout for an hour." Exasperated with herself, Sam looked up with an admiring smile. "You look at it for six seconds and it's perfect. You have a definite eye for balance, honey. Just like Lindsey."

"Or Dad," Erin corrected, immediately losing interest in what her mother was doing.

"Or your dad." Though it was tough, Sam maintained her smile, refusing to acknowledge the subtle challenge in Erin's expression. "You said Trevor gave you a message for me?"

At the change of subject, the challenge subsided. "He said one of the guys from the ranch is coming by the house to fix the back porch. You're supposed to order some screen."

"What?"

"That's all he said."

"What's his dad doing that for? Sending someone out, I mean."

"I don't know. I thought you'd talked to him about it." A hint of hesitation stole over her expression. Looking uncomfortable, and trying not to, Erin inched her chin up. "Is there something going on with you and Mr. Whitaker?"

Sam's expression mirrored her daughter's. "Going on? What do you mean?"

"I mean, are you two, well...*involved,*" she said, using a word she felt a woman of her mother's generation would understand.

Caught completely off guard by the question, not to mention the accusation lurking in Erin's tone, Sam simply shook her head.

"No, Erin." She hadn't talked to Logan in a week. She wished she could say it had been that long since she'd thought about him. "We're not involved. What makes you ask such a thing?"

Erin didn't answer. She merely reached for her backpack, using the excuse of slinging it over her shoulder to avoid eye contact with her mom. In a way she looked almost relieved, Sam thought. Or, she considered when Erin turned back to her, maybe the somber teenager merely looked preoccupied, which was pretty much how she looked most of the time.

Whichever, Sam couldn't say she was too eager to pursue the topic her daughter had raised.

Apparently neither was Erin.

"Can I go to Lindsey's house after I finish at her shop tonight? I want to help her design the costumes for the waitresses."

"What waitresses?"

"She thinks it would be cool to have the people working the beer garden dressed in Alpine stuff."

Sam doubted very much that Lindsey had referred to *liederhosen* as Alpine stuff. She was also amazed at her little sister's stamina. Lindsey already had more to do than she could keep up with. And she was always willing to take on more.

She had no idea what her sister did for sleep.

"You won't finish at the shop until seven. It's a school night, honey. Don't you have homework?"

"I did it in study hall."

Hating to be saying no to her, Sam offered a compromise. "I was hoping we could all have dinner together one of these nights. With you and me both working on the festival, the four of us haven't had a meal together all week. Why don't you ask Lindsey to come over so the two of you can work and we'll do cheeseburgers on the grill?''

The offer, including the mention of Erin's favorite meal, resulted in nothing more than a disheartened ''Never mind.''

Even bribery didn't work anymore.

Shoving her hair over her shoulder, Erin mumbled, ''I've gotta go. Lindsey has errands to run and she can't go until I get to the shop.''

''Wait! Take these with you.'' Snatching a stack of envelopes lying among the layouts, Sam snagged her daughter by the arm. As she did, she trapped a handful of her beautiful, waist-length hair. ''Drop these off at the post office for me?''

Sam lifted her hand from her daughter's arm, only to catch herself. Erin's hair still reminded Sam of spun silk. It was nearly as baby fine as Amy's and, as Amy liked to do now, Erin use to sit at her feet while Sam had brushed those long tresses, talking of little girl dreams...

Erin wasn't a little girl anymore. But she wasn't yet a woman, either.

''Don't be any later than ten,'' Sam said, because it was better for Erin to be with Lindsey than for her to sulk in her room. ''You need your sleep.''

Perhaps sensing her mother's ambivalence, or possibly remembering how close they'd once been, Erin quietly murmured ''I won't'' and took the envelopes Sam still held.

A moment later, with the faint tinkling of the bell over the door, Sam was left staring at the sunbeams coming through the window, wondering if she and her daughter would ever be close again. Wondering, too, why she hadn't asked her when was this person Logan was sending over supposed to stop by.

Sam recognized Archie Oakes the minute she opened her front door Saturday morning.

"Ma'am," he said, lifting his hat to expose his coppery hair. "You've got a back porch I'm supposed to fix. Like to take a look at it so I can see what I'll need to do, if you don't mind. I'm supposed to check out your sink, too. The one in the kitchen, the boss said."

Despite the eighty-degree heat so typical of southwestern days this time of year, the rangy cowhand wore his workshirt buttoned to throat and wrist. He also wore a smile that was decidedly self-conscious, his manner that of a man who wasn't entirely comfortable being in a place where potted petunias graced the walkway and lacy curtains fluttered on the windows.

Sam appreciated his discomfort. It was his mission she didn't understand.

"It's nice to see you, Mr. Oakes," she told him, meaning it because he'd been so helpful the day she'd gone to the RW in search of her daughter. "But I think there's been some sort of misunderstanding. You don't have to repair my house."

"Yes, ma'am. I do. Boss said."

"Is Logan here in town?"

"No, ma'am. He sent some of the boys to help out over at the school grounds, but he told me I was to come here." He stood a little taller, straightening out the bow in his legs enough to add another inch to his scrawny frame. Something that looked tellingly like pride flitted over his freckles. "The boss was real specific about what I'm supposed to do," he added, making it sound as if he was the only one Logan trusted with this particular task. "He said I wasn't to leave until I'd checked everything out real good."

"There isn't any need for you to do this," she insisted, too bewildered by Logan's gesture for her refusal to sound rude. "If you're willing, I'd much rather you spent your time over by the school grounds. They're clearing the field across from it to use for parking. I'm sure they could use the help."

Archie was shaking his head so vigorously his features nearly blurred. "Can't do that, ma'am. No disrespect, but the boss said I wasn't to mind your protesting. And he said you probably would, too."

"He did, did he?"

"Yes, ma'am."

"Did he say why I'd protest?" she asked, thinking she might get a clue to Logan's rationale from the man's response.

"No, ma'am."

She'd once thought Logan a man of few words. But Archie beat him hands-down when it came to reticence. Or maybe it was just the nature of men who spent most of their time either alone or in the company of other men to be less than loquacious when faced with a woman. What they lacked in communication, however, they made up for in stubbornness.

Nothing short of dynamite was going to blast Archie from where he'd planted himself on her porch. At least, not until she consented to what he'd been sent to do. Having neither dynamite nor the desire to have him camp on her doorstep all day, she caved in and told him to meet her around back.

Sam had her own mission to accomplish. A minute later, having handed the decidedly loyal and determined man a glass of lemonade because he looked as dry as the strawflowers in the wreath over her fireplace, she left him to contemplate the broken board in her back step and headed for the phone.

Logan wasn't available. According to the no-nonsense employee who answered the phone out in the barn, Logan wouldn't be back until tomorrow. "He took the helicopter to the west range, Mrs. Gray" he said, his tone becoming almost diffident after she'd identified herself. "I can try to raise him on the radio, but if he's already caught up with the herd and got him a horse from the string, I won't have much luck."

The matter was hardly an emergency. That being the case, she told him not to bother and was in the process of thanking him for his help when the back door cracked open.

"Did you by any chance order the screen for back here, ma'am?"

"No, I didn't," she told Archie, still tethered to the wall by the phone as she snatched up Spot before the gray-and-white puppy could dart through the tiny opening Archie had made in the back door.

"I'll need to call over to the hardware store, then."

Tilting her cheek away so the puppy couldn't nail her with its tongue, she motioned him in and called to Amy to come get her dog. The crack in the door widened, and an empty glass came through, followed by a shyly smiling Archie.

"Here," she said, trading him the receiver for the glass. Exasperation caused her cheeks to flush. "Ask your boss to call me when he gets back, will you?"

Archie gave her a cautious nod. Or maybe what she saw wasn't caution so much as uncertainty. Whatever it was, as Sam turned from where he was frowning at the plethora of colorful sticky notes that had grown beyond the refrigerator and now surrounded the telephone, she had the feeling that Logan's men didn't quite know what to think of her.

The hardware store didn't have what Archie needed. That being the case, he'd put in an order and, as he'd apparently been instructed to do, charged it to the RW account. He also told Sam he'd be back just as soon as the materials he needed arrived. But it wasn't Archie who brought the supplies a few days later.

It was Logan.

He was in town for his weekly supply run. But it was after five when he arrived at Sam's house, dog-tired and in no mood for the argument he suspected he might get. He'd slept on the range for the last two nights, out under the stars with his drovers. There was nothing unusual about that. Logan often went out to help move cattle. During roundup, when there was sorting, branding and castrating to be done, he'd be out for days at a time before coming in to catch up on chores and then head back out to help his men again. After so many years, he was certainly accustomed to the abuse inflicted on a man's body by wrestling a ton of mule-headed steer, or sitting on a horse for twelve hours, or sleeping on ground with as much give as a slab of reinforced cement. Such activities were bound to catch up with a man sooner or later. The aches in his bones got a little more vocal with each passing year, and when he was tired, he noticed them more.

Though it required a little more effort than usual, he sought to ignore the bruised feeling and push past the fatigue settling in his bones. Promising himself a long soak in a hot tub and a double shot of something fiery to finish what the soak started, he climbed out of his black pickup and lowered the tailgate.

He had pulled a five-foot-long roll of mesh screen from the loaded bed and hoisted it over one shoulder when he heard Sam's front door open.

Michael appeared in the doorway of the welcoming old house. His light brown hair was tousled, as if he'd been running, and his grin held more welcome than mischief. Right behind him was his mother. There was no welcome to be seen in her delicate features, however. Hesitation clearly marked her expression, and the way she protectively crossed her arms over her loose yellow T-shirt after she stepped outside had Logan bracing himself.

"What are you doing?" she asked.

Locking his jaw against the ache in his lower back, knowing now what Hank had meant years ago when he'd warned Logan he'd regret not adding those extra blankets to his pack to pad the ground, he looped his arm over the rolled screen. "Leaving this so Archie can rescreen your back porch. Hey, Mike," he called before she could ask any other questions he didn't want to answer. "Come help me unload this, will you?"

The slam of the front screen door had the windows rattling. "All of it?" the nine-year-old asked, bounding down the steps as he eyed the load of feed sacks and rolls of barbed wire.

"Just the boards and the two small sacks just inside the tailgate. I'll get the boards, if you'll get the rest."

"I can get the boards, too," Sam heard her son say as he loped past her. "They're not that big."

Amy's pink and purple trainer bike blocked the walkway. Skirting it, Sam saw Mike round the back of the truck, his expression full of anticipation when he grinned up at the man dwarfing him. More interested in keeping her son from hurting himself than in the fact that she hadn't yet agreed to what was going on, she was about to tell him to let Logan take care of the boards himself when she found her progress blocked.

Logan had stepped in front of her, his solid chest blocking her from her son. Though his eyes were shaded by the brim of his hat, she could still clearly see the lines of fatigue etched around them.

"They're only two-by-sixes," he said, his deep voice a low rumble. "They aren't heavy. Just awkward. Let him help."

Logan had spoken low so Michael wouldn't get the idea that he was countermanding his mother, a gesture Sam would have appreciated had she been thinking of anything other than the distance in his expression when his glance moved over her face.

"It won't hurt him," he added, then turned to the child checking out the heavy-duty shock absorbers on his truck.

"Here you go." He pulled the top board off with his free hand. "Take one at a time and lay them by the back porch. At the far end, so no one trips on them."

"Are you going to fix the broken step?"

"One of my men is going to," Logan explained over the clunk of the board hitting the tailgate. "He's going to fix the whole porch."

"How come you're not going to do it?"

"Michael!" Sam cut in, but both males, more interested in balancing the the narrow plank on Michael's shoulder, ignored her.

"Because the job will probably take a couple of days and I can't be away from the ranch that long right now. Archie's an old hand at this kind of thing. He'll do a good job."

"Can I watch?"

"If it's all right with your mom. And if you stay out of his way."

"I will," the boy solemnly promised, his sober expression making it seem as if it would never occur to him to cause even the slightest bit of trouble.

Baffled as much by her son's behavior as Logan's, Sam did what Logan had done moments ago and stepped between him and her son. "May I talk to you for a moment? Please?" she added, ever so reasonably.

At the quiet determination in Sam's expression, something that looked suspiciously like resignation passed over Logan's haggard features. Giving the child a nudge to get him on his way now that he was balanced, Logan muttered an unenthusiastic "Sure" and started toward the back of the house himself. "Grab that sack of nails while you're at it, will you?"

"Wait a minute! What I want to talk to you about is what you're doing."

"Then talk to me about it while we unload," he told her and kept on going. "I need to get back and I don't particularly feel like entertaining your neighbors."

It wasn't until he mentioned it that Sam became aware of their audience. Mrs. Gunther was across the street visiting with one of their elderly neighbors while the woman tended her flower garden. Both women, heads together and mouths moving, appeared far more interested in what was going on in Sam's front yard than they did the health of Mrs. Shuman's prize-winning dahlias.

Sam, perplexed, slapped on a smile and waved toward the ladies before heading, as nonchalantly as possible, after Logan. Picking up speed as soon as she'd escaped the women's view, she caught up with him and Michael just as they reached the strip of dirt along the back of the house where she'd intended to plant tulip bulbs this month. The bulbs had already been scratched off her list.

"I can't let you fix my house, Logan."

"Why not?" he asked without breaking stride. "It needs to be done."

"Yeah, Mom," Michael piped in ever so helpfully "You're always yelling at us to be careful of the bottom step. And flies won't come in the house if there aren't any holes in the screens. You go ballistic every time you see one."

"I do not go ballistic, Michael."

Trotting alongside Logan, Michael rolled his eyes, then grinned up at the big man. "Yes, she does," he said in that cheeky, conspiratorial way preadolescent boys seem to come by naturally. "She chased one all over the house last night with a rolled-up newspaper. She was standing up on the couch whacking at it and everything."

"Did she get it?"

"Yeah. I gave it to my frog."

Something that almost passed for a smile tugged at the hard edges of Logan's mouth. But he wouldn't let the smile form. Or, maybe, Sam thought, unable to deny the sympathy she felt for him when he released a deep, weary breath, he was just too tired to muster the effort.

Wondering why he pushed himself so hard, not wanting to care, she glanced toward the sagging screens and the step she had put her foot through two days after they'd moved in. The porch itself was wonderful, deep and wide and a great place to sit on balmy evenings, or for Amy to play in when the mosquitoes got bloodthirsty. It would be nice to have it fixed. And she planned on doing just that. Next spring.

"How about getting that other board?" From the corner of her eye, Sam saw Logan take the board Michael had carried and set it down with the roll of screen next to the latticework under the back porch. "And the sacks your mom forgot. Bring those, too."

Michael, who seldom showed much enthusiasm for anything that didn't involve something gross, had no sooner run past the fragrant clematis vine blooming by Erin's bedroom window, than Logan turned back to her. He did not look pleased.

"What is your problem with me doing this?"

"My 'problem,'" she repeated, hating to seem so ungrateful when he was going out of his way for her, "is that I don't understand *why* you're doing it. I can't afford to have any work done around here right now."

"I don't expect you to pay me. And I'm doing it," he went on before she could tell him she couldn't accept that, "because you're doing something I asked you to do. Look on it as my way of repaying you." He saw the softness he felt so compelling steal over her fragile features, her understanding removing her caution. "I don't like owing anybody."

The caution slammed back into place, seeming to rob the strength from her voice. "I'm not doing it just for you. I'm doing it for me, too. You don't owe me anything."

"Yeah, well that's not the way I see it."

"What the town is doing might not even work," she suggested.

"That won't be your fault. Look, Samantha, you've got some things that need to be done around here, and I've got the manpower to do them. In a couple of weeks, we'll be into roundup and I won't be able to spare anybody for an hour, much less for a couple of days."

He'd had a feeling she'd argue with him about this; if for no other reason than because she seemed so dead set on doing everything herself. Ever since he'd left here last week, he'd found himself wondering how she thought she could manage all she was trying to tackle without a little

more help. Between her job and her kids, she had enough
to handle. She needed someone to finish the painting
she'd started and to fix the sink he knew she hadn't had
much luck with, because he'd heard it dripping into a can
or bowl or something when he and Michael had corralled
his beetle. Her back porch wasn't anything she could
tackle on her own. Though, remembering his encounter
with her next to the plumbing at the hardware store, he
wouldn't put it past her to get a book on basic carpentry
and give it a shot.

It shouldn't matter to him that she was struggling with
so much. It shouldn't matter, either, that the look in her
eyes was causing him to feel bad, too.

"Samantha," he began, not sure what he'd said to rob
the light from her eyes. He lifted his hand to her cheek,
unable to deny himself that contact any longer. "This isn't
any big deal. Just let me take care of it. Okay?"

The man didn't play fair. At least, that was Sam's
thought when she felt his strong fingers nudge back the
strands of hair the warm breeze had tugged across her
cheek. His touch was gentle. The look in his eyes, suddenly, was not. Hungry and heated, his glance fell to her
mouth.

Sam's heart jerked against her ribs, the quick pounding in her ears nearly deafening her to the electronic war-
ble of the telephone ringing inside the house.

The ringing stopped a moment later. The pounding did
not.

Scarcely aware of how completely she was failing to
protect herself, her head tilted toward the warmth of the
callused fingers drifting along her jaw, her eyes locked on
the disturbing depths of his. He didn't want to owe anyone. To be obligated. To be committed. He'd told her that

every way he knew how. Yet, when he touched her, she felt a need in him that contradicted every word he said.

Or maybe it was only her own need she felt.

Her breath shuddered out as she lowered her head, forcing him to break the nerve-racking contact. It would have been so much easier had she never once known the closeness she craved. But as long as she focused on her children, she would be okay. If she started thinking about what she might need, she had the feeling she'd be lost.

"I'll accept your help," she said, her capitulation barely audible over the sharp crack of wood slamming together when Michael dropped the board he'd retrieved atop the one behind them. "For the kids. That step needs to be fixed before one of them forgets to be careful and gets hurt."

She didn't know if he realized how she was rationalizing or not.

Michael was completely hidden behind Logan, oblivious to what was taking place between the adults. Erin, however, had a totally unobstructed view from the back door.

Sam realized that, when she saw her daughter's disapproving glance bouncing between her and the man casually stuffing his hands into his pockets. "Aunt Annie's on the phone," she said before turning away.

"That's my sister."

"I thought your sister's name was Lindsey."

"Annie's my sister in Seattle."

"Go take your call," he coaxed. "I'm leaving, anyway."

Michael's head poked up from where he'd been inspecting the twine holding the roll of screen together. "Can't he stay for dinner, Mom?"

"No," Logan said before Sam had to look uncomfortable with the suggestion. "I've got to get back."

Michael's face crumpled. Ruffling the boy's hair, he finally saw a smile form. It was probably tough being the man of the house around here. "There are certain chores that don't get done when I'm away, and I've been gone for two days as it is. If I stay for supper, it'll just be that much later before I get to 'em."

It wasn't the chores that had him so anxious to get moving. Though he wasn't being dishonest with the boy about what was stacked up on his desk waiting for him. What had him needing to leave was the thought of sitting at Samantha's table. Seeing her smile at him across it with her kids gathered around, just didn't seem terribly wise somehow.

Nor did the thought of what he'd like to do with her once those kids were in bed.

"You are welcome to stay, Logan. You've got to eat, anyway, and it's the least we can do to repay you for what you're doing for us."

If she was trying to throw his words back at him, make it clear somehow that no one was going to owe anyone in this little arrangement—whatever it was—she was going to have to improve her technique. It would help, too, if she wouldn't look at him with that quiet concern she seemed to come by naturally.

"I appreciate the offer," he told her. "But I really do have to get back. Trev said he needs to talk to me tonight. About college," he added, because it felt right to tell her that. "He'll be starting winter term instead of waiting until next fall."

Logan's last words were overridden by Erin, their subtler import lost on Sam when her daughter called out an utterly impatient "Mom! Telephone!"

Not at all sure why Erin sounded so exasperated, wondering why she wasn't talking to Annie herself until she got there, since Annie would want to talk to all of the kids, anyway, Sam backed toward the door.

"Congratulate him for me?" she asked, because she felt sure Logan must be proud of his son graduating ahead of his class, even though at the moment he just looked more tired at the thought of having yet something else to do. "And be careful driving home," she added because he did look so weary.

Logan said he would, then turned to see her son rummaging through the sacks of nails, tacks and tape. Even before Sam made it through the back door to take her call, Michael was chattering away about Logan's truck. But it wasn't admitting how hungry Michael was for an adult male in his life that had Sam pacing after supper that evening. Nor was it the possibility that she might be doing her son more harm than good by letting him form an attachment to someone who could disappear from their lives any time he chose. It wasn't even how good the rough and rugged rancher had been with Amy when, just before he'd left, she had returned from her classmate's house with Spot bouncing along on his leash behind her.

What had Sam nursing the knot in her stomach as she stood outside Erin's bedroom door, was her oldest daughter's reaction to what she saw as her mother's betrayal.

Chapter Nine

Sam knocked on Erin's door, then reached for the knob. It was locked.

"Come on, Erin. I want to know what's wrong."

"Nothing's wrong," came the belligerent reply from the other side. "I just didn't want any dinner."

"Open the door," Sam insisted, refusing to believe lack of an appetite was at the root of Erin's attitude tonight. When Sam had come in to talk to Annie, Erin had sent her a wilting look and promptly stomped up the stairs to her room. She'd stayed there through dinner and the entire lineup of her favorite sit-coms. Now, she was refusing to open the door.

"Erin, open *up*."

The sound of feet hitting the floor with a thump was followed by equally irritated footsteps. Erin didn't open the door herself, though. She merely unlocked it before stomping back across the room.

Sam had the door open by the time the denim-clad teenager had plopped back down on the pink eyelet-covered twin bed. Sitting cross-legged in the middle of it, Erin had Pete, the threadbare stuffed rabbit she'd had since she was a baby, pressed beneath her crossed arms.

Moving into the relatively neat room, wishing her son the slob would pick up the neat streak his sister had somehow acquired along with her less desirable traits, Sam set the sandwich she'd brought next to the assortment of mousses and makeup on the white wicker dresser.

Erin eyed the sandwich with distinct distaste. "Dad wouldn't make me eat if I wasn't hungry."

"Dad wouldn't have been around at dinnertime to notice you didn't want to eat," Sam said, a little tired of hearing herself compared to Jim, something Erin had taken to doing with some regularity. Even when the children's father had noticed problems with the kids, he would have left Sam to handle the situation. He'd dealt with enough crises in his work. Because of that, Sam had tried to shield him from the minor ones at home. "I'm not going to make you eat, Erin. It's just there if you want it. You're the one who will suffer most if you get sick."

A blouse was draped over the chair at the desk. Picking it up, along with the T-shirt under it, Sam added them to the clothes hamper sitting beside the row of shoes in the closet.

Erin still had packed boxes stacked inside.

"You lied to me."

Sam whirled around, completely unprepared for her daughter's accusation and the venom behind it. "What are you talking about?"

"You came down all over me about how important it is to tell the truth so people can trust you, but you lied.

You said there wasn't anything going on with you and Trevor's dad.''

"There isn't," Sam retorted, incredulous.

"Then why did he touch you like that?"

"Like how?"

The look in Erin's eyes had no business at all on the face of a child protectively hugging her rabbit. It was far too old, far too knowing. And the moment Sam saw it, she knew exactly what her daughter was talking about. Erin had obviously seen Logan push back her hair as they'd talked outside the back porch.

There were degrees of involvement. For Sam to say nothing was going on between her and Logan was not exactly true. There was definitely something between them. Physical attraction, at the very least.

"Logan is my friend," Sam said, the description the best she could manage. "He wants to help."

"That wasn't what it looked like he wanted to me."

"Erin!"

"I'm not blind, Mother. And I'm not stupid. Trevor thinks his dad has a thing for you. And you're out at the ranch at least once a week."

"I've been to the ranch three times," Sam said, not sure why she was even having to defend herself. "Once to get you and twice for business."

"That's not what people are calling it. Katy Murdock's mom saw him kissing you when you were out there last week. That's not just friends," she insisted, her voice rising and her eyes growing suspiciously bright. "How could you do that? What about Dad?"

"What about him?" Sam insisted, only to realize that she finally had a hint of what was really going on here. "He isn't here anymore, Erin. But we are. And we go on because we don't have any choice. All of us."

"But were not supposed to forget him!"

"I'm not!"

"You are, too. If you still cared you wouldn't be interested in some other guy."

Sam crossed her arms tightly over the roiling sensation in her stomach. It was either that or shake the living daylights out of the girl glaring at her from the middle of her bed. This wasn't about Logan, though heaven knew Sam hadn't suspected the whole town was talking about them.

"You're sixteen years old, Erin. That hardly makes you an authority on human nature, much less on how I think or feel."

Despite the deliberateness of her words, Sam made her voice as calm as she could. She'd been through enough sessions with the psychologist to know he would say that Erin was only lashing out, that she was hurt by what she perceived as a betrayal by her mother of her father's memory and that the thought of her mother with another man made her feel threatened. He would also probably tell Sam to let the girl talk it out without judging, condemning her feelings or taking her anger personally.

The man had obviously never raised anything but houseplants.

"Do you want to talk about this without yelling?" she asked, willing to try, anyway.

"There's nothing to talk about."

"You're the one who brought it up."

Erin's glare was mutinous, but she said nothing—something she was very good at doing when it served her purpose.

"All right," Sam conceded. "You don't want to talk, and I don't know what to say to you that will make any difference. All I can tell you is that I honestly don't know what my relationship with Logan is right now. But if and when the time comes that I do get serious about another man, I would hope you'd try to be as understanding about it as I'm trying to be about you and Trevor.''

Erin didn't seem to know how to react to that. And since Sam didn't want to make the situation worse by telling her daughter to stop being so selfish and to start thinking of someone other than herself for a change, she left the room. Every person in this family was coping as best they could, yet Erin seemed intent on making life miserable for all of them.

It was after midnight before Sam heard Erin stop tossing in her bed. Every instinct told her to go and comfort her child. But she knew it would do no good, so Sam lay curled in a little ball in her own bed, staring at the pattern of shadows the lace curtains and the moonlight made on her wall. She lay that way for a long time, waiting to hear Amy's footsteps in the hall—until she remembered that Amy hadn't climbed into bed with her since she'd bought Spot for the kids. Tonight, though, Sam really missed the company. With Amy's little body curled up in her arms, she might have found enough comfort to sleep herself.

As it was, all she could do was lie there. And try not to think. Admirable as the attempt was, the only thing she managed to avoid was sleep itself—which was why, once fatigue finally won out, she slept right through her alarm the next morning.

Mornings were always harried. Starting out thirty minutes late made this one positively frantic. That was why, in the rush to make sure Michael was wearing matching socks, get Amy's hair braided, so it wouldn't be a knotted mess by the time she got home from school, and chase down change for Erin's lunch, Sam didn't get a chance to indulge her concern about last night's argument. Erin wasn't acting any differently than she did on any other morning—given that the girl had never been a morning person. But as hurried as everyone was, Sam forgot to ask her if she was working at the football field that afternoon or if she would be at Lindsey's shop.

That was why she had to call Lindsey later that day to ask if she knew what Erin's plans were. It was Wednesday and because Mrs. Gunther had bingo on Wednesday nights, Sam needed Erin to watch Michael and Amy while she attended a meeting. But Lindsey said Erin must be working at the school because she wasn't working at the shop this week, which Sam would have remembered had she not been up to her topknot in preparations for the festival.

It was only a week away. And the football field was humming with activity when Sam arrived. Between the pounding of hammers and the blare of a boom box pouring out a twangy lament, she could barely hear Bud Meiers's reply when she tapped him on the shoulder and asked if he'd seen Erin anywhere.

Shoving his baseball cap back on his bald head, the portly mayor abandoned his surveillance of the thirty or so people milling about and wiped the perspiration from his forehead with the back of his shirtsleeve. From what Sam had heard, he never did a lick of work when he came by to check things out. But he did spend a lot of time standing around handing out subtle criticisms with his glad-handing.

"Haven't seen her around here anywhere today," he told her, dabbing at his forehead as if he'd been working up a sweat right along with everyone else. "But listen, Samantha, I've been meaning to get an update from you.

About where you are with our business development," he declared, adding a grin. "I know you've been tied up with all this, and I'm real pleased with the way you got the ranchers cooperating, but we've got to start getting some commerce in here."

The grin that had once seemed so pleasant to her looked a little forced. Or maybe it was just that he was uncomfortable standing in the warm sun. Whichever, Sam was well aware of the fact that she hadn't been soliciting businesses as his plan called for her to do. She knew he knew it, too.

"I'd like to see something happening on that real soon," he told her.

Sam was sure he would. But she was too preoccupied with finding Erin before her meeting with Zoe's committee to mention that he might want to entertain a change of strategy on his development. As "forward thinking" as he'd told her he was, she felt certain he'd be willing to listen to new ideas—if the festival turned the profit she hoped it would. Unable to talk to him now, though, she promised to get back to him right after all the craziness was over. Then she snagged the shop teacher when he walked by to see if he'd seen Erin anywhere.

That inquiry turned up another zero. When two more turned up the same, she decided Erin must have gone home and headed there herself.

Erin wasn't at home, though. According to Mrs. Gunther, who practically backed out the door when Sam walked in because she didn't want to be late getting to the church, Erin hadn't come and gone while she was there, either. When Sam glanced into her daughter's room, it didn't appear that she had been home at all. There were no school books on the desk and her backpack was gone.

Sam was turning from the door, not sure whether to be worried or angry, when she noticed the closet. The door was open. Most of the clothes inside were gone.

So was the makeup from her dresser.

And the clothes from her drawers.

And Pete.

"Can we have bacon for dinner, Mom?"

Michael stood at the bottom of the steps, oblivious to how the color had just drained from his mother's face. In his right hand he held a pound of bacon. In his left he held the knife with which to open the package.

"Michael James," Sam said in a voice held tight for fear shock would raise it too much. "Put the knife back. Carefully. I'll get your dinner in a minute."

"I'm hungry now. Can I have some ice cream?"

"Michael, please," she begged, taking the knife herself when she passed him at the bottom of the steps. "Get an apple."

Stepping over Spot, who had designated the doorway of the kitchen his personal space because it afforded the best view of kitchen and living room, Sam snatched the receiver off the hook. Her hand shaking as she searched through notes on the side of the fridge, she found Logan's phone number and punched it out.

Amy, already working on an apple, wandered over to peer up at her mother. "Are you mad, Mommy?"

"No, baby." She wasn't mad. What she felt was more like panic. And worry. "I'm just...hello," she said, when a male voice answered the ringing on the other end of the line. "This is Samantha Gray. Is Logan there?"

She should have asked for Trevor. If anyone would know where Erin was, he would. That she hadn't hesitated to ask for Logan seemed telling somehow, but she didn't care to wonder why that had been. All that mattered just then was that it seemed like forever before she heard Logan's voice on the other end of the line.

"I'm so glad you're there," she said the moment after he'd said hello. "Is Erin there with Trevor? Have you see her?"

A moment's hesitation preceded his cautious "What's wrong?"

"Her clothes are gone. And Pete."

"Pete?"

"Her stuffed rabbit," she explained, needing him to understand the significance of the missing bunny. The fact that Erin had taken Pete meant she didn't intend this separation to be temporary. "As close as she is to Trevor, I thought maybe she was there with him. I know how she loves it at the ranch and after—"

"She hasn't been here since she came out last Sunday," he said.

Erin and Trevor had gone on a picnic. Sam had supplied the fried chicken.

Logan's response was not what she wanted to hear. "Are you sure? If she isn't in the house, maybe she's in the stable. Could you look?"

"I just came from there. She wouldn't be here without Trevor anyway, Samantha. And he's not here."

"He's not?"

For several disturbing seconds, there was nothing but the faint hum of static on the other end of the line. Static and an uneasy silence.

"Logan?"

"I'm here," he said, apparently catching the worry in her voice. "I'll get back to you in a few minutes."

"What's going on?

"I'm not sure. Just let me check something out. You're at home, aren't you?"

That Logan now sounded concerned, too, wasn't lost on Sam. But the terseness in his tone didn't allow for any more questions. He clearly had something in mind and, preoccupied with it, he wasn't interested in delays.

Not wanting any herself, Sam told him that she was home, not at the office, and that she would wait for his call. Praying fervently that it wouldn't take him long to do whatever it was he was doing, she added an additional supplication for patience with her son. He was behind her whining about hating apples while Amy coaxed a reluctant Spot to take a bite of hers.

Tuning out Michael, hoping the dog wouldn't get sick, Sam grabbed the phone again and called Zoe to tell her something had come up with one of her children and she wouldn't be able to make their meeting tonight. Zoe, having survived five children of her own, understood perfectly.

Five minutes passed. The kids got peanut butter and jelly sandwiches and carrot sticks for dinner. Then, to keep from going stir crazy waiting for the phone to ring, Sam wiped down the drainboards and put away the breakfast dishes from the drainer. When five more minutes dragged by, then ten, she tackled the sandwich crumbs on the table, wrapped the uneaten carrot sticks to recycle for tomorrow's lunches and caved in on the ice cream. By the time the kids were ensconced in the living room with their dessert and Logan still hadn't called, she'd decided enough was enough and called him back herself.

Logan wasn't there.

He was on his way to Austin.

The hum of the truck's powerful engine muffled the mournful lament of the country song coming through the speakers. Catching just enough of the melody to be irritated by it, Logan snapped off the radio and settled his hand back on the wheel. Normally his grip was relaxed, the way it was when he held the reins of a horse. At the moment his grip was considerably tighter than usual.

He trusted his son. He just wasn't sure what in the hell Trevor was thinking, taking Erin with him. If he was doing what he appeared to be doing, though, the boy was messing with something that held the potential to all but ruin his future.

The kid had turned eighteen last week. For a number of very good reasons, he had no business with a sixteen-year-old girl in his hotel room.

A thread of guilt tugged at Logan's conscience. He knew what it was to want a woman. Heaven knew he'd spent enough time under the icy spray of a shower himself lately, so he wasn't faulting his son his hormones. Trevor was a normal, healthy male. He was also well acquainted with the facts of life. The boy had, after all, grown up on a ranch where breeding was the lifeblood of the entire operation. There were just a few facts Logan hadn't passed on. All of them having to do with protecting priorities when a woman entered the picture.

It was that failure that forced his actions now. He would be the first to admit his parenting skills were questionable at best. That Trevor had survived his father's well-intentioned efforts at raising him was testimony only to the kid's resilience. But, man-to-man, Logan should have warned the boy about how a man's physical need for a certain woman could interfere with even his best intentions. That need could be so strong it could make a guy abandon his common sense. And endanger his dreams.

Logan didn't want that to happen to Trevor. The boy had dreamed of being a vet since he was old enough to hold a bottle to an orphaned colt. With his grades and determination, there was no reason he couldn't accomplish that goal. Provided he didn't do anything foolish in the meantime to jeopardize it.

The way his father had.

The road curved to the left, dipping down to cross the bridge at Haven Creek before straightening out to lead to the freeway. He took the road to the right. The one that headed into Leesburg.

Edgy with his thoughts, it did little for his mood to have to take Erin's mother with him.

Within seconds of hearing the truck pull up in front of the house, Sam was at the window cupping her hands against the glass to see who was there. Logan had barely cleared the front fender before she had the door open and was watching his strides make short work of the walkway.

He was dressed much as he always was: chambray shirt, denims and boots. Except the shirt was crisp and the jeans had only had a few washings. The boots weren't the rundown and dusty ones she was accustomed to seeing him wear, either. These were much newer. Made of black leather, they looked hand tooled and very expensive.

Her glance jerked to his face when those boots hit the top step. Beneath the brim of his black hat, this one not nearly so battered as his gray one, he looked as hard and unapproachable as the day she'd met him.

"You said you were going to call."

Reaching for the screen door, he pulled it open. "I tried. Twice. Your line was busy."

The call to Zoe, she realized, backing up when he walked in without another word. From the nick in his chin, it appeared he'd just shaved and showered. He smelled of soap and shaving lotion, leather and fresh air. As grateful as she was to see him, she didn't bother to worry about why she had become so fond of that particular combination.

Logan didn't enter a room. He claimed it. Closing the door with a solid click, he tossed his hat on the entry table as if that were where it belonged and took the three steps that brought him to where she'd backed up.

His glance barely touched her pale features before it settled on the kids pressed to the front window. Michael grinned at him. The little girl with the white bows in her hair and the lavender balloons on her T-shirt looked as unhappy as the day she'd had to give up her kitten.

"Let's go into the other room," he said to Sam.

She didn't budge. "Do you know where she is?"

Realizing he was going to miss something, Michael had pitched the electronic game he'd been playing onto the sofa. He now materialized behind his mom.

"Erin ran away," he announced, his matter-of-fact tone designed to let Logan know he was already privy to what was going on so there was no need to cut him out of the conversation. "If she doesn't come back, I'm going to ask for her room. It's bigger than mine."

"She is coming back!" Amy shouted, causing her startled puppy to start yipping at Michael in defense of his little mistress. "She's just on a sleep over."

"She is not."

"She is, too!"

"Not."

"She is, too. Isn't she, Mommy?"

"Kids, please." Needing very much for calm to prevail, Sam bent to silence the puppy by stroking its head, then carried that soothing touch to her daughter by pushing back her feathery bangs. "This is all going to be okay. Let's not make it worse by getting upset with each other."

"Erin is coming home, isn't she?"

"Maybe not tonight," she told the child, not wanting to give assurances that might not materialize. "Let me find out what's going on. Okay?"

"What if she went to New York?" Animation sparked beneath the thoughtful expression on Michael's face. "Or that place in that movie where those sleezoids sold those girls to that slave thing..."

"What movie?" Sam gasped, not sure which was worse—that her son was bringing up the very things making her nauseous with worry, or that he'd been watching the sort of program she never allowed on in the house.

"It was on over at Brandon's. They have cable. It was really gross the way these guys..."

"That's enough, Mike." Logan stepped forward, dwarfing the boy as he placed his big hand on the child's skinny shoulder. Sam looked as if she were about to lose it, though he seriously doubted she would. Not in front of her kids. "Your sister isn't in New York. She's in Austin with my son. Now, keep an eye on your sister in here while I talk to your mom. Think you can handle that?"

Because it was Logan who asked, Mike didn't even balk. Or maybe he cooperated simply because things weren't sounding as interesting to him as they had a few moments ago when his pre-adolescent male imagination had been turning his mother gray.

Whichever the case, he more or less did as Logan asked and plopped down in front of the television with the remote control. Amy, with her mother's encouragement and the promise that her mom wouldn't be far away if she needed her, reluctantly followed.

"What are they doing in Austin?" Sam practically demanded as soon as she and Logan cleared the kitchen door.

Logan was ahead of her, his head bent as he worked at the knotted muscles in his neck. He'd scarcely made eye contact with her since the moment he'd set foot in her house. He didn't now, either.

Acutely aware of the leashed power in his body, she stared at his back and waited for his words to ease the knot of nerves tangled in her stomach.

"Trevor went up to check out the university and talk with a counselor," she heard him say, his voice low so the little ones couldn't hear. "He wasn't at the hotel when I called, but the guy at the desk said there was a girl with him."

"But if they weren't there..."

"They'd probably gone out to get something to eat," he suggested. His hand fell, his tension seeming to increase when he turned to her. "He hadn't checked out, and he's not due to check out until tomorrow."

It had been easier staring at his back. The expression in his eyes was as forbidding as Sam had ever seen.

She forced her chin up. "Which hotel?"

"It's one downtown. It's where I stay when I have business there." He lifted his head toward the living room, his jaw tight. "Is there anyone you can leave Mike and Amy with?"

Mrs. Gunther was already at bingo. "I'll try my sister," Sam said, too busy hoping she could reach Lindsey to consider that neither of them had questioned what they would do—or that Logan looked brittle as a branch ready to snap.

There was only one way Sam could cope just then. Doing what she'd learned to do when faced with a crisis, she simply blanked her mind to anything beyond what needed to be done at that moment.

That was why, after she'd reached Lindsey in the workroom of her shop and explained the situation as best she could, she hurried up the stairs and threw pajamas, toothbrushes and a change of clothes into an overnight case for the kids.

"We're spending the night at Aunt Lindsey's?" Amy asked, practically running behind her mother as Sam towed her toward Logan's truck minutes later. Logan was just ahead of them carrying the overnight bag. Michael had Spot and the dog dish.

"Yes, honey," she told the little girl, handing her up to the seat while Logan dropped the bag behind it then held the door for her to get in, too. "I don't know how late we'll be, so you can sleep in her four-poster. How about that?" she asked, forcing a smile to make it sound like a treat.

"Are you going to sleep with him?"

Logan stood at the door, preparing to close it. Amy's small finger was pointed directly at his chest.

Brown eyes locked on blue. Despite the brooding in his dark features, Sam could have sworn she saw his left eyebrow arch.

The knot in her stomach seemed to change quality as, unable to break his visual hold, she folded her hand over her daughter's and drew it to her lap.

"No, sweetie. Big people… No," she said more firmly, canning the explanation Logan seemed rather interested in himself. She simply didn't have the energy to answer those kinds of questions right now.

The door closed with a solid thud, and Sam let out her breath. This would all be easier to deal with once the kids were safely stowed with Lindsey. Much easier, she told herself.

Or so she thought.

Within a minute of dropping off Michael, Amy and Spot, it became apparent how much of a buffer the children had been. Without them, there was no one to distract Sam from the man brooding beside her in the dark confines of the truck's cab. Logan hadn't said a word since they'd left Lindsey's house, and the brittleness she hadn't wanted to consider while she'd hurried about was now impossible to ignore.

He turned at the Y, leaving the lights of Leesburg, such as they were, behind. Certain it wouldn't take long for the silence to grate on her already touchy nerves, Sam glanced at the digital clock on the dash and asked how long it would take them to get where they were going.

"About an hour and a half."

"Can you go any faster?"

The look he slanted her was tolerant at best. "It won't do us any good to arrive in pieces. I'm ten miles over the speed limit now."

Already feeling as if so much had slipped beyond her control, his tight-lipped response only made her feel more powerless. "I just want to get there before anything happens."

"Like what?"

"Just...anything," she concluded, not caring to get that specific with him. Wishing she could pace, she settled for worrying a loose thread on the sleeve of her shirt. His tension seemed to be feeding hers.

Or maybe it was the other way around.

"How involved do you think they are?" she finally made herself ask.

After a moment's hesitation he said tersely, "I have no idea."

"Trevor hasn't said anything to you?"

"If he had, I wouldn't have just said I didn't know. Would I?"

"That's not helping, Logan."

"Yeah? Well, you're not helping much, either. What is it you're more afraid of, anyway? That Erin took off? Or that she and Trev might be sleeping together?"

"I'm worried about both," she informed him tightly, understanding that he had reason to be upset but seeing no call to take it out on her. "Erin's not . . . experienced. And Trevor's . . ."

"Trevor's what?" he challenged, daring her to say anything against his son.

"Trevor's very mature. And very . . . virile," she concluded in a tone that was remarkably matter-of-fact.

In the light from a passing car she saw the hardness in Logan's expression melt to an uncomprehending frown.

"Virile?"

"Oh, please, Logan. You know what it means."

Sure he did. But her response was not at all what he'd anticipated. He'd expected her to blame Trevor for Erin's running away, or for taking advantage of her. At the very least, he'd thought she might even blame *him* somehow. After all, it had been he who had insisted they would be doing more harm than good by keeping the kids apart.

He was learning in a hurry that Sam wasn't the sort of person to assign fault. When something happened, she simply dealt with it as best she could. He, on the other hand, seemed to have an uncanny knack for making whatever she was dealing with that much harder.

From the corner of his eye, he saw her press the tips of her fingers to her forehead.

"I just don't want her starting out the way I did," he heard her say, her quietly spoken words barely audible over the hum of the truck's engine. "I know she's angry and she's upset, but I know she thinks she's in love with your son." Lindsey had told her as much, and she couldn't discount her daughter's feelings. "I can see where she might think of him as her escape.

"That doesn't mean she doesn't really care about him," she told Logan. "Or that she's using him. What she feels for him could be very real." She pulled at the thread of her jacket. "I was fifteen when I fell in love with Jim, and barely eighteen when we married. No other man existed for me but him. I have a feeling Erin could be that same way."

Though Erin would probably rather eat sand than admit it right now, she was very much like her mother in many respects. Her loyalties were fierce, and when she cared, she cared with all her heart and soul.

"If she does feel that way, then I know she'll want his babies. But she's just a baby herself." She rushed on, thinking she probably should have just kept her fears right where they'd been—even though she knew she and Logan were concerned about the same thing. "She needs to give herself a chance to grow up first. Having a baby so young makes a relationship harder than it needs to be."

She remembered the fights she and Jim had. About money, because there was never enough. About him being able to spend time with his friends, and her being stuck in the house all day with a baby. Jim had come around, eventually. He'd grown up, as she'd had to. But it had been hard. "I don't want Erin to have to struggle like that."

"I don't want Trevor to struggle like that, either," Logan muttered, thinking Jim Gray had been one hell of a lucky man. "He has his whole future ahead of him. The last thing he needs is to have all of his choices taken away." His voice dropped another notch. "He has no idea what he's getting himself into."

This time it was Sam's protectiveness that surfaced. But before she could defend her daughter—no matter that in theory she agreed with every word he'd said—she realized that, like her, Logan was relating what was happening to his own experience. His wife had walked away from their son. From him. And when he'd come back to his ranch, he had to give up the very dream his son now sought.

She was truly at the mercy of the defenses he'd cultivated because of that betrayal of trust. Now, she wondered if it would ever be possible to breech them.

She needed to try.

"Our children aren't us, Logan. Maybe we should try to remember that."

She had no idea what to make of his narrow glance, or of his silence when he turned his attention back to the road. His expression provided no clue, either. With only the green glow of the dashboard lights to provide illumination, she could see little in his profile—other than that he wasn't interested in continuing their conversation. He kept his focus straight ahead, his gaze never moving from the road and his right hand gripping the top of the steering wheel.

That grip finally eased.

"Family has always been important to you, hasn't it?"

She had no idea where the question had come from. But she told him that, yes, it had. Always. Then added a quiet, "Why do you ask?"

"It just seemed that way from what you said. And I've seen you with your kids and your sister."

Whether he realized it or not, he had just managed to accomplish what she had not. He had found their common ground.

"I think it means lot to you, too," she ventured. At least, the idea of family was. The continuity he sought in his life spoke of a need for roots. And he kept the ranch going as much for his brothers as he did for himself and his son, even though it appeared that his brothers couldn't have cared less about the family home.

"You know, Logan," she said, because he'd remained so stubbornly silent. "There's nothing wrong with saying you care. It's not like it's a weakness or something. Even if it were, you're allowed one or two."

She'd meant to encourage him. All she'd done was make herself more aware of the tight rein he held over himself. As far as humanly possible, Logan was not a man who allowed himself any weakness at all.

"I have more than one or two," he informed her, ignoring the rest of what she'd said.

He'd deliberately avoided confirming her insight. Wondering if he thought he'd choke if he said he cared about something like home and family, or if he even knew how to express himself, she asked, "Like what?"

For a moment he said nothing. Then, looking toward her, his glance skimmed her mouth before he turned back to the road. "You," he said in a voice as flat as the long stretch of highway.

"Any more questions?" he asked at her quiet intake of breath. "Or should we get back to Erin and Trevor."

Sam swallowed. "I think we should talk about the kids."

"Good idea." He tightened his grip on the wheel, letting the dangerous comment pass. "How do you want to handle this with them?"

Chapter Ten

The hotel where Logan stayed when he had business in Austin was not at all what Sam expected. The Hancock had once been a gentleman's club. The staid, three-storied building seemed out of place among the modern glass and cement structures that had grown up around it. Yet, when Logan ushered her through the lobby and past small groups of nicely dressed women and men in Western-cut suits sitting in a lounge with deep red leather booths, brass railings and a gleaming mahogany bar, Sam couldn't imagine Logan staying anywhere else. The atmosphere was decidedly masculine. It was also one of quiet wealth; of money that knew its power but didn't find it necessary to impress anyone with it because every one here had as much as the next.

These were all cattlemen.

And this was a private club.

Sam had heard rumors of Logan's wealth. What had impressed her more was how unaffected Logan was by it. Now, wondering at how hard he worked when he could have easily afforded more help than he employed, Sam watched him return the deferential nod of the uniformed gentleman guarding the elevator and lead her past a wide, red carpeted staircase. A house phone sat on an antique table near a grouping of leather chairs.

"What are you doing?" she wanted to know, since the means of getting to the hotel's rooms were now behind them.

"Calling Trevor. Things are going to be awkward enough without walking in on them. If they're even there."

He was right, of course. In her present frame of mind, Sam wasn't thinking of anything other than getting to Erin. The situation would only be worse if they walked in on something . . . compromising.

The muscles in Logan's broad shoulders bunched beneath soft blue chambray when he reached to pick up the phone from the claw-footed table. Trevor had given him his room number when he'd called to let him know he'd arrived safely that afternoon, and Logan now punched it out on the telephone.

With his back to her, Sam could hear the impatient clicks and Logan's deadly calm voice.

"Step out into the hall, Trevor," he said without preamble. "I want to talk to you. That's right," she heard him say after a moment. "I'm here."

The receiver clicked back in place. "Come on." Jaw locked, he held his hand out for her to precede him. "Let's get this over with."

He fell into step beside her, checking his longer stride to match hers as they headed for the stairs. Sam could feel his hand at the small of her back, the heat of his palm seeping into her spine. The gesture was meant only to guide her, but it also spoke of the united front they had agreed to present. United on the surface, anyway. The only agreement they had actually reached was that Erin was going back to Leesburg with them tonight—a trip Sam was not looking forward to in the least.

Trevor had just stepped out of a room halfway down the wide, burgundy-carpeted hall when Logan and Samantha turned into the long hallway on the second floor. Pulling the door closed, he turned to face them, only to pause when he saw the woman at his father's side.

Crossing his arms over the number thirty-two on the Houston Oilers jersey tucked into his jeans, he met his dad's eyes evenly. "What are you doing here, Dad?"

"I was just about to ask you the same thing."

Confusion flashed over the young man's handsome features. "You know what I'm doing. I toured the campus this afternoon, and I've got an appointment with a counselor in the morning."

"I mean, what are you doing with Erin? She's here with you, isn't she?"

Trevor's eyes revealed far more than Logan's. Lacking the cynicism that made the older man's so hard, Sam could easily see his discomfort when he looked uncertainly toward her.

A faint hint of pink crept upward from the boy's collar as he looked back to his dad. "She's here. She came up with me this morning."

"Why?" Logan bluntly asked.

"Because she needed a ride. Look," he muttered, frowning. "It's not what you're thinking."

"Damn it, Trevor . . ."

"Come on, Dad. She called this morning saying she needed help. She needed a ride up here and I gave it to her." He nodded toward Sam. "You'd have done the same thing if her mother had asked you to help *her* out."

"Whether I would have or not," Logan replied, refusing to let his son confuse the issue with that bit of truth, "is not the point. Didn't it occur to you that she might be doing something she wasn't supposed to? Or that her mother would be worried about her?"

The discomfort returned to the young man's expression. Along with it came a certain protectiveness.

His father hadn't raised his voice. If anything, his deep drawl had grown dangerously quiet. Now, Trevor's voice quieted, too, so much that Sam barely heard him when he turned to the side and said, "Can I talk to you alone?"

Nerves raw, Sam cut past his attempt to cut her out. "I'll leave you alone to talk to your father," she told him. "Just open the door so I can see Erin."

Easily six feet tall, Trevor already towered over her. When he straightened to look directly at her, the set of his jaw making him appear as protective as his father had been about him not so long ago, his size seemed even more impressive.

"I'll tell her you're here, ma'am, and if she wants to talk to you, that's her business. But I can't just let you in without..."

"Warning her?" Sam offered when he let the sentence trail off.

He had the decency to look chagrined. He did not, however, back down.

Had it not been for the fact that he stood between her and her daughter, Trevor's quiet, unyielding stance would have earned a major share of Sam's respect. Her daughter trusted him, and he didn't want to jeopardize that trust. On the other hand, Erin was her daughter and he had no business keeping her from her.

Afraid she wouldn't phrase it too nicely if she pointed that out, and not interested in creating a scene in the hallway of a hotel, she tipped her chin up and, as politely as possible under the circumstances, met his unwavering glance. Heaven only knew what Erin had said to him to make him think she had to be protected from her own mother.

"Would you please warn her, then?" she asked. "I'm not leaving here without her."

Seeking a more sympathetic audience, Trevor looked to his father. Finding no encouragement there, he let out a deep breath. "Erin doesn't want to go home. She wants to go to her aunt's in Seattle. We just got back from buying her a ticket for the bus in the morning."

"She wants to go to Annie's? I thought she wanted to go to L.A. That's the only place she's ever talked about going."

Trevor hesitated. From where Sam stood, it looked as if he were trying to decided the best way to help his girlfriend without incurring the further disapproval of the man he clearly respected. It was not an easy decision to make.

Logan offered an assist. "She's sixteen, son. That's too young to be on her own, if that's what she has in mind. If you want to help her, tell her mom what you know."

Running his fingers through his hair, the young man shot his father a dubious look. But he was worried about Erin, too.

"She did want to go to L.A. She called a couple of her friends, but it didn't work out," he explained, the muscle in his jaw working the way his dad's sometimes did. "I think it was Shawna who said Erin couldn't stay with her because her mom didn't want to get involved in a family problem. And Mindy has a new boyfriend. Whatever that has to do with anything.''

That he looked confused by Mindy's rationale wasn't surprising. Sam doubted there was a male alive who understood how fickle some teenaged girls could be. Sam understood it, though. The new boy in Mindy's life was simply more important to her than an old friendship.

Sam could only imagine how Erin must have felt after she'd placed those calls. Erin had held on to the idea of going home, of going back to her old school with her old friends and living her old life, since the day they'd arrived. To finally be faced with the realization that going home was no longer just something her mother was preventing her from doing must have been devastating.

Closing her eyes, she willed herself to believe there was a way past all this. But all she could think about was that the destination apparently no longer made any difference to Erin. She wanted to leave home. Period. With L.A. no longer a option, she'd simply go to Seattle.

It will be all right, Sam tried to tell herself, much as she so often told her children, but her supply of optimism had grown abysmally short. The conviction, this time, just wasn't there. Erin hated the home she'd tried to make for her, and Sam didn't know what to do to make her like it any better.

She was pushing her fingers through her hair, certain Logan could see them trembling but not knowing what to do about that, either, when she heard the click of a handle being turned.

Erin appeared in the slit between the door and its frame. For the briefest moment the thought of all the worry the girl had caused resurrected a healthy dose of anger at Erin's thoughtlessness. But seeing the alienated, distrusting look in the girl's eyes, Sam felt the fight drain out of her. She didn't know what else to do for her daughter. How to give her back what she needed to make her happy. Or how to compensate for the ways she'd failed her. She knew only that she didn't want to make matters any worse than they already were. At least with Annie, Erin would be safe.

"Hi, Erin," she said in a voice that lacked the strength she'd hoped for. She searched her daughter's face, needing to reassure herself that she was all right. All Sam could see was unhappiness. "I know you won't believe it, but I've been worried sick about what might have happened to you."

Holding the door just wide enough to see the trio in the hall, Erin rested her head against the edge of the door. With her bottom lip caught between her teeth, she didn't say a word.

"Trevor said you want to go to Annie's," Sam continued, though she suspected Erin had heard every word that had been said, anyway. "Have you called her?"

Erin released her lip. "I was afraid she'd call you if I did. I was going to call her when I got there...and have her call you then."

It helped to know that. A little. "Don't you think we should call her now?"

Erin's eyes narrowed as she lifted her head. She didn't open the door any farther, but her eyes darted immediately to where Trevor stood almost shoulder to shoulder with his father, watching them. Her glance stumbling over the bigger, more formidable man, she looked at Trevor as if she didn't believe her mother was really being so reasonable.

That same doubt was in her expression when she looked back to where Sam held herself so stiffly by the door. "You'll let me go?"

"What choice do I have? It's either that, or try to keep you in a place you hate. I'm not going to do that."

Erin had tried to run away once now. As unhappy as she was, she'd undoubtedly try it again. Especially now that Trevor wasn't going to be around.

Feeling as if she were about to shatter, but knowing she'd only have to pick up all the pieces by herself if she did, Sam fought off the wave of hopelessness demanding to be felt. If only someone could tell her what else she could do, she thought, and felt her helplessness compound itself.

"If Annie says it's okay, you can go. If she can't take you for some reason, we'll call Grandma and Grandpa."

Still dubious, Erin pushed back the golden braid that had fallen over her shoulder. "I thought Grandma and Grandpa were in Europe."

"They got back to Florida last week."

"I'd rather go to Annie's."

"Fine," Sam conceded, preferring that idea, anyway. Since her parents had retired, they were usually home only long enough to do laundry and repack for another trip. Heaven only knew where Erin would wind up if she went with them. "But I'll put you on a plane. It's safer than a bus."

Dragging in a deep breath, Sam looked up at the man at her shoulder. "Would you mind taking us to the airport?"

Logan didn't hesitate. He simply shook his head to indicate her request wouldn't be a problem and moved his hand to the small of her back.

Neither of the kids saw what he had done. But Sam felt his hand linger at her waist, that silent offer of support meaning more to her at that moment than anything he could possibly have said.

Only two airlines had remaining flights to Seattle that evening. One was boarding even as Sam spoke with the ticket agent, using the phone on the hotel room's desk while studiously avoiding the rumpled-looking bed. The other flight left shortly before ten o'clock and stopped in two cities in between. After speaking with a very concerned Annie, who immediately agreed to Erin's coming to stay, Sam booked Erin on the milk run.

Trevor didn't accompany them to the airport. While he and Logan carried a subdued Erin's bags to the pickup, Sam overheard the young man tell her daughter that he wouldn't be going with them. His dad would just have to bring him back to the hotel if he did, and he and her mom already had a long enough drive ahead of them.

To Sam's surprise, Erin didn't argue the point with him. She simply said okay as if she always deferred to his practicality, then started to cry when he kissed her good-bye on her forehead.

Sam, standing several feet back, looked away. Hurting for her daughter, hurting for herself, she didn't know what else to do.

Quite deliberately, Logan stepped in front of her, blocking her view of their kids. "We'd better go," she heard him say and looked up to see something that looked almost like concern shadowing his eyes. "After we put her on her plane, I'll buy you a drink. You look like you could use one."

He was steering her to the truck a moment later and motioning to Erin that it was time to go. He was sure she didn't want to miss her plane, he told her, then added to Trevor that he would talk to him later. The way he clapped his son on the shoulder as he passed him was as much a gesture of assurance to the boy that all was well between the two of them, as it was one of affection.

Sam could only hope Erin felt the same reassurance Trevor had when she wrapped her daughter in an awkward hug just before she boarded the plane forty-five minutes later. It was apparent that Erin wasn't comfortable with the gesture, but she endured it because she had to. There was no way Sam could have let her go without it.

From behind her, Sam heard Logan say, "You'd better call your sister," as the plane backed away from the gate. "To let her know she made it on."

His reflection towered over hers in the huge window where Sam watched the nose of the plane recede. She met his eyes in that reflective surface. "Please don't think she's a bad kid, Logan. She's been through a lot."

His fingers curved over her shoulder. "I'm hardly in a position to criticize. I have a brother who did the same thing. Only he didn't have family to go to." Turning her around, he tipped her chin up. "Call Annie."

Feeling a little sick, but mostly numb, Sam nodded. She didn't question that she hadn't thought of calling Annie herself just then. Nor did she question the way Logan slipped his hand around hers to lead her to the telephone when several seconds passed and she hadn't budged. She thought only that it felt good to have something so solid to hang on to—and that she hoped Annie could, somehow, help Erin. Annie was younger than Sam by six years, but Sam had always thought her the voice of reason and the strongest of the lot. She only hoped her sister could help Erin understand that her mother was on her side.

As grateful as Sam was for Annie's help, by the time she and Logan were back on the freeway, it was what she felt for the man who'd remained beside her for the past few hours that finally helped her make it past the worry. Logan hadn't said a single word about the inconvenience Erin's defection had caused him. Nor did he appear as resentful as he could have of the distress he'd suffered himself where his son was concerned.

In the flashes of street lamps, she studied his strong profile. The respect Trevor had for his father had been apparent. So had Logan's for his son. "I'm really sorry about this, Logan. About all the trouble we've caused you tonight."

"You haven't caused any."

The breath she drew brought the familiar combination of fresh air, leather and warm-blooded male. Already aware of him, the scent shimmered along her nerves. "I can't let Erin take all the blame for this. We had an argument last night. I didn't realize how upset she really was." She took another breath, needing desperately to maintain the precarious hold she had on herself. All she managed to do was give her nerves another jolt. "I shouldn't have let her clam up on me. I should have made her talk."

The strain in her voice had him frowning. "What did you argue about?"

She glanced away, toward the night-blackened window. "You. Actually," she continued, when his head jerked toward her, "I think it was more about what you represent. She doesn't like the idea of me caring for another man." Her fingers lay intertwined in her lap. She didn't know when she'd stopped seeking the comfort of the ring that was no longer there. But she had. "Did you ever have that problem with Trevor?" she asked, looking back across the wide expanse of bench seat. "Was he ever upset because you were involved with someone?"

As distraught as she was, she didn't realize what she'd just so innocently admitted. She knew only that she needed to make some sense of what had happened in the past twenty-four hours and that Logan, having raised a child alone, too, might have some answers.

It was a moment before he replied. When he did, his response was measured. "The problem never came up. I was never involved with anyone. At least, not with anyone from around here." There had been a woman in Austin who would warm his bed when he'd had business there. The arrangement had worked fine—until she'd started complicating it by talking about settling down. He figured he was as settled as he was going to get. "And not for a long time."

"So Trevor never met her."

"No."

Her chin edged up in acknowledgement. He had been alone for a long time. As imposingly, potently male as he was, it should have been difficult for her to picture him living the life of a monk. Still, she found that picture forming with no effort at all. Emotionally Logan isolated himself. He even isolated himself physically, by spending all but a few hours a week surrounded by miles of range land, his men and his cattle.

Yet, as hard as Logan fought to keep from being involved with most people, she wondered if he'd noticed how enmeshed he'd become in her life. This wasn't the first time they had faced a common problem together. Nor was it the first time he'd been there for her.

Not willing to consider how very much that meant to her, she conceded only that he had succeeded where she had so apparently failed. "You did a good job with him," she said, and hugged her arms to herself. "You're a wonderful father."

It was the crack in her voice that gave her away. In the dim glow of the dashboard lights, Logan saw her shrink into herself. Her eyes were straight ahead and unblinking, but he had the feeling that what lay behind her compliment, gratifying as he so unexpectedly found it, was what she regarded as her own inadequacy.

He didn't doubt for a minute that she was in the middle of a knock-down drag-out battle with herself, trying to figure out where she'd gone wrong with her daughter. She was a great mom. The best he'd ever seen. Yet, he was pretty sure his opinion would hold about as much water as a sieve since the only mothering he'd seen done in the past sixteen or so years had been by his cows. That was why, knowing that nothing he could say would make a bit of difference to her right now, he did the only thing he could do.

He might not be able to do anything for her himself. But he knew of a place where a person had no choice but to let go of what preyed on his mind. That was why, instead of returning her to her house and the responsibilities waiting for her with her other two children, he tightened his grip on the steering wheel and nudged the speedometer up another notch. Ever since the night he'd felt her melt in his arms, he hadn't trusted himself to be alone with her. He'd intended to keep the distance he'd deliberately maintained, too. But his intentions right now didn't matter. Tonight, she looked very much as if she needed a break.

The freeway between Austin and San Antonio was only lit in a few places. In the dark, that long stretch of divided road didn't vary by more than a gentle curve or subtle dip. The two-lane country roads rolling over the hills had little to identify them from each other, either, except for the occasional milepost that would reflect back the beam of the headlights. That was why, lost in her troubled thoughts, Sam didn't notice that Logan took a freeway exit north of the one for Leesburg, or that they were coming into the RW on a back road. At least, she didn't notice their destination until Logan had cleared the copse of trees at the top of a rise and the lights of the ranch appeared just ahead of them.

"Why are we here?"

"I want to show you something."

"But it's almost midnight."

"That's the best time to see it."

"You have to be up in a few hours, Logan. And I have to get home. The kids—"

"Are asleep," he said, knowing sleep wouldn't come easily when he could think of little beyond how her slender body had once trembled at his touch. "At least they should be. Lindsey told you to just leave them the night, since we didn't know how late we'd be. They're fine.

"Come on," he coaxed, when he saw her brow lower as if there should be some other reason she couldn't take a few minutes for herself. "I'll pour you that drink I promised you. But there's something you need to see first."

The porch light was on at the house. Another light burned in the entry, making the window glow a soft, pale yellow. Logan didn't take her into the house, though. After parking the truck and leading her to the walkway, he left her by the gate while he strode up to the porch. Reaching inside the unlocked door, he flipped the switches on the inner wall, and the lights went out.

There was no moon. At least not enough of one to provide any illumination. The silver sliver she had noticed earlier wasn't even visible, with the trees and the house blocking it from view. As dark as it was, Sam could only see half a dozen feet in front of her.

The steady thud of Logan's boots on the walkway joined the song of crickets. Hugging her arms against the chill of the night air, she glanced toward him when he stopped beside her, a large, solid shadow in an even darker night.

"Where are we going?"

"We're there."

"We are?"

"Look up."

She did, and felt herself draw a long, deep breath.

Stars. He'd wanted her to see the stars, and what she saw were trillions of them in a vast swath of indigo sky. The great masses of tiny twinkling lights were so dense they actually whitened great streaks of the fathomless heavens.

With nothing to obstruct the view, with no light pollution and air so clear she could literally see forever, the Milky Way shimmered and shone and stretched endlessly on.

"Pick one."

"Pick one?"

"A star. Just pick one out and focus on it," he told her, his voice as quiet as the night surrounding them. "Let me know when you have one."

"Okay," she said, giving a slight nod to let him know she'd done what he asked.

"Now turn around and look at the fence behind you."

He was standing so close she could feel his heat radiating into her. Craving that heat, she tightened her arms around herself to keep from moving toward it and glanced at the shadowed lines forming the low fence.

"Now what?"

"Find your star."

She knew she wouldn't be able to do it even before she turned back and tipped her head up to find the bright little light she'd selected. There had to be a million stars jammed into the area where hers was. Finding that one star when she wasn't even sure she was looking in quite the same spot as she had been before was hopeless. "I can't. It's lost."

"It's there," he assured her. "Keep looking."

"This is silly, Logan. Trust me. It's lost."

His glance skimmed her upturned face, the strain he knew was there hidden by the night. Anyone else would have simply said she couldn't find it. Not that he had ever brought anyone else here to know that for certain. But Samantha had insisted it was lost, and that was when he knew she would understand exactly what it was he'd wanted her to see.

"It's lost," he repeated. "Or you are."

Sam felt herself go still. His perception was unnerving. As unnerving as the feel of him standing so close to her. He wasn't touching her, but he was near enough to make her wish desperately that he would.

"Is this what you do to put matters into perspective? Or to remind yourself of how insignificant something is?" She had the feeling she knew what he was trying to do. And she appreciated his wanting to help. Under other circumstances she might even have been more receptive to the usual comparisons to celestial bodies. It might have actually lessened the awful lost feeling he had so unerringly identified. But right now she wasn't feeling terribly philosophical. "What happened tonight might not be all that significant in the overall scheme of things, but it matters very much to me."

"I'm not suggesting it shouldn't," he said, more aware by the moment of how tightly she held herself. "If something's on my mind, I'm not too apt to think it's insignificant. When I come out here, it's to keep whatever is concerning me from making me overlook something else that's just as important. Sometimes we lose sight of things just because of everything else that gets in the way."

The way the other stars did, crowded as they were around the one she'd chosen and making it nearly impossible to find.

"What have I lost sight of?"

"What a good mom you are."

She didn't know of anything else he could have said at that moment that could have mattered more. Or that could have caused her to feel so completely unprotected.

"If I'm all that great, why is my family falling apart? You were right, Logan. Do you know that?" She stepped back, turning away. Only to turn right back again because she didn't know where to go. "You'd said that keeping Erin from her only friend was a mistake. I shouldn't have grounded her for as long as I did. Or I should have backed down and not grounded her at all. Maybe if I had let her see Trevor more often, she wouldn't have had time to build up so much resentment toward me."

She went silent only because her voice cracked. But it was the burning at the back of her eyelids that annoyed her the most. She was trying to hang on, and he was making it so hard.

So damned, impossibly, hard.

"Your family's not falling apart, Sam. Erin's with your sister. If she really resented you, she'd never have wanted to go where you could find her."

He sounded very much as if he knew what he was talking about on that score. And what he'd said did relieve her. A little. It was the kindness in his tone that made the hurting inside so much worse. The compassion.

It made no sense at all, but if he said one more thing to her in that gentle tone, she was going to lose what little was left of her composure, and she'd never forgive him for that.

He didn't say a word. But what he did made hanging on harder still.

He took her hand, his fingers wrapping around hers, and tugged her forward. Settling her hand at his waist, he pulled her into his arms.

He felt warm. He felt strong. And when he slipped his fingers through her hair to hold her head to his chest, Sam felt her throat grow so tight it hurt.

"I don't know what to do," she whispered against the steady beat of his heart.

The pain in her voice tore at him. Or maybe it was the small sob she muffled against his shirt that had him tightening his hold. "Don't worry about it right now," he told her, because he didn't know what she should do, either. "Just don't worry about it and lean on me for a while."

"I can't do that, Logan."

"Which." Drawing his hand over her hair, he slipped his fingers under her chin and lifted her face to him. "Not worry. Or lean on me."

Both, she thought. "Lean on you."

"Why not?"

"Because I want to so much."

The admission was not what he had expected. Nor had he expected his own reaction to it. She tried so hard to make everything work for everyone else—for her children, for the town. And she never seemed to think of what she might want or need.

"Do it anyway," he whispered and, without thinking of the consequences, he lowered his lips to catch the tear glistening at the corner of her lashes.

Her eyes drifted closed and he pressed a kiss to her eyelid, tasting the salt of her tears. If he kissed her the way he wanted, it wouldn't be what she needed that he'd be considering. So he steeled himself against the hard jolt of need that slammed into his gut and carried that tender kiss to her temple, rubbing his thumbs in circles along the smooth cords in her neck to relieve the tension she carried there. Hearing her soft sigh, he trailed his lips to the hollow of her cheek, then on to the corner of her mouth.

Snaking his fingers upward through her hair, he tipped her head back and lifted his.

His eyes glittered hard on her face.

He thought he saw longing. Or maybe he only heard it. She whispered his name, the sound half plea, half promise and the control he'd thought to maintain snapped with no resistance at all. His mouth covered hers. Gently at first, then drinking deeply when she gave in with a tiny sigh and opened to him. He had so little control where this woman was concerned. And while he hated that flaw in himself, he could no more deny himself the feel of her than he could have denied himself his next breath.

He was making her do what she'd said she could not.

That thought filtered dimly through the haze of heat flowing through Sam as Logan drew her against the solid wall of his body. *Lean on me,* he'd said, and she'd felt what little strength she had left slowly leak from her.

Don't worry, he'd said and, with the touch of his lips, every other thought had fled.

Now, every breath, every stroke of his tongue over hers, brought the scent of him, the taste of him. That essence filled her, becoming part of her heated blood and pounding heart. His gentleness had undone her, but it was his strength that she craved. She needed it. She needed him. And that realization shook her to her core.

Curving her hands over the corded muscles in his forearms, she drew away.

Logan didn't try to pull her back. Nor did he release her. He simply stood with his hands on her shoulders, his breathing as uneven as her own while he searched her shadowed features.

"What's wrong?" she heard him ask, his smoky voice flowing over her like a caress.

Her hair was mussed from the thrust of his hands. She felt the tangles when she pushed her fingers through it and shook her head. There wasn't anything about this man that failed to seduce her. "I have to go."

She took a shaky step back, nearly stumbling in the dark.

His hand shot out to steady her, only to fall to his side when she stiffened at his touch.

She inched back farther. "Please take me home, Logan."

"Samantha..."

"Please. I need to get back to Michael and Amy."

"Michael and Amy are fine. Tell me what's wrong."

Logan could read little in her stance and nothing in her expression. Not in the dark with a half dozen feet separating them. But he definitely recognized her caution. He felt it himself. Along with a truckload of other equally sensible instincts that he was prepared to disregard. He wanted to be with her. He wanted her. Period. He wanted her naked in his bed, those luminous eyes glowing with pleasure. He wanted to hear her call his name and feel those small, soft hands running over his body. But more than anything else, he wanted her to be honest with him.

She hadn't answered.

He moved closer, more relieved than he could have imagined when she didn't seek to put that distance between them again. "What is it? Didn't you want me to kiss you?"

"No," she said softly, shaking her head. "I mean, yes. I wanted you to. It's just late and..."

"Don't tell me you need to get home. You know as well as I do that there isn't any reason you have to leave here right this minute. That's just an excuse."

"Logan."

"Isn't it?"

"Yes!"

"Why don't you just say it?"

"Say what?"

"That you're afraid. You don't need excuses, Samantha. I don't want you to go. But I'll take you home... if that's what you really want."

Chapter Eleven

You're afraid.

Logan's words seemed to echo in the silence, a silence filled with the sounds of the night. Crickets. The hoot of a barn owl. The rustle of tall grass and leaves as night critters moved through them. Sam scarcely noticed the sounds. They were barely audible over the heavy beat of her heart.

Logan was little more than a blue shadow in the night. But she saw him offer her his hand. He would do as she asked and take her home. All she had to do was slip her hand in his.

Reaching toward him, she felt her hand disappear in his strong grip. If only she could disappear like that for a while, and be held in that warmth. After the emotional upheaval of the day, to face the night alone...

Logan felt her hesitation. Torn between his aching need to drag her back to him and the voice in his head that was telling him to let her go, he said nothing. The decision had to be hers.

"Haven't you ever been scared?" he heard her ask, her voice a small, thready whisper.

"Of course I have." Only a fool would deny such a thing. "I just don't want you to be afraid of me. Ever."

It wasn't him she feared. It was what he made her feel that frightened her so much, because what she felt for him was something she feared he could never return. Yet, more frightening than that was the possibility of never again feeling as whole…as safe…as she felt when she was in his arms.

"It's not you, Logan. It's everything else that scares me. But when I'm with you, it doesn't all seem quite so overwhelming."

At her quiet admission, he stepped closer. "I make it easier?"

It didn't sound as if he could comprehend how such a thing was possible, but when she nodded, he laced his fingers through hers.

His hand tightened. "Then don't go."

His low, seductive drawl was as soft as the feel of his lips when he brushed them over her mouth.

He kissed her once. Then again. And again. Each time he lingered just a little longer. Each time he took, and gave, just a little more.

Only their hands touched. And their mouths. Yet, when he lifted his head the last time, she could feel his tension radiating into her as surely as if he'd pressed her to the hard length of his body.

Reaction shivered through her.

"You're cold."

She no longer even noticed the damp night air. "Not when you kiss me like that."

The corners of his mouth quirked up. She felt it when he brushed his lips over hers before he slowly, thoroughly, repeated what had left her nearly breathless. "Like that?"

She thought she nodded. She knew she said "Again."

He sucked in his breath, the sound as raw as his groan when his mouth came down over hers and he wrapped her in his arms.

Sam felt a shudder rip through him the moment her tongue touched his. It seemed incomprehensible to her that she could affect him as deeply as he affected her. The knowledge that she did only fueled the desire he'd awakened in her. Something inside her grew liquid and heavy. The sensation intensified with the feel of his big hands moving over her shoulders, her back and down to shape the curve of her hips. But when he pulled her closer, drawing her up to press her to the bulge straining against his jeans, it felt as if her blood had turned to steam.

Gritting his teeth against the fierce pleasure ripping through him, Logan pulled her even tighter. "Last chance," she heard him grate in her ear. "We leave now, or you're not going anywhere."

She was trembling. Shaking like a dry leaf in a brisk wind. She realized that, when she lifted her hand to the hard line of his jaw. If she had the brains God gave a grasshopper, she would heed his warning before he worked himself any deeper into her heart. "I'm not going anywhere," she told him, because it was already too late.

For a moment Logan remained perfectly still, his heart thundering against hers. The night seemed to close in around them, magnifying the sound of her uneven breathing and the faint rustle of fabric when he set her back to see her face.

She would never cease to be astounded by the gentleness that kept his strength in check when he touched her. His fingers barely skimmed her cheek when he brushed back the hair clinging to it. As if she had suddenly become so fragile she might break, he touched his lips to her forehead, her temple.

"I want you too badly to keep my hands off you. I mean it, Samantha." His breath feathered warmth over her skin. "You stay and you'll wind up in my bed."

She leaned closer. He made her feel so precious, so desired. "I know."

His voice became little more than a guttural rasp. "Put your arms around my neck."

The muscles beneath the soft fabric of his shirt quivered as she brushed her fingers upward over his chest. No sooner had she locked them around his neck, than she felt him bend to lift her into his arms.

He carried her as if she weighed no more than a sack of thistle down. Nudging the screen door open with his boot, he shouldered it wider and kissed her again as they crossed the threshold. The house was dark, but she knew he had wandered its halls for over three decades. From the steadiness of his stride, he needed no light to find his room.

He turned into a doorway at the end of the hall, the thud of his boots on the hardwood floor suddenly becoming muffled as he crossed a large rug. A moment later, he'd slowed to a halt by an open window. He didn't set her down as she thought he might. Instead, he buried his face in her neck and began trailing a line of kisses over her jaw and down her throat. To ease his way, she dropped her head back. She felt him raise her higher, his mouth creating utter havoc with her nerve endings when he shifted to carry those debilitating kisses down her throat and over her blouse to the soft swell of her breast. His breath felt hot and moist through the thin cotton, and when he nipped at the tight bud straining against the fabric, she felt the sensation clear to her core.

She thought her legs would wilt beneath her when, long moments later, he lowered her legs to the floor.

Keeping one arm around her waist, he reached over and pushed down the window. A moment later, fabric rustled as the curtains were drawn. There was a lamp on the nightstand behind him. It came on with a quiet click.

Raw need was carved in his features. His eyes glittered with blue fire, that primitive light as exciting to her as the possessive feel of his hand working up her back, drawing her closer.

"I think I'm nervous," she heard herself admit.

The feel of his hand was mesmerizing, almost soothing as it roamed up her side. "There's no need to be."

"I've only made love with one man in my entire life."

His hand slowed, then went still. "Is there a ghost in here with us?"

He was talking about Jim. "No. No," she repeated, because this had nothing to do with anyone but her and Logan. And what she felt belonged solely to him. "It's just been a long time."

Something shifted in his eyes. The need was still there. Hot and aching. What softened it was understanding. "It has been for me, too. We'll just work through this together. Okay?"

Together.

He made it so easy.

"Okay," she whispered with a trembling smile.

He framed her face with his hands, his lips descending to hers once more. The weakness in her legs seemed to compound itself. He knew how lost she'd felt. He'd known when he'd shown her his stars. And now she wanted nothing more than to accept the respite he offered and forget for a while that she so often felt as if she were floundering alone in the dark. Just for now, just for tonight, she didn't want to think of all she had to face tomorrow. Not that rational thought was possible with him touching her.

His mouth worked over hers, teasing, taunting as his hands slipped down to work her shirt up and over her head. His lips returned to hers and her bra drifted to the floor, followed by his shirt. Her skin was cool, but his chest felt hot when he pulled her against him. His hand felt hotter still when he settled his palm over one breast, making it swell, then making it ache when he bent to take her nipple into his mouth.

It was all she could do to remain standing when, having left them both trembling, he started working at his buckle. Over the thundering of her heart, she heard the rasp of his zipper and the rustle of denim as he tossed his jeans toward the foot of the bed.

The bed was huge, a massive thing made of dark wood with a forest green comforter tangled among clean white sheets. The evidence of his restless night was pushed aside as he backed her up to the edge of the mattress.

She didn't have time to wish she owned something sexier than the sensible panties he exposed when her slacks landed atop his jeans. Something of sheer lace instead of plain cotton. In the time it took his heated gaze to run the length of her body, the gleam in his eyes had turned from raw need to pure hunger.

Guiding her to the center of the bed, he leaned over her, refusing to let her hide her imperfections from him by drawing up the sheets. He wanted to see her. All of her, he told her, and made her believe she was beautiful because he told her so.

But it was he who was beautiful, she thought, kissing a bruise on his shoulder and smoothing her fingers over the calluses on his big, scarred hands. His body looked as if it were molded of bronze, every muscle rock hard and delineated by years of hard, demanding work.

She raised her arms to him, pressing her lips to the pulse hammering at the base of his throat, and heard him suck in a deep, ragged breath. But he wouldn't let her touch him the way she wanted. When she kissed him, seeking him as greedily as he sought her, he snagged her hand and entwined her fingers in his to keep her still.

Hunger swept through her, matched only by the desire to make him feel the mindless need he created in her. Stretched out beside her, he drew his palm over her breasts, her ribs, her stomach. His mouth crushed hers, drinking in the small sound she made when his hand drifted farther. He whispered to her, speaking words that enflamed as he sought her. He told her how she felt to him, how she made him feel, how they would feel together. The words he spoke made her feel as powerful as they did powerless, and he was caressing her so intimately she could hardly bear it.

She whimpered, wanting him to stop. But he wouldn't. He just kept repeating her name, encouraging her and telling her it was okay to let go, to trust him. He would take care of her.

"Please, Logan."

"I know, honey," he soothed, her plea nearly undoing him. "It's okay. Just stay with me."

It was all he could do to hold himself back. Every time her thigh rubbed against him, the pleasure was so intense it nearly felt like pain. And the one time she had managed to fold her small, soft hand around him, he'd nearly lost what little control he had. He wanted nothing more than to sheath himself in her warmth, but it would be all over if he did. It had been too long since he'd been with a woman, and the ten seconds he'd last wouldn't be enough to satisfy her. He told Sam that, too, whispering the words against her mouth while he continued to stoke her warm flesh. Just the thought of slipping inside her had him gritting his teeth. But he forced himself to hold off, to think only of her—until he felt the tension in her body turn to a shudder.

"That's it, honey," he soothed, drinking in her ragged breaths. "That's it," he repeated as, his own body beaded with sweat, he shifted his weight over her.

He entered her in one smooth stroke, and managed one more before he felt his mind shut down to everything but the feel of her wrapping herself around him.

They fell asleep with the light on.

It was a little before four o'clock in the morning when Logan woke. Samantha was in his arms, curled to his side. It must have been her movements that had awakened him, for a gentle, almost shy smile formed on her lips when she saw him open his eyes.

"You need to take me home."

He knew she was right. But with her looking so beautifully soft in the pale lamplight, her hair all tousled around her sleep-warmed face, he couldn't let her go just yet. "What I need," he told her, cradling her head between his hands when he trapped her beneath him, "is this."

The smile was still on her lips. He felt it when he kissed her. But that smile vanished within seconds, her mouth softening beneath his and her arms winding willingly around his neck. He'd awakened wanting her. Like before, it took nothing more than the thought of her for need to hit him, hard and swift. But this time, the debilitating urgency wasn't there. In its place came the exquisite intimacy of exploration as he learned every curve and contour of her body and she, in turn, learned his. And when he entered her this time, it was to guide them together to a fulfillment that left him stunned by its intensity—and more shaken than he'd been in his entire life.

He was thirty-eight years old. He'd lost his virginity at sixteen. He'd had a wife. He'd had a lover. He knew what sex was all about. Or so he'd thought.

This he wasn't so sure about. What he'd shared with Sam went far beyond the need for physical release. The physical need he understood; that burning in his belly that could be so strong that he hurt. It was the need underlying it, the need to be there for her, that he didn't trust.

The sun had just crested the hills, turning the sky shades of pale blue and pink along the horizon, when Logan pulled up in front of Sam's house a little before six o'clock. Snagging her hand the moment he stopped, he dragged her back across the seat.

"You sure you don't want me to take you to Lindsey's?"

"I'm sure," Sam replied, liking the possessive way he looked when he brushed his thumb over her lower lip. Her mouth felt bruised from his kisses, and she flushed just thinking of what they had shared a while ago in his bed. And in his shower. "I need to change clothes and dry my hair."

She lifted her hair from her neck. A blow dryer was not an appliance found on a ranch in an all-male household.

At least not Logan's. She'd toweled dry as best she could, but she was still damp underneath.

Tipping her chin up, he kissed her. Hard.

"Let me know what you hear from Erin."

"I will."

He turned away then, looking as if he might follow her inside if he didn't get away from her soon. Taking the hint, she slid back across the seat and stepped down to the curb.

When she turned back, his jaw had locked and the muscle in his cheek had developed a definite twitch.

Wanting to believe that dour expression was nothing more than preoccupation, she hurried up the walkway, digging her keys out of her purse as she went. Hank had come in the back door of Logan's house to have his customary cup of coffee with his boss just as she and Logan had been preparing to leave. At five-thirty in the morning there was little reason beyond the obvious why she should be walking down the hallway from his boss's bedroom. But the grizzled old man had been a perfect gentleman. After offering her a polite "Morning, ma'am," he'd told Logan he'd catch up with him later about their plans for the day and headed out to the bunkhouse to have coffee with the men. She was sure Logan hadn't seen Hank grinning, just before the door had slammed behind him.

She felt pretty sure that Logan was just impatient to get back to the ranch and his chores. Yet, when she turned to catch one last glimpse of him before he pulled away, she realized that it wasn't just impatience causing his mouth to pinch. It was the sight of the elderly woman in the poppy print bathrobe across the street openly watching them. Claire had her newspaper clutched to her chest with both hands, and her mouth was hanging open like an old hound.

"You should have come here instead of having him drop you off at your house, Sam. My neighbors are field mice. They don't talk like people do."

"I'm not going to worry about it," Sam insisted, not because she didn't care what her nosy neighbor had mentioned to Louella over at the café. She was just maxed-out on things to worry about at the moment. "By now everyone in town knows that Logan brought me home at six o'clock in the morning. They also know he took me to Austin because of Erin. They just don't know that we didn't come straight back to my house."

"Have you seen him since then?"

Leave it to her little sister to plunge right to the heart of the matter.

Sam shook her head. "He's shipping cattle this week."

"And last week?"

"I've *talked* to him, Lindsey. It's not like it was a one-night stand."

She hoped.

Frustrated, hurt, Sam turned to the boxes of balloons waiting to be taken over to the town square and inflated with helium—if the tanks ever arrived. She was up to the pearl studs in her ears with preparations for the opening of the festival tonight. On top of that, Michael had a cold, Bud Meiers had called twice to remind her that she needed to get going on his plan the minute this festival was over, and when she'd talked to Annie last night, there had been a strain in her sister's voice that had belied all of her assurances that Erin was doing just fine. There was something Annie wasn't telling her. She was sure of it.

Lindsey, having talked to Annie herself a few days ago, had concurred. Annie had definitely sounded stressed.

"Is Logan coming this weekend?"

"He won't be able to make it."

The look in Lindsey's eyes was as protective as it was militant. But the last thing Sam wanted was to suffer her sister's sympathy. She didn't deserve it because she had no business being hurt. Logan might have been around for her when she'd needed him before, but she wasn't going to fool herself into believing he'd always be there. He'd made it clear that he was content with his life as it was, and he was not a man who invited change. That had been evident from the moment they'd met.

"He'll still be shipping stock," she explained when Lindsey wanted to know why he couldn't get away. "Ranch work doesn't stop for anything."

"Zoe said most of the other ranchers are planning on bringing their families. It's the biggest event around here in years, Sam. He can't take off one day?"

"Apparently not," Sam said before she forced a smile and turned her sister toward the door. "He has work to do and so do we. Let's get over to the square and see if they were able to cover up the missing slats in the bandstand. That thing is falling apart, but Essie thought she could drape it with bunting and hide the bigger gap."

It was with no small amount of relief that Lindsey took the hint and dropped the subject of Logan Whitaker. But Logan was all Sam thought about as they joined the people who, for the most part, now greeted her with smiles instead of simply speculation.

The man was a hypocrite. When she'd tried to hide behind an excuse, as she had the other night by insisting she had to get back to her children, he'd called her on it and made her admit what had frightened her. But work was just an excuse for him. For everything. The reason he wasn't coming to the festival was because it wasn't something Logan would ever do. He didn't see himself as being a part of the community. Even though he'd contributed his money and his men, he still kept himself separate.

The way he was keeping himself from her.

As it turned out, Sam wouldn't have had any time herself, even if Logan had been able to get away. Because of the hoards of visitors her advertising had drawn, she was so busy filling in wherever she was needed that weekend, that even Michael and Amy had to attend the event with the families of school friends. Yet, despite the toll the project took on the locals, by the time everything had been torn down and cleaned up the following Monday afternoon, the festival had been declared a success. All that week it was *the* topic of conversation in town—especially after Lindsey and the town treasurer tallied up the receipts. It appeared that the school would, indeed, get new sprinklers, and a decent start was made on a fund to repair the bandstand and the library.

Under any other circumstances, Sam would have been glowing with that success. But with Erin away, she couldn't make herself feel as good as she should have about it.

She told Erin that, too, when her daughter surprised her with a call as she was trying to get her new proposal ready for the town council meeting the next evening.

As hard as Erin had worked on the festival, Sam wasn't surprised that Erin asked about it. What caught her so off guard was that she had called on her own—and the nature of the questions she asked.

"Are you going to do the same thing next year?"

"I don't know," Sam told her, putting everything from her mind but the sound of her daughter's voice. Erin's tone was subdued, as it often had been. Still, there was a difference. There was no exasperation, no belligerence. Just a lot of hesitation. "A lot depends on what happens tomorrow night. Most of the people I talked with seem to like the idea of doing things like this a few times a year."

"Like on the Fourth of July, you mean?"

"That's been one of the suggestions. Why, honey?"

Sam could almost see her daughter's mouth twist as she contemplated her answer. "I just wondered. Mom?"

"Yes?"

"Things are kinda weird around here. Can I come home?"

Gripping the receiver as if it were her child's hand, Sam closed her eyes and sank against the back of her chair. She had no idea what Erin meant by weird. With her, it could mean anything. She knew only that Erin's last four words were some of the most beautiful she'd heard in her entire life. "Of course you can. When?"

"Tomorrow?" she asked, sounding as if she wasn't entirely sure she was welcome. "Aunt Annie booked a flight for me tomorrow afternoon, but if you've got a meeting, I can come Thursday morning."

Sam wouldn't hear of it. If her daughter wanted to come home, she wanted her there as soon as modern aviation could arrange it. Barring that, she'd settle for tomorrow night. But after she hung up from Erin, instead of calling Essie or Bud to bow out of the meeting so she could pick up her daughter, Sam decided she would make her own gesture of peace. Instead of picking Erin up in Austin herself, and knowing her daughter would like to see him, she decided to ask Trevor if he would be willing to pick Erin up at the airport and bring her home.

Sam reached for the phone to call the RW. Even as she did the nagging anxiety she felt every time she thought of Logan reared its ugly head. She still hadn't seen him since the morning they'd returned from his ranch. That had been nearly two weeks ago. It had also been three days since he called, wanting to know how the festival had gone. He'd sounded pleased that all had gone well, and when he'd asked about the kids, she'd had the strange feeling that he actually missed them. But the call had been a quick one and he'd said nothing about if, or when, he would see her again.

She hadn't heard from him since. Not that she'd expected to just yet. He had told her he would be out on the range for a while. By now, she knew that when he went out to help his men, the work often kept him away for days at a time.

That was why she didn't expect him to answer the phone.

She hesitated the moment she heard his voice, her heart swelling at the rugged sound. "Logan?" she said, afraid to consider how very much she'd missed him.

His hesitation caused her smile to fade.

The only thing she couldn't tell from the uneasy pause that preceded a guilty-sounding, "Hi," was how long he'd been back.

He didn't ask how she was, or if she had finished her proposal—something she knew he was interested in, because it would put an end to the mayor's plans for development. He didn't even ask if she'd heard from Erin, which he always had before. And when she asked if Trevor was there, because Erin had called and she was coming home, he merely said, "I'm glad to hear that," then added that Hank was waiting for him, so he'd call Trevor to the phone. After that, came the click of her line being put on hold.

It only took a minute for Sam to make the arrangements with Trevor after he answered. But by the time she hung up, she was feeling more uneasy than ever. It was entirely possible that Logan had just been preoccupied. Heaven knew she'd seen him that way often enough. And he might have just returned from the range, so he hadn't really had a chance to call her, much less get away to come into town. She knew he didn't care for telephones, anyway. Not once had she ever had a phone conversation with him that lasted over two minutes, and even then he'd always sounded anxious to get off.

The excuses were reasonable. They were also just that. Excuses. As Sam paced her office with a death grip on her coffee cup, she knew exactly why she was making them, too. She was doing it because it was easier than admitting that she'd fallen in love with a man who had no intention of allowing her any further into his life than she was already.

The truly frightening thought was that he might not want her there at all. Maybe what he was doing now was simply letting time deliver the message he didn't care to deliver himself.

Sam was trying her level best to not think about Logan, when she left for her meeting the next evening. As it was, she'd spent half the night and most of the day vacillating about asking him point-blank if he really needed to be working as hard as he was, or if he was simply avoiding her. Lacking the guts, she decided to do nothing. With Erin coming home tonight, she had enough to deal with—which was why she wasn't anywhere near as enthusiastic about her presentation as she wanted to be.

Not that it mattered. Bud wasn't interested in hearing it. Because her ideas were hardly a secret, he already knew what she wanted to present. But the matter of the town relying on tourism rather than development wasn't on the official agenda, so he overruled it, conceding to those who protested because *they* wanted to hear what she had to say by putting it on the agenda for the following month.

It soon became apparent, however, that he had no intention of letting her present her proposal at all.

The moment the meeting broke up, he mentioned to Sam that he wanted her to stay behind. Anxious to get home to see if Erin was there yet, staying to listen to the man she was now coming to think of as pushy rather than motivating was not high on her list of priorities. Especially since she thought she knew what he wanted to talk to her about.

She was only partly right in her assumption.

"I'm not happy with this idea of yours," he told her the moment they were alone in the sickly mint green library meeting room. "I want you to drop it. You can't possibly implement your ideas and mine, too. With all the time you spent on the festival, you didn't have any time at all to do your job."

Slowly Sam straightened. "Part of my job is getting people to cooperate. That's what I've been doing."

"But you haven't done the rest of what you were hired to do," he said in a tone that bordered on condescending. "You were hired to bring in light industry."

"I was hired to bring in money," she said, suddenly knowing she was prepared to fight to keep the town as close to what it was as possible. "If everyone agrees on an alternative, what difference does it make where it comes from?"

The difference was that it wasn't his idea. The mayor, obviously miffed that his plan had taken a back seat, wasn't interested in alternatives.

He wasn't interested in discussing it any further, either. "It's clear we no longer share the same vision. I made a promise to these people, and I intend to carry it out the way I said I would."

"But what if they want something else?"

That was, apparently, the wrong question to ask.

"I'm sorry, Samantha," he said, though he didn't look sorry at all as his hackles rose. "You're fired."

Chapter Twelve

Losing her job was only one of the worries on Sam's mind while she wandered through the house the following evening turning off lights. She was now worried about Annie, too. Erin had told her last night that Annie and her husband weren't getting along very well, and that she caught her aunt close to tears several times while she was there.

"It's just the same old argument," Annie had explained when Sam had called her. "You know, the one where Rob doesn't think we should start a family as long as he's test flying experimental craft, and I want a baby before I'm old and gray? But don't worry about me, Sis. You've got enough going on without adding me to your list."

Knowing how badly Annie wanted children, Sam worried anyway. Anyway, it was what she did best.

For her children's sake, however, she was trying not to let those worries show.

That was why she hadn't intended to say anything to Erin about being unemployed until she'd had time to figure out what her options were. The prospect of another change, should they have to move again, might pull her daughter from her once more—and they were just now beginning to talk. But Erin had heard Sam tell Lindsey this morning about being fired. To Sam's relief, the girl who had returned home last night looking as if she weren't at all sure of her welcome, hadn't asked any of the questions Sam couldn't answer. Such as "What are we going to do for money?" She'd just looked at Sam with a strangely sympathetic expression, then asked if she could go see Trevor.

That Erin's first thought had been to turn to the young man came as no surprise to Sam. There was something about the Whitaker men that made a girl want to lean on them. Or, maybe, what they did was make her feel stronger than she thought she was. Whatever the reason, Sam understood Erin's reaction completely. There was a Whitaker she badly wanted to talk with herself; to seek his advice, his comfort. But Logan was making it as clear as he knew how that whatever it was they'd had was over.

A truck door slammed out front. Thinking it was Trevor bringing Erin home, Sam continued turning out lights and picking up toys and socks on her way to the linen closet.

The knock sounded on the door just as she started for the stairs and the long, hot bath she'd promised herself. Thinking her daughter had forgotten her key, she changed direction and flipped the lock on the door.

A moment later she went stock-still.

Logan stood in the light of the porch lamp.

"I thought you were Erin," she said, caught so off guard she didn't know what else to say. "Is she with you?"

It was impossible to see if her daughter was coming up the walk. His jean-jacketed frame completely blocked her view. As it was, she found herself taking a step backward when Logan, looking oddly hesitant, reached to open the screen door.

"She was still helping Trev polish tack when I left. I imagine they'll be along in a while."

He stepped inside, quietly closing the door behind him, and drew a breath of air that smelled faintly of cinnamon from the kitchen and wildflowers from Sam. He assumed from the towel she held that she might be on her way to her bath. The thought of what she might, or might not, be wearing beneath that very modest pink robe had his palms itching to reach for her.

He kept his hands right where they were. One relaxed at his side, the other tightening around the brim of his hat.

He knew she hadn't expected to see him. He knew, too, that she didn't trust his presence here now. He didn't trust it himself. But he was more concerned with her at the moment. The wariness that had been in her eyes so often before was as marked as the shadows beneath them.

Erin was right. Her mom looked awful. Beautiful. But awful.

"Where's Mike and Amy?"

"In bed. Asleep," she added, though she couldn't tell if he'd asked because he'd wanted to see them, or if he wanted to make sure they weren't around.

He gave her no clue, either, before he muttered, "Are you okay?"

"I've been better. Why are you here?"

He deserved her caution. And her coolness. Such as it was. Though she stood with her arms crossed over the towel and the soft pink robe that covered her from neck to peach-painted toenails, she could never pull off the starchy stance she strove for. There was too much vulnerability in her expression. Too much hurt.

"Do you want me to leave?"

Sam closed her eyes and drew a deep, trembling breath. Slowly letting it out, she dragged her hand through her hair and looked back up at him. "No, Logan. I don't want you to go. It's just that I haven't seen you since... I mean, I haven't heard... I don't know what I mean," she concluded, and let her hand fall.

She didn't have to say another word for him to know what she was talking about. The last thing in the world he'd wanted to do was hurt her. But he hadn't known of any other way to put an end to what had been happening between them other than to simply stay away. He couldn't count the number of times he'd wanted to go to her and take her to his bed; all those restless hours he'd spent working himself to exhaustion just so he wouldn't have to think about the fierce pleasure he'd taken in her.

But it had been other thoughts, thoughts his basic principles had demanded he consider, that had made him keep his distance. Thoughts of what he would be doing to a good woman's reputation. She didn't deserve the kind of talk that would develop by having an affair with him. Her kids didn't need that kind of shadow hanging over them, either. No one knew better than he how talk could hurt. It had been over twenty years since he'd paid any attention to the buzzing that went on in town, but the things he'd heard as a kid about his father and his family, after his mom died and the family had gone to hell, were still burned in his mind.

He didn't think he was being noble at all. The way he looked at it, a noble man wouldn't have jeopardized her to begin with. He didn't feel at all comfortable with what he had to do, either. But concern for her was what had brought him here after Erin had told him what had happened last night. That and his sense of responsibility.

Setting his hat on the entry table, he took the two steps that put him squarely in front of her. Unable to stand her wariness, he reached out and cautiously skimmed the smooth, soft skin of her cheek. When he felt her almost imperceptible movement as she turned to his touch, he slipped his hands to her shoulders and pulled her into his arms.

It was only when he felt her sag against him that he realized how afraid he'd been that she might not want him near her.

"Erin told us about losing your job. I'm sorry about that, Sam. I really am."

She felt his hand move over her back, gently stroking, soothing. Wondering what had happened to her resistance, she let him gather her closer. She had no resistance where this man was concerned. As upset as she was with herself for loving someone who seemed to have so little need of her, he was always there when she needed him most.

The denim of his jacket felt rough against her cheek. Sam didn't care. She cared only that he was holding her. That he was here. "Erin told you?"

"She was talking more to Trevor than to me. But, yeah, she did." The calming motions of his hand suddenly ceased. "That's what I came to talk to you about."

She felt his muscles tensing. Warned by that, she pulled back, leaving her fingers curled around his forearms. "About Erin?"

He shook his head, his dark hair brushing his brow as he did. "About what happened last night." Reluctance swept his features, accompanied by the more familiar hardening of the muscle in his jaw. "It's my fault you got fired. I'm the one who sidetracked you. If I hadn't pushed you, you would have gone on with what the mayor hired you to do, and you'd still have your job."

"And the town would change."

"That's not what we're talking about right now. The point is that you came here looking for security for your family, and I've messed that up. There's no other job around here that'll pay you what you need to get by. The way I see it, I can best make it up to you by taking care of you myself." The muscle in his jaw jerked again. "I'll marry you, and you won't have to worry about putting a roof over your kids' heads."

His hands rested at her waist, and her own still clutched his forearms. Not sure she was breathing, Sam felt her fingers slide down his jacket sleeves. She didn't remember stepping back from him. She must have, though. His hands were now at his sides and she was staring at him from an arm's length away.

He'd said he'd marry her. He hadn't said a word about love. About caring. About need, or affection. He'd given her no reasons for his offer other than guilt and practicality.

"I don't need to be taken care of," she heard herself say, hoping she didn't sound as hurt as she felt. "I appreciate the offer, but I can think of a number of reasons why that wouldn't be a very good idea."

He frowned. "Such as?"

"Such as the fact that marrying you wouldn't be fair to either one of us."

"Why not? We get along fine." Heat joined challenge, his glance moving possessively down the front of her robe. "Better than fine."

He had her there. It took no effort at all for the look in his eyes to remind her of the volatile physical effect they had on each other. That he had so easily robbed her of any restraint with him had been as freeing to her as it had been bewildering.

Just the thought of what they had shared in his bed was enough to warm her skin. But it was the thought of sharing his life, as they had already shared so much, that forced its way past the immediacy of her reaction. Knowing him as she did, it was entirely possible that a deeper reason lay beneath his practicality.

A heavy dose of caution colored her tone. "Don't you think we'd need more than that?"

"I don't know what more would matter."

Hope flattened to a dull ache. "So getting along is enough," she concluded.

"It helps."

"And you've thought about how this would affect you?"

"There'd be some adjustments," he admitted, not seeming to trust her calm questions enough to let his defensiveness go. "But there's plenty of room in the house. I'm not there most of the time, anyway."

She was sure he'd meant his last remark as some sort of assurance. All Sam felt when she heard it was a dulling sense of loss. Until that moment, she hadn't realized how completely Logan had shut himself off from emotional commitment. She'd suspected it. She'd even warned herself of it—for all the good it had done her. But not until that moment did she understand how high were the fences he'd built. He spoke of marriage to her as if it were nothing more than something he was prepared to do to make amends.

"It wouldn't work, Logan. Even if you did owe me something . . . which you don't," she quietly emphasized, "an obligation is hardly a basis for a marriage."

"As far as I'm concerned, it's as good a basis as any. At least as good as the land trade that accompanied my parents' marriage."

She looked at him in disbelief. "Has this always been your attitude about marriage?"

"What's wrong with my attitude?"

His incomprehension fed hers.

"You really don't know, do you?" There was sadness in Sam's tone. For herself. Because all she wanted was someone to share with, something he would be perfectly capable of doing if he would just open his heart and let go. Every time he started to get close, he pulled back. He did it with her. He did it with the kids. She felt sad for him, too, because the man had no clue what a real marriage was about. He'd probably never even seen a good one.

"I can think of only one reason two people should promise to spend the rest of their lives together. Because it's what they *want* to do. They want to do it because they love each other, and life is better for them together than it is apart."

Together. The way they had already done so much.

"You know that, Logan. I know you do," she told him, yet even as she said the words, she also knew better than to expect him to admit he cared for her. He wouldn't risk himself that way; wouldn't make himself that vulnerable. Already, he had distanced himself.

His eyes had grown shuttered, his expression cool and remote. For several long seconds, he said nothing. He just stood there, towering over her with his eyes steady on hers.

An empty ache had centered in her chest, when she heard the slam of a truck's door.

Erin was home.

Logan apparently realized that, too. His hard mouth looking even harder, he muttered, "That's the best I can do, Samantha," and picked up his hat. "Sorry it's not good enough."

She'd turned him down. He'd offered what he could and she'd said no. There was nothing more he could do.

That was what Logan told himself as he dumped the dirt in his shovel and attacked the ground once more. For three days he'd been telling himself the same thing. He was hoping by the end of the week he'd have himself convinced, and his life could return to normal.

Behind him, the steady cadence of horse hooves changed from gallop to walk. A moment later the rhythmic beats ended with a loud snuffle when Trevor drew Express to a halt a few feet away.

"Why are *you* doing this, Dad?" the young man asked, pushing up the brim of his hat as he frowned at the back of his father's sweat-stained shirt. "Hank will send one of the men out to ride fence if you want it done right now."

Logan didn't look up. Putting his back into his task, he jammed the shovel into the hard-packed earth once more.

He hit a rock and swore. "I'm doing it because it's what I want to do," he snapped, attacking from another angle.

With all the other jobs requiring his attention—bank statements to be reconciled, payroll to finish, analyses to be run—he had no business fixing fence himself. He had a dozen men who could do it just as well or better. But the thought of being cooped up in his office, doing paper-work or down in the lab, had him feeling like climbing walls, and he was restless enough as it was.

With the creak of saddle leather, Trevor slid from his horse. Pulling a pair of leather work gloves from his back pocket, he walked his bay to the Jeep Logan had driven out and tied him to the bumper. After retrieving another shovel from the back of the vehicle, he joined his dad by a sagging section of barb wire fence.

"Ready for rocks yet?"

"Yeah," Logan muttered, yanking off his hat to wipe his brow with his shirtsleeve, then slapping his hat back on again. With his own gloved hand, he jerked the badly listing fence post upright. "I think I've got it dug out enough."

A rock the size of a soccer ball was set in the hole at the base of the post. "I'm going into town for a while," said Trevor as he reached for another stone. "I'm taking Erin to the football game."

Logan shoved two more rocks in with his boot, doing his level best to avoid thoughts of the house his son would soon be driving up to. "She doing okay now?" he asked, when what he really wanted to know was if Trev knew how Sam was. Not that he wasn't concerned about Erin. He truly felt for the girl. "Any more talk of running off?"

Picking up a shovel now that the rocks were in place, Trev scooped dirt from the pile to add to the hole while his dad kept the pole steady. "Not anymore. I think she's okay with her mom now." The caw of a crow joined the sharp swoosh of the shovel sliding into loose dirt. "Things weren't like she'd remembered them being at her aunt's, either. I guess she and her husband are fighting, or some-thing like that. It was better at home."

"Didn't like the change after all, huh?"

Logan meant his comment as conclusion. Picking up his own shovel now that the pole could stand on its own, he started alternating scoops with his son. But even as dirt filtered between the rocks, then buried them, Trevor kept talking.

"All the changes were the problem to begin with. Like losing her dad and moving and all that." Metal rang as the tip of his empty shovel grazed the pole on the way back to the pile. "I think they scared her because there wasn't anything she could do about them."

Logan glanced at his son. He had always felt that Trevor possessed far keener insights than a person would expect of someone so young. It was one of the traits that made him so good with his animals. His compassion allowed him to see what others might miss. Jett, Logan's youngest brother, had been like that, before their father had bullied the compassion out of him.

A frown formed on Logan's brow. Not from thoughts of his brother. From his son's conclusion. Something in his words had struck a familiar chord. But his concern for what Trevor might be doing to himself was more important at the moment than trying to figure out what that something was.

"I'm not much on advice, Trev. You know that. Just be careful where Erin is concerned, will you?" Back aching, he tamped down dirt. "I'm not speaking against her. I'd just hate to see you complicate your future by getting in deeper than you should right now."

Trevor didn't even blink. "Nothing's getting in the way of school, Dad, if that's what you're talking about. I like Erin, but I'm not what you'd call serious about her. Not serious the way she wants to be," he added, making it sound as if he might be feeling a need to back off from the relationship. "And nowhere near as serious as you are about her mom." His frown held first confusion, then what suddenly looked like exasperation. "Why don't you just ask her to marry you and get it over with?"

Logan met his son's knowing glance quite evenly. He *had*. And it hadn't gotten him anywhere at all.

He wasn't up to mentioning that at the moment, however. Nor was he feeling particularly good about the fact that his son had a better handle on his love life than he did.

His scowl felt as if it was becoming permanent. "What did you come out here for, anyway?"

"To check on you." Taking his shovel with him, since the hole was now filled and the fence straight, Trev headed for the Jeep and his horse. "Hank said you looked loaded for bear when you headed out here. I don't know how he's missed it, but you've looked that way ever since I saw you leave Erin's house the other night when I took her home."

The shovel landed in the back of the truck. A moment later Trevor was swinging his strapping frame onto his horse and asking if there was anything Logan needed from town.

All Logan needed was another hole to dig. Lacking that at the moment, he settled for restringing a section of barb wire, managing to scratch the hell out of his arms in the process, and made it back to the ranch in time to help unload and stack the three hundred bales of hay Sharkey's delivered.

It was eight o'clock before he stripped off his dirty clothes and stood under the stinging spray of the shower to wash off the sweat and the grime; eight-thirty before he opened a can of stew for his dinner and shoveled it down with a quart of milk and half a loaf of bread. And it was almost eleven o'clock when he found himself on his front porch listening to the crickets because he couldn't sleep.

He couldn't keep doing this to himself. He'd practically driven himself into the ground with work, and he still couldn't shake the hurt he'd felt when Sam had turned him down. And he did hurt. Bad. But he didn't understand at all what he could do about it—until he stepped into the darkness and looked up at the stars.

Haven't you ever been scared? Sam had asked the night he'd brought her here.

They scared her because there wasn't anything she could do about them, his son had said of the changes in Erin's life.

Scared.

That's exactly what he was, he thought—and standing under the stars, wondering at how lost he felt, he suddenly realized what it was about Trevor's insight with Erin that had felt so familiar.

It was the lack of control, the lack of power over the changes that had scared Erin. And it was fear of that same lack of control that had made him hold back from Sam. As long as he'd kept his emotional distance with her, nothing had really changed. She had no power to disappoint or hurt. Without that power he was in control. But he'd had no more control than Erin, and everything had changed anyway.

He hurt.

And he'd hurt Sam by offering so much less of himself than she'd shown him he could give.

Tuesday was Logan's day to come into town. Knowing he usually arrived mid-afternoon, Sam had been pacing a path between the kitchen and the living room wall she had finally finished painting, now that she had more time than she knew what to do with, when Essie arrived with a box of doughnuts.

Essie started to expound the moment she walked in the door, barely pausing for breath. So the doughnuts wound up on the dining room table and Sam postponed her debate over whether she had the nerve to be hanging around the feed and hardware store when Logan showed up there later today. She needed his friendship too much to let him end their relationship this way.

Since it was only ten in the morning, she had plenty of time to decide just how brave she was feeling.

"Then I talked to Glen over at the gas station," the snowy-haired lady continued, brandishing a long yellow pad, "and he said he'd be more than happy to sign it. Louella got thirty signatures just this morning from folks coming into the café. The only one who wouldn't sign was Rudy Baker. But Rudy works for him at the market, so that's to be expected."

Essie stopped in front of Sam's reproduction of *Blue Boy* and tossed the pad of paper she'd been waving like a wand onto the table. "We're not going to let him get away with it, Samantha. There's 107 signatures there, and we'll get more."

For a moment Sam didn't know what to say. She just stared down at the names her friends had gathered. Lindsey's was at the top, the boldest of the lot. And while the sisterly support made her smile, it was seeing all the other names following it that made her throat feel just a little tight.

"Isn't recalling the mayor a little drastic?" she finally said, touched by the number of people supporting her. "I'd settle for just getting my job back."

"You still have your job as far as the rest of the council is concerned. Bud needs to be taken down a peg or two, anyway. Ever since he was elected, he's been acting like he owns the place." The woman, who now bore a stronger resemblance than ever to a fairy godmother, pushed her hands into the red wool jacket she'd thrown on over her white dress and apron. "Can I help you put on that coffee?" she asked, only to have her pleasant smile fade to speculation when she caught glimpse of a vehicle pulling up out front.

Sam couldn't see it from where she sat. But she recognized the rumbling sound just before the engine was cut. It was a truck. And it belonged to a Whitaker. Michael could have told her which one without batting an eye.

Sam couldn't differentiate between the sound of the father's truck and the son's, however. She could only tell herself it couldn't possibly be anyone but Trevor, though she couldn't imagine why he would be here this time of day.

The sharp thud of boots on the porch preceded a heavy knock. It was that sound that caused her heart to jerk against her ribs as she excused herself to Essie and started for the door.

There was only one thing she could think to say when she saw Logan standing there with his hat in his hand. "Why are you in town so early?"

He didn't seem to understand why she would ask. Puzzlement joined the strange unease in his expression. "I figured the kids would still be school. It'd make it easier to talk."

He didn't open the screen door and walk in as he had always done. So Sam pushed it open, too unnerved by his unexpected appearance to notice the blatant interest on the cherubic face of the woman behind her. Logan was wearing the same denim jacket he'd had on the other day, and when he passed her, she caught the familiar scent of him clinging to it. Its effect on her was as profound as the agitation radiating from his big body.

She was closing the door when he saw the local baker.

His hesitation was immediate. "I didn't realize you had company."

"Oh, I'm not company," Essie said, smiling up at the burly rancher taking up most of the entry. "I'm just a friend. And I'm on my way out."

"The coffee..." Sam began.

The look Essie sent Sam could only be described as tolerant. The woman had heard every word Logan had said. Unless a person was as dense as a primeval forest, it was pretty apparent that the man had something specific on his mind.

"I'll take a rain check. I have more signatures to collect, anyway. We're getting Sam her job back," the woman said to Logan with a friendly smile.

Picking up her pad of paper, and leaving the box of doughnuts, she turned that smile to Sam. "I'll let myself out," she whispered as she passed her, and proceeded to do just that.

The house had never sounded so silent as it did in the moments following the quiet click of the door when it closed.

Fortunately Logan didn't let that silence last long.

"You're getting your job back?"

"Essie seems to think I will."

"I suppose congratulations are in order then." He lifted his hat, but he didn't toss it on the entry table. He simply let it fall back to his side. "Considering that, maybe what I've come to say won't matter."

She couldn't imagine not caring about whatever it was he had to say. But she understood his uncertainty. She felt it herself. "There's something I wanted to say to you, too. It might not matter, either. So, I guess we're even."

She wished he'd smile. She knew he was capable of it. She'd seen him do it before.

As if to remind him how it was done, she tried it herself. "Do you want to come into the kitchen?" she asked, finding her effort meeting minimal success.

He would rather have gone outside. But he settled for the kitchen because, though it wasn't as big as his, there was room enough to pace if he needed it. That was exactly what he felt like doing, too, as he stepped over Spot lounging in the doorway and hung his hat on the back of one of the chairs at the table. Now that he was here, he didn't know where to start. Or even how. Buying time, he leaned against the counter to watch her open a canister shaped like a mushroom.

She was preparing coffee—which was the last thing he wanted, restive and anxious as he already felt. She didn't need it, either. He could see the fine tremor in her fingers when she tried to separate a fresh filter from the stack.

She was as nervous as he was.

He couldn't stand it.

He was at her side in two long strides. "Come on," he said, taking the filters from her and dropping them on the counter. Grabbing her hand, he led her across the room. "Do you need a jacket?"

"Where are we going?"

"Outside."

The sweatshirt jacket she'd kept for quick dashes to the woodpile now that the temperatures had finally cooled, hung on one of the pegs near the door on the back porch. Slipping it on while she followed Logan across her rescreened porch and down the steps she no longer had to worry about one of the kids hurting themselves on, she kept her eyes on his broad back.

She hadn't recognized the uncertainty she'd seen in him before. But she was definitely familiar with his impatience. At least, she thought it was impatience until she came up beside him at the bottom step. He'd waited for her there before continuing on.

Watching his shoulders rise when he drew a deep breath of crisp fall air, she realized he'd just needed to escape the confines of the house.

Now that he had, he seemed a little less edgy. At least she thought he did, as she matched her step to his deliberately measured stride. Leaves crunched beneath their feet as they moved into the shadow of one of the huge pecan trees sheltering her secluded backyard.

"How are you and Erin doing?"

He posed the question quietly, almost sounding as if he'd considered it before saying anything at all.

"Better. We've had some good talks," she told him, trying for an ease she couldn't quite manage. Logan had a reason for being here. After the last time he'd shown up so unexpectedly, she wouldn't let herself even imagine what that reason was. "I don't think she's blaming me for everything that's happened anymore."

"For having to move here you mean?"

The air was cooler beneath the branches of the tree. Pushing her hands into her pockets, she shook her head. "I think it was more because I couldn't prevent what happened to her dad...because I couldn't keep everything as it had been."

"How could she expect you to prevent things like that?"

"I'm her parent. I was supposed to protect her."

A twig snapped beneath his boot. He picked it up, contemplating the three slender orange-gold leaves still clinging to it as they walked from shadow back into the bright November sunshine. "From all the changes, you mean."

She gave him a faltering smile. "Something like that."

He didn't return the smile. Not that she'd expected him to. What he did do was come to a halt, his eyes fixed on the six-inch-long twig the wind had blown from the brilliantly colored tree behind him. With his dark head bent as it was, he looked almost as if he were trying to figure out why the three bright leaves were still clinging so stubbornly to the doomed bit of wood.

"I think I understand Erin a little better than you think I do, Sam." The leaves trembled as he slowly twirled the twig in his fingers. "She just came around sooner than I did."

"What are you talking about, Logan?"

"Being afraid."

Disquiet settled over her as she watched him deliberately tear away one golden leaf.

"More about how we both handle it, I guess," he added, snapping off another leaf to join the brilliant bits of foliage scattered over the lawn. "The way Trev sees it Erin was frightened by the changes she had no control over, so she rebelled. I was afraid and just tried to pretend the changes hadn't taken place."

But they had. Without his even being aware of it, he had fallen in love with the woman watching him so guardedly—and that had already changed everything.

The twig joined the leaves.

"I'm not following you," she said. "I mean, what you say about Erin makes sense, but what were you afraid of?"

"Of you," he told her bluntly, wishing her caution would go away. He wanted her to look at him the way she had the night he'd made love to her, as if she trusted him with all her heart. "Of everything you made me remember wanting. A real home. A wife. Kids." Of all the things he'd never let himself try for because he couldn't bear to risk, yet again, losing that dream. She had known he'd wanted them. She'd even told him so. "I don't blame you for turning me down," he finally said, because that was what he really needed to say. "You deserve better than that."

Logan was not a man accustomed to speaking of what he felt the deepest. He'd always let his actions speak for him. If Sam understood anything about him at all, she knew that much. Yet, as he quietly searched her face, she knew, too, that what he felt the deepest was part of what she loved so much about him.

He deserved better than he'd been willing to settle for, too. "I hope you're not going to apologize for what you offered."

"Not for that. For doing it the way I did. I wanted you without risking anything of myself. It was just easier... safer," he amended, since that felt closer to the truth, "to ask you to marry me if I thought I was doing it only because you needed me." Denim rustled as he stepped closer. "Now that you've got your job back, I don't know if it even matters."

He'd just come as close as he ever had to admitting how he felt about her. He was also giving himself an out by mentioning the job. But they both knew as they stood in the dappled sunlight with nothing separating them but their own fears, that the job had nothing to do with anything.

Swallowing against the beat of her heart in her throat, she stripped away that pretext when she murmured, "It matters, Logan. It matters very much."

His hesitation was marked, but the relief her words brought him was almost tangible. Searching her face as if he needed to be sure he could trust what he saw there, he rested his hand at the side of her neck. "I wanted you to need me, Sam. But it's me who needs you." He'd thought he'd wanted to avoid entanglements, but she had stirred something inside him that had been long dead. He needed the life and vitality that surrounded her.

He told her that, too, his words spoken simply, as if his need for her were nothing more than a matter of fact he should have acknowledged long before now. But not until he brushed a kiss over her lips and stood with his thumb tracing the line of her jaw, did Sam get a chance to tell him she needed him, too.

When she did, the motion of his thumb slowed to a stop. "How much?" he needed to know

Wondering if he had any idea how beautiful he looked staring down at her with the quiet question echoing in his eyes, she rested her palm against his chest. Beneath the heavy denim she felt the steady beat of his heart. "More than I should."

"What does that mean?"

She lifted one shoulder in a resigned shrug. "I love you, Logan."

The smile that slowly lifted the hardness from his face started in his eyes. With it, years of loneliness seemed to wash away.

The words came easier than he'd thought they would. "I need us together, Sam. Like you said. We're better that way. I'm better," he told her, drawing her against him. "I love you, too." His breath feathered over her cheek as his mouth hovered over hers. "I really do."

He crushed her to him, turning her knees weak and her mind to mush with a kiss that threatened to burn the ground where they stood. The man could reduce her to nothing but nerve endings in seconds. But it was her heart he touched when, long moments later, his kisses gentled and he held her head to his chest. He was crazy about her, he said, pressing a kiss to her forehead.

"And your kids," he added, his big hands roaming her back. "I'm crazy about your kids."

His jacket was open and her head rested against his chest, muffling her response. "They'll be glad to hear that. They're pretty fond of you, too."

"Even Erin?"

"Even Erin," she responded, smiling against his shirt.

"I always thought we got along okay," he said, sounding satisfied. "But knowing for sure will make it easier."

"Make what easier?"

"Living in the same house."

Her head came up. "What are you talking about?"

A pained expression crossed his rugged features. "You're not going to make me ask you again, are you?"

Sam couldn't stop her smile. "You never *asked* the first time."

She had a point. And Logan did want to do this right. So he pushed the hair back from her forehead, looked her straight in the eye and felt his heart swell. "Will you marry me, Samantha?"

She was still smiling. He felt it when she pulled his head down to hers and met him with a kiss he hoped to heaven the kids wouldn't walk in on. It was a while before she got around to answering him, though. But when she did, it was with a heartfelt "Yes."

Epilogue

It had been years since Logan's house had seen the activity of a typical Thanksgiving. Sam had been afraid he'd find the invasion of his space daunting, but he'd made it clear when she'd shown up with the advance crew at the crack of dawn this morning that the sooner it was invaded, the better. As he'd also pointed out while moving some of her things over a few days ago, it made no sense to put together a big meal at her place in town when she'd just be coming back that night anyway.

Therefore, while Logan and Trev tended the chores of ranching that knew no holiday, Sam, her daughters, her sisters and their mother spent the morning peeling, paring, stuffing and concocting. By noon, the scents of roasting turkey and spiced pumpkin pie filled the house, but it would be a while before the meal would begin. When it did, it would indeed be a time of family and sharing and counting one's blessings—for Sam and Logan were getting married today.

If Logan had had his way, they'd already *be* married.

Logan had wanted to elope. As far as he'd been concerned, once Sam had accepted his proposal, there'd been no reason to wait. Sam loved him for his impatience with wanting to make her his wife. But the holiday had been only a couple of weeks away at that time, and her parents had already announced their plans to spend it with Lindsey and Sam and their grandchildren. Since her parents were already coming, she'd wanted to wait until Thanksgiving so they could be there for the wedding.

Sam didn't choose the Friday or Saturday of that weekend, however. She chose Thanksgiving day itself. Logan had once told her that the holidays meant very little to him; that they just came and went, much like any other day in the week. She never wanted him to feel that way again. Starting with this Thanksgiving, she would see that he remembered them all as special.

Fortunately, friends and family alike had pitched in to help with the preparations. Sam's neighbor, Claire, had provided the glorious autumn flowers Annie had fashioned into a centerpiece for the festively appointed dining table and into Sam's bouquet. Essie had contributed the three-tiered cake, a gorgeous creation of vanilla icing swirls, and Lindsey had made the simple, old-fashioned gown of pale, cream colored satin Sam now wore with their Great Aunt Kathleen's pearl earrings. Their mom had brought the earrings with her, along with the new blue blazer that made Michael look quite grown-up as Sam took his arm to step from the front porch.

Her son had asked to give her away. Not for keeps. Just to Logan.

The early afternoon air was as warm as the shades of crimson and gold burnishing the meadows. The minister stood on the lawn with his back to the flame colored hills, his dark robes fluttering in the faint breeze. Gathered to one side of him, all smiling at the sight of her, were Sam's mom and dad, Lindsey, Erin, Amy and Annie, who had come alone. Sam had the feeling that all was not yet right between Annie and Rob and would have understood if Annie hadn't been able to make it, but she was glad her sister was there. Her family was important to Sam. It was important to Logan, too. But only his youngest brother had come.

Jett Whitaker, a leaner, hungrier version of Logan, stood near Trev. No one had heard from Cal. The middle Whitaker brother hadn't responded one way or the other to the invitation. While Logan had said he hadn't expected to hear from him, Sam knew he'd wanted him to be there. Lindsey, too, had sensed his disappointment. Though her sister hadn't said anything specific, Sam suspected Lindsey was, even now, trying to figure out how to get Cal and Logan together. Lindsey, always the arbitrator, never had been able to stand it when people weren't getting along.

It was always something, Sam thought, then felt herself smile when she saw Logan's dark head turn toward her. Her life was never dull, filled as it was with so many people to care about, and she wouldn't have it any other way. Especially now that she would be sharing it forever with the man who'd taken her and her children so completely into his heart.

The breeze tugged at cream satin as Sam took the step that brought her to stand in front of Logan. If she lived to be a hundred and five, she'd never forget the look on his beautiful, rugged face when his eyes moved from the baby's breath in her hair and settled on hers.

"Thank you," she heard him softly say.

"For what?" she asked, her voice just as quiet.

For breathing life back into this place. Back into me.

"For today. I love you, Sam," he whispered, and reached out to take the hand of his bride.

* * * * *

Look for Book Two of
THE WHITAKER BRIDES,
THE REBEL'S BRIDE, coming later this year
from Silhouette Special Edition.

Silhouette®

SPECIAL EDITION™

COMING NEXT MONTH

#997 BABY'S FIRST CHRISTMAS—Marie Ferrarella
The Baby of the Month Club/Celebration 1000!

When Marlene Bailey opted for an artificial way of conceiving a baby, she never thought she'd later find herself in a custody battle. But helping with the birth soon had semi-dad Sullivan wondering if he shouldn't marry the new mom—just in time for baby's first Christmas....

#998 MORGAN'S RESCUE—Lindsay McKenna
Morgan's Mercenaries: Love and Danger/Celebration 1000!

Years ago, Pilar Martinez discovered a mercenary's life was never easy when she was forced to abandon the only man she ever loved. Leaving Culver Lachlan meant he might never know his daughter...until Morgan Trayhern's kidnapping brought the lovers together again.

#999 THE BRIDE AND THE BABY—Phyllis Halldorson
Holiday Elopement/Celebration 1000!

It might have been more than luck that brought Mariah Bentley to the aid of a child in distress. And when she met the babe's attractive and available uncle, Aaron Kerr, it soon looked as if Christmas wedding bells would ring!

#1000 THE PRIDE OF JARED MACKADE—Nora Roberts
The MacKade Brothers/Celebration 1000!

Nora's eightieth Silhouette is also Silhouette Special Edition's book 1000! Jared MacKade was a man to be reckoned with, but *he* hadn't reckoned on Savannah Morningstar—a woman who could make a man forget his own name. And a woman with a past....

#1001 A CHRISTMAS BLESSING—Sherryl Woods
And Baby Makes Three/Celebration 1000!

Pregnant and caught in a blizzard, widowed Jessie Garnett turned to the only person she knew could help—her husband's brother, Luke Adams. The birth formed an unshakable bond between Jessie and Luke, but could the baby help bring them together when they felt their love was forbidden?

#1002 MR. ANGEL—Beth Henderson
Celebration 1000!

Kevin Lonergan thought he was nobody's angel—but tell that to Rella Schofield and her three kids. He'd appeared out of nowhere when they'd needed him most...and now they were determined to make their temporary daddy a permanent one!

Silhouette
SPECIAL EDITION ™

Holiday Elopements

He was a miracle Christmas baby....

It may have been more than luck that brought
Mariah Bentley to the aid of a child in distress. And
when she met the babe's attractive and available
uncle, Aaron Kerr, it soon looked as if Christmas
wedding bells would ring!

Don't miss
THE BRIDE AND THE BABY
(SE #999, December)
by Phyllis Halldorson

It's a

Holiday Elopements

—the season of loving gets an added boost with a
wedding. Catch the holiday spirit and the bouquet!
Only from Silhouette Special Edition!

ELOPE2